Samuel

The sastel legacy

Nadia Marsoli

Book Formatting by Derek Murphy @Creativindie
Book and Cover design by Nadia Marsoli.

ISBN: 978-1-7396137-0-9
Library of Congress Control Number: 202291052

Samuel

The sastel legacy

Nadia Marsoli

Listen to the full playlist;

Broken – Anson Seabra
Trying my best – Anson Seabra
IDK You Yet - Alenxander 23
If you're meant to come back – Justin Jesso
Fight Song – Rachel Platten
Nightmare – Lillian Hepler
Rise up – Andra Day

And much more on Spotify, an exclusive playlist created by Nadia Marsoli, inspired on Samuel and Ruby.

PROLOGUE

Samuel

June 2000, Edinburg

The bedroom is dark, warm, but it has his fresh scent. He might be sick, but he always smells the same, a mixture of leather and mint.

Rosita has called me at boarding school. Grandpa needs to talk to me. I was two weeks away from summer break, but this seems it can't wait.

"My... boy..." he can't barely speak.

I step closer, take a seat on the old leather chair by his side. He tries to stand with his hand, but I hold it before he loses the little energy he has left.

"I need to talk to you," he murmurs.

What could happen that he will lose all his energy?

"Grandpa, whatever it is, please just rest," my voice breaks.

"My boy... this is important... this will be the last time we talk..."

"Grandpa, please, don't say that." I need him.

"You listen my boy." His voice is getting rough, a hard whisper.

I push the armchair closer

"Do you remember my night walks?" He asks, giving himself a break after every word.

I remember seeing him a few times, walking around the house, moving things around, but I never understood what was happening. Many times it's like he disappeared into thin air.

"You know the small corridor heading to the kitchen?" He asks. I just nod again. "There's a..."

He stops the story when someone opens the door—I turn to find my father standing there.

"Father, you must rest," he orders as usual. "Samuel, please leave your grandfather. You will have time to talk later."

My grandfather holds my hands, shakes his head, but a rough cough is a simple order for me to leave the room.

Once the door closes behind me, I can hear his monitor screaming like a siren, and he is gone.

There is no point in me going back in. I can feel it. I just lost him, the only person I could talk to, I could trust—he is gone, and I am left here surrounded by ghosts, traitors, and strangers.

I walk away from the door when Stella rushed in, screaming at his side, shouting for my father to leave, but is too late.

Heading straight to my bedroom I take a well-needed shower, put on my black full suit, and head downstairs, find our favourite spot in the garden, and sit there, letting the summer wind surround me, the sound of the birds, the soft branches moving.

I close my eyes and I let my head travel back in time, when I was a little boy, before they took me away from his side.

***

It's the day of the funeral. We've just returned from the graveyard when my father calls me to his office.

We won't talk about Grandpa—nobody talks about him—it's like he never existed.

All his belongings have disappeared. I asked Rosita, but silence was her most frequent answer.

Stella is a ghost floating around the house, but she is gone, in silence, hidden somewhere. That is not an option for me.

"Collect your belongings. We will travel to London immediately," he orders.

Standing straight, rolling my shoulders back and slightly raising my chin I confront him.

"Father, I am not coming." I answer firmly, my fist tight on each side, anger fills my veins.

Turning around ready to leave the office, he stops me by holding my biceps.

"Son!" He exclaims.

I shake away his hold, but he firms it up, forcing me to turn, and my right fist hit the wall exactly by the side of his head, he doesn't blink, as if he would understand and take the punch.

I might hate him with all my soul, but if I hurt him, I will hurt myself, or worst my mother even more.

"You have no power over me," I argue, extremely close to him, his blue gaze glued on me. They are two empty oceans like mine, but I feel no mercy for him.

He should suffer as much as we all did. He separates us— he disrespected us, that this is what he deserves.

Loneliness, hatred, suffer paying the consequences of his actions for the rest of his life.

My knuckles are on fire, *fucking old thick wood panels.*

I walk into the dining area, trying to control my temper. My beautiful mother is having lunch alone day dreaming. I step closer to her shoulder—she can feel me, but she doesn't look at me.

"I love you, mother," I whisper in her ear after dropping a kiss on her beautiful, perfect cheek.

She doesn't move—she doesn't respond, she just freezes there.

I turn around, leave the dining room, and keep walking until I reach the front door. My black leather suitcase is there. I grab it tight, turn the handle, and step outside.

Fresh air hits me. I can smell the grass, the mountains, and the gravel that is under my shiny black shoes.

Jeremiah is standing by the back door, holding it open for me, and without a second thought I jump in.

Driving away from this dark castle, never looking back.

CHAPTER ONE

Samuel

Present day, London.

My olive skin feels warm, my upper arm covers my swollen eyeballs, while the light tries to get through the heavy curtains.

I roll over and sit up in bed, my vision is blur and my head is heavy, seems like a constant hungover, one that happens every day.

The clock on the black marble night table reads 5 a.m. I haven't slept at all, but tiredness, pain and loneliness don't bother me anymore.

Encouraging myself to rise, I grab some shorts and move to the gym downstairs.

There aren't shades here, so the sun hits me through the glass walls facing the rear garden, while I follow my daily routine, one that will wake every muscle on my body and make my blood pump around it as it should, the only way to make me feel alive.

After a while, sweat drips out of every pore, I stand

viewing the fresh cut green grass and the blue sky with a few transparent clouds floating around, a beautiful end-of-June morning, while past images, conversations, and familiar feelings run through my system. Today twenty-two years ago, my mentor, my hero, my best friend left me. He took my entire soul and left my corpse, an empty shell with a lack of emotion or feelings, surrounded by a darkness that traps anyone who dares step close enough.

Unaware of how long it has been, I return to the bedroom.

I take my time getting ready, following my daily ritual to wash away my sleepless nights. Fresh water to get the sweat off with my favourite soap — eucalyptus and mint. I comb my black thick waves aside, apply some cinnamon oil over my face and thick-dark stubble and put some eyedrops to clear the unpainful redness that surrounds my turquoise eyes.

Pleased, I adjust the towel around my waist and step out towards my shiny marble desk where the work of weeks is.

I see what I'm seeking for—the speech Helena and I have been preparing — rehearsing it while I walk into the closet to pick out the suit; I stand and face the rail filled with armors', the only thing capable of making me feel more human. As respect gesture to my Grandfather Mr Scott senior, I choose a black Armani, dropping all on the now tidy and smooth mattress. The murmuring stops when I find a wrinkle on the jacket.

"Fucking unbelievable!" I growl through my teeth.

I toss it away and walk back to face the line of suits.

Let's try with the Hugo one instead. My mouth curls and I hang it.

Someone's having fun with me today. Is it possible that there won't be a perfect one to wear?

I stand in front of my reflection in the wall mirror, struggling to control everything, as my fingers mess up the effort I put into my hair about ten minutes ago.

Something in the mirror causes me to stop. It's a fresh, spotless, dark three-piece, light grey shirt and narrow black tie, with shiny ebony shoes resting below.

There's a card hanging out of the breast pocket:

They would be proud,

R x.

I put on my fresh and perfectly ironed Dolce; it fits my six feet four like a glove, buy my shaky hands make me redo the knot on my tie over five times, nailing it at the next trial. My fingers brush my waves, glad as I study myself on for the last time, brushing my thick stubble, making sure the ideal mask is on.

Grabbing my great-grandfather's 1815 'Homage to Walter Lange' special edition watch from the drawers on the way out, I have a peek and it tells me is 8:25 a.m., perfect, Matteo should be here any minute now, if he leaves on time.

The reason I spent the night at my Belgravia apartment, to avoid the central London traffic, mixed with Matteo's usual unpunctuality.

Taking a last look at the briefcase to make sure everything is in place. A gentle knock, Rosita appears by my suite door.

"Your ride is here," she announces. Well aware today is one of those when everything should run smoothly and quietly. I don't give a fuck on others' opinion over my business or how sorry they may feel about my family dramas. I am here for a reason, and as soon as I fulfil it, I expect space and respect. But this woman, to her I owe her my life, Rosita, has taken care of my sister and me from babies. Taking over our mother's busy travelling schedule. Turning into our guardian when we lose our parents at eighteen and twenty.

Becoming the owner of a multibillion-pound empire at that age wasn't my plan, but hard work and consistency, gave me the respect and loyalty of multiple partners and clients, all under the close supervision of my father's right hand and best friend, Mr Rolland.

"See you for lunch," I add, bending to kiss her cheek. "Wish me luck."

"You are breathtaking, *hijito,*" she says, and I walk away.

I open the front doorway. Matteo is waiting by my spotless Black Badge, moving his frame, and opening the door.

"*Buenos días* Matteo," I offer the briefcase. "I'm walking to the office," I inform him.

He has been my best buddy since we were eighteen; we found each other on the magnificent roads of Rome; we had the best time around the world. He knows I require the breath of clean air today.

He taps on my arm, jumps into the driver's seat, and drives off.

I pull out my mobile and start going through my emails and messages, immediately calling Helena for updates on the upcoming meeting.

"Morning Samuel. I was in the conference room," she says.

I hear the clicking of her heels running around the office.

"Everything is on the screen. The folders are on each seat. Catering is in place. And you should be here on time."

I end the call and place the mobile in my trousers, struggling to focus as someone distracts me across the street.

I can only get her profile. She has a messy bun of dark thick hair on her nape. Skin like the snow, enormous eyes with endless eyelashes, a pointing nose, and those lips.

Fuck, she's the perfection in person, wearing a fitted summery floral-print maxi dress that brightens up her pale skin.

Observing she is not alone, there's a girl crying.

The breathtaking beauty squats to cuddle her, comfort her, kissing her temple, rubbing her palm in circles on her back, and whispering in her ear, making them giggle.

Eager to see her closer, I move across the avenue, blending with the tourist and neighbours walking, and rushing around.

I lean on a wall, but I glue my gaze on her, on every movement, on how she stands and, looking away from the child, taking a deep breath, she finds me. An additional to her angelic figure are her eyes, bright blue, glued on me when a perfect soft frown appears over her forehead. I can't look away. She sees me, and I see her. Breaking the connection, she looks down at the pushchair facing her. Is not the little girl's. There's a little boy who rises and calls her *mama.*

Both kids have her hair, but a darker tone of skin.

Carrying her daughter in the arms, she turns towards me, a few steps more and she will cross over me.

My body is tense, my throat block, my brain empty. I step forward, ready to cross paths with her, but an older couple of tourists blocks my way.

"Palace?" She asks in a hard Eastern European accent.

I am incapable of avoiding them, as she is placing a giant map under my nose.

I spot Buckingham Palace and point at it for her.

"Just straight and turn right, when you..." I start. For some unknown reason, I am talking to these people. It might be my stupid empty brain functioning wrong.

I see how they frown at me. And the beautiful creature tries to hide a gorgeous grin when she walks by.

"No, English," they answer, making me laugh.

Have I just laugh? What the fuck!

Turning my head, I observe how she looks back at me and smirks, taking part in a secret joke.

What is she doing to me?

"Follow me," I gesture to them, walking away, right behind her. I might dislike other people's company, but I need to follow that angel.

"Tour guide?" Asks the gentleman, as we arrive at the crossroad, causing the beauty and me to laugh.

I haven't laughed like this before. We stare at each other. She is playing crazy games with my mind and body and I should look away.

I won't let go, but she does, as the traffic light changes, everyone cross, pushing themselves forward and something inside me awaken, when she struggles to walk across, stepping closer, I extend my arm and open a path, my other hand rests on the lower part of her spine, we both jump, frightened by what that slight contact has done, my palm is on fire and my entire body has received an electroshock.

Her gaze glues to mine, her lips apart, and her breath slows. I can hear her heart humming in her chest from this distance.

The path gets tighter — her shoulder brush my chest, and that is when the pain comes to my chest.

What is she doing to me?

I inhale, trying to take all of this weirdness way. When her scent hits my nostrils, she smells like a field of wildflowers and a bakery.

The path narrows and I grab her by the waist. Her eyes meet mine and my entire body becomes alive, all in a mixture of pain and loneliness.

After a few more seconds, we arrive at Wellington Arch where she steps aside and emptiness comes to me. *Fuck, that hurts!* I can't break our gaze, and neither can she, but I put back my armor and mask when I feel someone has touched me. The tourists, who instantly regret that slight approach as I burn them with my ugly gaze.

"That street, Constitution Hill, Palace," I say sharply.

"Palace!" The woman cheers, and they both laugh while she searches in her purse.

"That is unnecessary," I clarify and turn.

When I do so, the beauty isn't there anymore. She has

crossed and is staring at me from the gates of Hyde Park Corner, putting her little girl on the ground, and holding her hand, walking towards the park.

I pull my mobile up, focusing on her and shout, "have a wonderful day!" She turns and there is her angelic smile again. She is blushing too.

Taking a picture that made my entire being shake when I notice how stunning she is.

Alarmed of what this woman has done to me I arrive at my building in Knightsbridge, walking in and joining the lift upstairs, unable to stop checking her photo, ignoring anyone passing by or greeting me.

On my way to my office, I pass the Helena's desk. She sighs when I avoid her, sit, and spin my leather armchair to the glass wall.

But she doesn't follow me. She has learned there is time for everything. Right now, words should be few and privacy is a must.

Helena's clicking heels quick me off my daydream and I turn. "Samuel, they are here." I turn and face my gorgeous assistant-secretary-friend. She is a fake blonde beauty, almost as tall as me, skinny as a post, and gentle dusky eyes. I always wonder how no guys ever sent flowers, cards, or any other presents.

Until a few years ago, I found a stunning red-haired woman, that explained everything, picked her up.

"Let's get on with this." I say, passing by her side, heading to the conference room.

"Good morning, welcome to the century publication

session." I welcome the members of the board, taking a seat at the head of the table, over thirty gazes glued on me.

"Everyone, please opens the folders."

They all found Helena's elaborate presentation.

"For decades SaStel has followed a traditional approach to develop stories, interviews, and promote businesses."

Some of their fathers and grandfathers have been here since 1922.

"We need to settle on the future of this country, the current entrepreneurs. We selected the best of the best, allowing one the opportunity to be our cover," I inform them.

A low murmur starts. Mr Rolland gives a light cough, and the room become silence again. Nobody talks when I am. They are used to common faces and topics for the major story, not a bunch of nobodies with fresh ideas, but I won't be following their path anymore.

"After that, another five businesses will receive a quick interview and sharing their services." I explain. "The particular change is, it will be available online and printed," I announce. "And we will publish it earlier than planned."

"What are you trying here, boy?" Mr Rolland asks in a low voice.

"Members of this board," I say standing, seeing how everyone become uncomfortable in my presence. "Some of you have been here for decades. All of my teams are ready to create what the recent readers crave. It will only be possible if we join the current trends and adjust our focus." I explain, opening the door and giving way to the illustration, press, and editorial teams to join us. "Everyone must put aside what our traditional readers need. They will not be here forever." I say, resting my hands over my chair. "Thank you for joining me today. In a week's time, we will meet again for the touch-ups. Please get back to me with the new drafts," I say directly to Isaiah, head of the illustration team. I fix my blazer and leave.

Matteo is waiting for me when I exit the building. I haven't called him, but Helena must have. He wants to talk—he wants answers, but I can't do questions right now. I need some fresh air to get my thoughts clear and ready to visit Scott.

"Is everything okay?" He frowns at seeing me walking again.

"I need fresh air. I will see you on Monday."

"As you wish, *hermano.*" He just shakes my hand and jumps into the car, driving away.

I walk around the roads in pain. My entire body hurts, my broken soul has been painless for decades.

What is happening to me?

It was that woman, for the first time, someone has stepped close to my darkness not scared or absorbed by it, she has actually shown me a spark I haven't seen before, what is wrong with me?

My pain, loneliness and I made peace long ago, incapable of settling down or attached to anyone. Never been interested in it, anyway, but this woman.

Damn you angel.

The sun is lower when I head back home. Rosita isn't here anymore.

Packing a quick weekend suitcase, I head straight to the garage, jump on my McLaren Speedtail and ride as fast as I can.

I reach Stella's house by 5:30 p.m., a perfect time for dinner as planned.

She moved to Blue Valley a few months ago, never a London lover.

Here it's quiet, safe, with lots of green area for Scott to practise outdoor activities, and for Mr Wrinkles to run.

He is five months old, an Old English Mastiff, not a cute little puppy anymore.

I step out of the car and have a minute observing this place, is the smallest property we own, her new hide away from the high-class lifestyle.

I can't blame her. She wanted to disappear after her husband died a couple of years ago. We held her in London, but there wasn't much we could do. I wouldn't give a second to her if it wasn't for Rosita's care and now for Scott's sake.

As I knock, Scott opens the door and jumps over to me.

"Uncle Samuel, you are here!" He exclaims cheerfully. I'm still a human because of this little man. He came to us and my world was upside down. I never knew how much I needed him until they moved away.

We head to the kitchen, following an unfamiliar smell.

"What is that little monkey?" I ask, twisting my nose as an unpleasant scent hit me.

"She was cooking all afternoon," he whispers in my ear, using his hands to avoid my sister hearing him.

"Hi stranger," she sings.

She looks a complete disaster. Her fake blonde waves are in an ugly nest, resting on the top of her head, cheeks and arms are full of flour, way more visible because of her olive skin.

I help myself to the cupboard, taking some wine glasses and a cup, pouring some red for us and juice for Scott.

"I think we all need a drink," I announce, gulping a full glass at once and pouring another.

Resting her glass on her side where she is murdering some vegetables, that is not the normal noise knifes make as they meet the board.

I give her a little kiss on the cheek, getting the taste of flour and corn-starch on my lips.

"Dinner should be ready in ten." I nod and walk away.

"I have a little surprise, my boy," I say, entering the family room and Scott runs behind me.

We sit on the couch, ready to play a new game Rosita bought for him. She knows dinosaurs are his favourite.

It's been over ten minutes, but I say nothing—she might give up and order some delivery. I haven't heard the knife or doorbell in a while.

"Dinner is ready!" She calls.

"You owe me another round," Scott sighs, using his serious, bossy voice.

"After dinner," I assure him, holding my hand out so he can give me the remote, and walking behind me to wash our hands at the toilet near the kitchen.

The table is full, there are more dishes than during Christmas lunch. Scott's face looks alarmed, but I just squeeze his shoulder and we both sneer at the scenario.

She has cleaned up, changed clothes, and come back to be the normal Stella perfection, but she is relaxed and smiley.

I catch a new spark in her eyes, is not from the wine, but I won't ask in front of Scott.

We talk a lot during dinner, more than usual. Stella is asking more questions about this morning's meeting.

"Our great-grandfather built an empire, grandpa brought it to the world, father kept it alive, and I'm just trying to adjust it to the new, young people," I assure.

"Where will you find excellent businesses worthy of SaStel magazines?" She asks.

"There's an incredible market out there," I say.

"Have you met them?" She asks curiously.

"I trust Helena on the ones she has found already, and that soon we will find the perfect cover business." I answer and she rolls her turquoise eyes on me.

"Ambition is wonderful, but you need to be cautious. This is an old empire to come and fu... damage it now," she sends me a wink, knowing she was about to use her forbidden language. "Besides, if this edition is so special to you, why you need to put your secretary into it?"

"Because that is why I pay her for," I say sharply, standing and placing Scott and my plate on the counter.

I send Scott to brush his teeth so Stella and I can have a minute. There is something going on. This has nothing to do with grandpa, she can't hide it from me.

"What's wrong?" I can't help but sound irritated.

"This isn't what I was expecting," she says.

Ungratefully, as usual.

"You choose this place, this house, this fucking hidden life, grow the fuck up, Stella."

"I am trying to live a simple life. Take my son for activities after school, do mum life," she says with a miserable sigh. "Kids don't want to play with Scott. Moms share a hi, smile and turn away," she says, facing me, and I can see her eyes fill up with tears.

"Have you considered they know who you are?" I ask. Nobody wants to be around us. People will share nothing more than monosyllables with us. So what is she stunned about?

"I just want to be a mom that can invite her friends for coffee, playdates and birthday parties." She never had real friends, just annoying people looking for fame and gossiping.

That's when I understand this conversation. Scott's birthday is a few weeks away, and she knows he has nobody to invite, just her fake friend's children.

"What if I take Scott this weekend to the park?" I hate to socialise, but I know the effect I create over women, and in this case I will do my nephew a favour. "He will make some friends and have mates to invite."

"I can't even find a skilled baker," she says, giving a pathetic attempt to sad face.

Tired of her pathetic attitude, I grab her laptop from the counter and take a seat on the island.

As usual, Samuel to the fucking rescue!

"Baker, party organiser," I mumble, searching online. It can't be so hard.

Over a million searches show up in front of me, but as I change it to closer locations, I have around twenty. My eyes spot one in particular. "How does Ruby Sweet Dreams sound?"

She turns around with a weird smile on her perfect face.

Why is she smiling that way?

"She is a local baker. Her calendar says she will be available for the party," I inform her, pushing the laptop aside.

Her expression changes and I rise, eager to run away.

What is going on with this woman?

"I will take Scott with me, contact her, book her and stop whatever is going on there," I say, pointing at her pretty face.

"Yes, boss." She says, cleaning away her tears, walking to the laptop and having a peek at Ruby Sweet Dreams' page. "Maybe she could be your front page." She says, giggling.

I ignore her sarcastic comment and the tingles on the back of my head.

This a serious matter.

Stepping out of the kitchen, I head to Scott's bedroom. He was reading one of his new books, all about wizards and potions. I sit on the floor with him, resting my back on the pillows that surround his little bookshelf, in the reading corner.

"What if we pack a small bag and take Mr Wrinkles to *Little Castle*?" I ask a silly question.

He places the bookmarker on the page he was reading and puts it back on the self.

Rushing to his closet and bathroom preparing a quick sleepover bag.

I stand on the door frame, observing him. This kid is not a normal one—is like Donnie, his father, inside-out, same light brown hair, green eyes, charming smile.

Gosh, I miss that man.

He left us too soon, but made sure his then five years old was an excellent copy of himself, someone attentive to detail, someone with a bright soul and big heart, able to make all of us content and calm. The years we spent with Donnie were the greatest. I used to smile and laugh back then; I used to care for and enjoy others; he transformed me, but he left us too. Shaking those memories away, we walk downstairs and say our goodbyes to Stella, collecting the leach and into the car.

After a ten-minute drive, we arrive at the biggest property in the neighbourhood. It has an extensive front gravel space, is across from the main park entrance, and except for a cottage on the side, it has no other neighbours by the side in at least twenty feet, giving privacy and space for the back garage, where mostly my biggest cars and bikes are parked now.

It was a little countryside castle from over a hundred years ago, and I didn't want to change a bit of the outside when I bought it a few months ago.

Walls with dark brown rocks with creepers growing in and out of them. Thousands of flowers have blossomed in the past few weeks and it is not a dark castle anymore.

Before I put the key in the lock, Rosita opens the shiny wood heavy door.

"My sweet boy!" She cheers way louder than I appreciate it.

Scott runs to cuddle her and Mr Wrinkles circles them,

guiding them to Scott's bedroom.

Stella and he have been working on renovating this room. It's a significant improvement. The walls are like a jungle, so real it makes the room endless. There're dinosaurs drawn everywhere, and they look real.

The bed looks placed in the middle of nowhere, surrounded by dangerous creatures. The carpet is brown to match the walls, and Mr Winkle's house is a small wood cabin that matches the room.

Scott is in bed quicker than I realise and Rosita is nowhere to be seen. "Good night, my boy," I say, dropping a soft kiss on his forehead, making sure the blanket is in place before I leave the bedroom, walking back to my gloomy reality.

CHAPTER TWO

Ruby

Naima and Aidan are having a bath while I clear up after dinner.

It's all giggles and screams when my mobile rings and I pick it up from the island as I see Louise's—my social worker's name on the screen. "Hi, Louise." I say, cleaning the counters.

She was at the court office this morning, guide us through the entire trial and stay slightly longer trying to find more information.

"Ruby, there's something you need to know," she says.

"What happened?" I ask. My voice trembles, and panic grows in my core.

"Advik's lawyer has pleaded for a reduction in his sentence," she says.

"What do you mean?" I ask, in shock.

"After your testimony, his lawyer gave a speech to the judge. The lawyer and governor fear for Advik's life."

"That's impossible," I say in a panic. "The judge can't do

that."

What type of judicial system do we live in?

"Ruby, the governors protect and prioritise inmates who are suicidal or in danger from other inmates." Suicide? For what I care, he can hang himself. "The lawyer proposed he could finish the rest of the sentence in a community center, doing some services and therapy. And under control that he doesn't break the restraining order..." is *that all?*

"He can't be free!" I say, I'm trying to keep my voice low, but this is boiling my blood.

"I understand your frustration," she says, her calm voice and measured speech making me even more anxious.

"You don't understand," I say—a part of me is packing already. "Have you agreed with it?" I ask, thinking I could trust her. "He almost killed me! Try to kill my daughter! He doesn't deserve freedom!" I say, growling through my teeth.

"On those matters, there's nothing we can do. It's all under the judge's decision."

I hang up, holding myself on the island. My head is heavy, my heart is at my throat, and my entire body shakes. I take a few deep breaths and try to calm down.

Focus to finish a few orders that will be collect it soon. I pack two boxes of eight cupcakes each, princesses and superhero themed, for twin's birthday party. I also pack twenty-four shortbread biscuits for the moms and fifteen mini sandwiches.

Next is a five-inch chocolate cake with strawberry filling, covered with a green fondant turtle, for little Malcom's birthday.

They look outstanding, but the packing, the pickup can be a tricky process.

Before I can finish with Malcom's cake, a soft knock announces my customer has arrived from work to collect the twins' desserts.

"Good evening, Susie," I greet.

She is shorter than me, has black hair and dark eyes. In her midthirties, kind and funny.

"My beautiful Ruby," she calls, stepping in and giving me one of her awkward hugs.

"I will get your order." I say sharply, walking back immediately.

After Susie leaves, I check on the kids and help them brush teeth, combing their hair and changing into pj's.

As I walk back to the bathroom with their towels, another soft knock calls my attention. The children are already sleeping, London trip was exhausting and has help for the bedtime. Daniel, my customer's husband, is at the door straight from work. He is a handsome Irish man with ginger hair. Kind and polite when we met and glad to help with this collection.

"Hi Daniel."

"Hi Ruby, you alright?" He sounds tired.

I nod and rush to picking up the cake.

"There you are," I say, opening the lid. "Enjoy your party tomorrow and send me pictures of Malcom and the cake."

"Take care Ruby, we will see you soon," he says.

I get back to the bathroom, remove my maxi floral dress,

and jump into the shower. I put on a t-shirt and headed back to the kitchen.

Pouring some fresh cold lemon tea and grabbing the phone on my way to the garden. It's a beautiful night. The streets are quiet, and the darkness of the rear garden calm my agitated being.

I take my time to upload the pictures and videos of the orders picked up earlier on my social media accounts, delete some emails and reply to some customers' messages. I reach a new email. Her name is Stella and has a party coming up in few weeks. She wants cake, biscuits, cupcakes, and salty appetizers. This will be a big deal.

***

Good evening, Stella,

Thank you for your enquire. I am available for your son's birthday party.
A first meeting will take place in the next few days. We will go through colors, flavors, type of food allergies, or special menus.
I have attached the link to my social media. Over there, you will find original designs I had created.

www.rubysweetdreams/birthdayandweedingsalbum/2341z

Sweet Dreams,
Ruby. ☺

***

Appreciate the quick response, Ruby.

You are a lifesaver.

My son loves dinosaurs, so I would love a party with that theme!

And he loves lemon cake, lemon custard, anything that has lemon flavour or colour.

I will need a menu good for everyone.

Please send me your availability for the first meeting.

Thanks so so so much, Stella. Xxx.

***

Dear Stella,

I could book you in for tomorrow morning and go through all the details.

Lemon and dinosaurs sounds good to me.

Would 10 a.m. work for you?

Sweet Dreams,

Ruby. ☺

***

10 a.m. will be perfect.

Thanks again, looking forward to meeting you.

Stella. Xxx

***

Dear Stella,

That is all booked for tomorrow Saturday June 25th at 10 a.m.

My address is Apartment 3, Daisy Road.

Sweet Dreams,

Ruby. ☺

***

I walk inside, grab my events folder, and take a seat at the stole on the island.

Few weeks ago I did some dinosaurs cookies, and I have different colors of cakes to show as a sample.

Researching in *Pinterest,* I found great ideas, save them, and attach them on an email to Miguel—the owner of the printing shop round the corner.

At 11 p.m., I lay exhausted by Naima's side. This isn't tiredness, this is emotional exhaustion after Louise call, it didn't surprise me though. That monster won't ever leave us, not until he finishes the mission he started over a decade ago.

I can smell home, my riding boots walking through the fields, the sun warming my pale skin.

Something is behind me. When I turn, there are only mama sunflowers surrounding me. A movement between the wheat made me turn the other way.

He is here, somewhere. I can feel him. He rises between the wheat fields, a bouquet of sunflowers in his hand, a mischievous grin growing by the side of his lips. Those that long ago I badly adore.

Slowly approaching me. There's something different in his eyes. They look glassy, almost believable.

Holding my wrist, he places the bouquet in my palm and closes my finger around it.

His other hand brush my cheek, through my jaw, until it is resting on my neck, my breath stops, ready for what is coming, moving to my nape, and brushing his fingertips around, almost tickling my skin, but his hold become harder, almost painful, pulling me closer to his face, one that long ago I couldn't take my eyes away from.

Resting his forehead on mine, I can smell the liquor, making my stomach twist, pulling me even closer until his lips touch mine.

"You are mine, now and forever sweet girl," he growls on my lips.

I jump in bed, cover in cold sweat. My entire body is stiff, scared, alert.

Tiptoeing out of bed, I made it to the bathroom. I take a long, warm shower.

Walking back to the bedroom I grab my comfy dress, get dressed and prepare some strong fresh coffee, shocked when I see the kitchen clock marking 3 a.m., plenty of time until the kids wake up, but as well enough for me to recover from my nightmares and get ready Stella's visit.

The 8 a.m. alarm rings, and it's like a *GO!* Signal to the kids. They are jumping in the mattress—who is screaming for help.

"Little monsters, stop for a second," I say, taking them to

the kitchen.

I am calm now. Everything is ready for breakfast and the meeting.

"Eat babies. Mama is going to get your clothes. We need to print something." I say, serving the crepes and fresh orange juice.

It will be a warm day, so I have picked flower dress for Naima and navy blue and brown t-shirt for Aidan, and mom short jeans and white oversize shirt for me.

Perfect for the meeting and my afternoon surprise—a picnic at the park.

"Let's get you dressed and let's go." Before I even finish talking, I am already removing their pj's and getting the clothes on. Doing everyone's hair is easy. It's a messy bun for all.

At 9 a.m., we are on our way to Miguel's printer shop.

He has been supportive and helpful since we arrived, never asking questions, and always doing as much as possible.

Miguel is finishing putting the board outside his shop and getting things ready for a short Saturday working day.

"*Buenos días señor* Miguel." I greet.

I adored it when I found out I could practise my long-abandoned Spanish. Advik forbid it since I left home and I know mama would be upset to know I can't have a conversation anymore.

"*Hola* Ruby," Miguel says.

He is a short gentleman, with black hair, tan skin, a thick mustache, and a big round nose.

"*Hola* Miguel! Can you please help mama to get ready for an important meeting?" Naima asks.

I couldn't stop talking about it all the way here.

"Does mama have an important order coming up?" Miguel asks. I am sure he already saw my email.

"Aha! Someone was working late," he says, looking over his small round glasses, raising thick black eyebrows at me once he found the extensive amount of pictures I have to print.

"She is having her son's birthday organized and wants me to cover the entire menu," I say worried. My heart is pumping so fast again.

"Ruby, you cook like an angel *mi hija*," he breathes.

He has ordered multiple times already—I keep bringing him things to be tasted all the time too.

"Your food is excellent—she will love it, same as all her guests and puffff." He raises his hand to the sky like a rocket flying away. "You will be the best caterer and baker in the neighbourhood."

"I'll need a bigger kitchen," I argue back.

"Keep working hard and you'll own that little cottage," he says, pointing to the other side of the park, to the house Naima calls *one step closer to heaven*.

Miguel's serious voice stops me before I stress myself more with my insecurities.

"Take this and show that lady what an incredible baker you are," he orders.

He hands me over twenty pages, while Aidan and Naima cheer and thank Miguel for the quick last-minute help and words of support.

At 10 a.m., a soft knock makes me stop moving the pictures again.

"This is mama's client." I say to the kids that are now playing in the garden.

I take a deep breath holding the door handle, put on my business mask, and open the door.

"Good morning, Ruby?" Stella is so pretty, she is tall, with olive skin, long blonde waves fall on each side of her face, breaking on her waist, beautiful turquoise eyes, and a perfect white smile.

"Please come in Stella," I say.

Stella takes a seat at the little dining table, where everything is on display.

"Some coffee?" I ask.

"Yes, please. You have children, wonderful," she says, looking around, probably spotting the toys, and back to the table moving the pages around.

"There it is." I said, leaving the mugs on the table.

"You have made an incredible presentation on a short notice," she says, when I take a seat by her side.

"When is the party?" I ask, opening my notebook ready to start my notes.

"Saturday, the 16th of July," she replies.

That gives me almost three weeks to get ready.

"How many people are attending?" I ask.

"It's uncertain yet," she replies, placing some hair behind her ear with shaky hands.

"We're new to the neighbourhood." It has replaced her

beautiful smile with an uncomfortable one.

"Let's say fifty. Those are at least my friends from the city." She confirms, giggling.

"I can do enough for fifty guests. I will need you to confirm by Thursday. How does that sound?" I ask and she just nod.

"You mentioned a dinosaur theme. I was thinking of a small two-layer cake. The bottom can be brown and the top green—representing the jungle, and either just flat or 3D figures around the cake," I explain, pointing to several images. She just looks shocked for a moment.

"Can we do flat ones as background view and a T-Rex in 3D?" She proposes.

"I assume the T-Rex is your little boy's favorite?" I ask, taking more notes when she nods.

"Would you like a colorful sponge, or just a soft yellow with lemon flavor?" I ask.

She just raises her shoulders, "on the sponge the flavour is more important, but outside it is more presentation than taste," she says, and I know that is every customer's thought.

"There are two options," I assure, "we can make tasty outside too, or just traditional fondant," I explain. "But let's be honest, no one wants to eat fondant."

"Tasty outside?" She looks confused. Taking a deep breath, I explain everything.

After an hour, I add all the images to a folder that matches the designs we have agree and take the last notes.

"I would like your full dedication, help with the food, decorations, and set up before the guests arrive. And of course, you can enjoy the party with us. Let's say you are my party planner, baker, catering, and guest," she says giggling, one that makes me feel uncomfortable.

She gives me the check and I hold my hands at the table. "Are you okay?" She is smiling and her hand holds mine. "You accidentally add some extra zeros," I say. "No, it's correct," she says, peeking at the check. Money does not seem to bother her.

"Am I doing some kind of celebrity party?" I ask.

I can prepare a regular party, but if we are talking high standards, the quality and type of food will have to be different. That would explain the thousands of pounds for food and decoration; high quality comes with a high price.

"He is a member of the third richest family in the world," she says.

Holy macaroni, I wasn't expecting this.

She stands, thanking me for the great service, and leaves.

As soon as the door closes, I can't resist and start screaming, rushing to the garden and rolling the kids around, kissing their faces, while they giggle.

"Everything okey?" Naima asks.

"Give me two seconds baby," I'm too nervous to explain.

I run back to the table and take my mobile, dialing Grace, our real estate agent. Louise put me in contact with her months ago, to make me aware that a person in my circumstances could get a fresh start, at a reduced price.

"Good morning, Grace Thompson. How can I help you?" She greets.

"Hi, it's Ruby." Well, she might not even remember me.

"Ruby, how are you? I've been waiting for your call," she says.

"Well, I just finished a meeting with a new customer." My throat is closing with every word, and my vision is becoming blurry. I didn't realize how emotional I was until I verbalize it. "I've got the money you asked for."

Not capable of holding them in any longer, my tears wash my make up free skin.

"Well done. Are you interested in the cottage we spoke of?" She asks.

When we meet months ago, Grace showed me a few properties in the neighborhood. That cottage is the closest to perfection for us.

It's a modest, cozy, rural place, it has a colorful garden at the front, lavender, roses, and bushes bright up the path, there's an arch orange wood door that opens to a hallway, cream walls, an antique bronze mirror rest in the wall, and a rustic wood cupboard rest underneath.

Double crystal doors that will take you to the kitchen at the end, everything is in beige and light-yellow shades, it has way more space than this apartment, a double the size fridge, one that reminds me of back home, an oven that will help me bake faster and much more space in the counters and island.

And to make it the perfect house, it has two family rooms and three bedrooms.

Our heaven dream castle is the one next door and both of the properties somehow share the entrance.

I asked Grace, but she could never determine the

correlation of the properties. The new owner has something to do with the builder.

"Is it still available?" A sense of worry grows in me, thinking someone might have got it during these months.

"It's available," she confirms. "I've been a little naughty and kept it for you, convincing the owner a few people were interested and making offers." That's great news.

"Thanks, Grace, for your patience and support."

"I will call you by Monday. They are desperate to sell." She confirms and hung up.

Naima and Aidan were waiting on the couch, hearing my phone call, ready to ask all short of questions.

"Do you understand what I just talked about?" I ask. Naima nods and Aidan looks confused. "Mama just called Grace, making an offer on the cottage we loved so much a few months ago. Do you remember?"

"The one next door to our dream house?" Naima asks with a bright smile.

"That one baby!" I exclaim.

"Can we visit again?" Naima asks.

"We will ride by on the way for my afternoon surprise."

The distraction must have worked, as their faces brighten up again, and they jump, ready to leave.

Everything is ready, so I just get the bike loaded, seat them in their carrier and head to the park.

CHAPTER THREE

Ruby
6 months ago, London

I can't breathe. I've been sleeping for so many hours.

Can't figure out if I'm still dreaming, but when my body is urged to turn and lean my back on the mattress, forcing my drowsy eyes to open wide in pain to discover my death sentence.

The liquor odor is making me sick. In the dusk, I can't look at his face.

But I recognize who is squatting on my waistline. I can't leave. My palms fly around, one diverting him, the other reaching for my phone, my old, cracked iPhone that will at least save the children, resting on the night table.

Punching my cheek when my fingers squeeze the side button many times—calling the emergency services.

I bury it under the pillow so he can't get it while the alert sounds, and I raised my voice.

"Help!!! Help!!!" Continuous fists are tearing my skin.

My knickers get ripped apart. He pushes himself in.

I can't turn, but I don't cease shouting.

His mission is to kill me, especially after the fight we had hours ago, after he slapped Naima for talking without permission. I was so naïve to think he left us.

I can't hold my eyes open anymore. My arms are in pain from protecting my face. My whole body aches.

I can hear some footsteps, unknown voices, and growls.

Everything stops. He isn't on the bed anymore — the kids are screaming at the top of their lungs, their voices are getting closer, until they jump in my bed, I hug them as strong as I can. My chest is wet from their tears. I keep dropping firm kisses on their heads.

While my back rests on the wall, they are in the small gap between my legs and my chest. My arms try to make a shield that no one can break.

I listen to the strong footsteps getting closer and I can't help but tremble. Is this help or more pain coming on our way?

"Everything is going to be okay," I whisper to their trembling heads. It's a significant promise because of the situation, but I will try my best.

"Ma'am, I'm Officer Clark and I'm here with my partner Officer Lewis," his voice is gentle, kind, but I can't see them. "There's an ambulance downstairs. We will escort you and help with the children."

"They are okay with me. I will hold them." I assure.

I step out of the bed, never letting go of the children. With every step, my hold gets tighter, and so does theirs.

"Ma'am, my partner and I will guide you. We will hold you, if you need us," he informs and I just nod.

I give one step after another, slower than usual, and leave the bedroom.

My eyelids are so swollen I can't open them. They have been through two rounds of hits in less than 72h. I can sense the hallway lights and my feet feel the change from carpets, the one in the bedrooms is softer, then is when I meet the metal underneath that means we are at the edge of the stairs.

Someone tall and strong is in front of me, bracing my forearm. He is too close, but that will make sure that one wrong step won't make us fall. He is holding us.

The other officer rests his palm over my shoulder, tapping every other step that comes our way.

We have like ten steps, but in these circumstances, they seem like two hundred.

We reach the bottom, and the chill of the night hits my bare skin, but a heavy and thick blanket gets placed over my shoulders.

"Ma'am, I'm going to help you up to the gurney. Just stay still," another male raspy voice informs.

Huge hands and enormous arms hold my shoulder and my legs.

He lifts me up like if I'm a feather, rest and covers us on the gurney, getting out of the house.

I know we are outside—people are murmuring, gasping, and sobbing.

My eyes burn, I can't breathe from my nose, and the taste of blood hasn't left my mouth. He tries to control me, manipulate me, but this was a murder-me situation.

We reach the hospital before I realized it. I must have fallen asleep with the movement and the sense of security. The doors of the ambulance open, and that's when I get anxious. There are so many voices around us.

"Ma'am, I am head nurse Wan," she says in a calm, low voice, "I will accompany you inside where my team and Dr Lopez would take care of your examination," she says and I just nod.

I can feel we are moving, the noise of some automatic doors opening and the warmth of the inside. They stop and nurse Wan informs me she will be back.

Someone else gets closer. I can hear heels clicking the marble hospital floor.

Without announcing themselves, try to open my blanket and get the kids. But I can hear hard boots stomping on the floor, which calms me as he speaks.

"Please, don't do that!" Says Officer Clark. He must have followed the ambulance. "They will remain with her at all times."

"Officer, there are rules and policies to follow." A hard woman's voice makes me tense, thinking she can come and have the allow order to take the kids away.

"I'm well aware, but my colleague and I will be around and help with them as much as possible." He is trying to sound firm, but I can sense the nerves behind his rough voice,

"Thanks ma'am, but Social Services won't be need it here." Nurse Wan says, followed by multiple footsteps and murmurs.

Why would Social Services be here? I have done nothing wrong, anyway they show up now?

What about the multiple other times we were here, or at our GP's office with minor wounds?

That time we didn't need them?

They move us to a further place, here is warmer, quieter, but I can feel each and everyone in the room, how plastic packages are being open, how Crocs move around the shiny slippery floor, but nobody said a word.

"Evening Ma'am, I am Dr Lopez," he is an old man, his voice tells me, but the calm tone tells me, this is not the first time he has been in this situation.

"Ruby,... I am Ruby," I whisper, my throat burns after all the screaming.

"Ruby, it's nurse Wan, I know you are worry, but my nurse team has brought two beds and we will need you to let us take the children," just by hearing that, our hold tightens, "that way we can examine you better, they won't leave the room, I can promise that, we have some food, books, and toys." She says, trying to convince the three of us is not a separation situation.

"Mama is here babies, the doctor just to clean mama up," I said. Naima stands, placing her soft palm on my wounded cheek, and I feel how she holds Aidan up.

He doesn't say a word. Just leave my chest and I feel empty for a moment. A soft woman's voices are speaking to them and I can hear paper bags opening. That must be the food.

"Let's get you in a gown," another woman's voice informs, gently taking the blanket and t-shirt off, covering my body.

"Please rest sideways. We are going to start with these

wounds," Dr. Lopez's voice says.

Last night lashes cover my entire back and bottom, even the back of my head and arms, it happens while I was protecting the children under me, the reason I couldn't sleep on my back and I woke up as soon as my back touched the mattress before.

"Everything is going to be okey," nurse Wan whispers, holding my hand, when a cold cloth touch my flesh and everything become a blur of the pain.

I take a deep breath and let go, give them the time to clean all my wounds, and cover myself.

CHAPTER FOUR

Samuel

Walking out of the suite I pull a black T-shirt over my head, my mobile rings and Thomas' name pops up on my screen.

"My man! How are you?" he says. I have known him for over ten years. He has worked over the offices, my apartments in London and even in Stella's. "Saw your email, man! That house is a dream come true."

"I need you to start today," I order.

"How about noon? A couple of my boys are in the area. We will come, take pictures, measurements and bring you some materials. How does that sound?" He asks.

"Noon, not a minute later—my nephew is with me." I demand.

I enter the kitchen. Where Scott and Rosita are getting the picnic bag ready for later when my phone rings and Stella's name is on the screen.

"Stella," I greet sharply.

"Oh my God, Samuel, you won't believe it!" She exclaims.

I need to pull the mobile away from my ear to don't end up deaf.

What is wrong with this woman?

"Do you mean it went well?" I ask.

"I found an angel, Samuel. She is perfect, professional, beautiful, and kind. She needs help, and she's helping me." Stella explains.

"How so?" I ask rolling my eyes at her comment.

Something is being planned on her head and it's irritating me, Stella never compliment or speak nice about people, specially other woman.

Thomas arrives before I can find out what she had done.

"This kitchen is amazing, man!" Thomas exclaims, followed by six employees and too much stuff. I knew every single inch of this house would surprise him.

Thomas takes possession of the dining table with all what I send last night while I roll my eyes and whisper *Stella*, making him shake his head.

My sister looks adorable, but it can be a big pain.

"I will help," Rosita murmurs.

I just gesture for the boys to go on with her because I can't leave this call.

"Continue," I order, stepping out into the rear garden.

Let's hear the brilliant plan.

"I paid her twelve thousand pounds for exclusive service." I choke on the water I am drinking.

"What?" I ask, I knew giving her freedom on finances wasn't a great idea, here is why.

What type of party is she organising?

"You should see her ideas, her passion. She would do an

incredible job." She can't stop talking.

Pulling the mobile away, I take a breath and try to listen to her again.

"Oh Samuel! That will send her business to another level, don't you agree?" She asks, while my mind is processing the fortune this lunatic just spent on a ninth birthday for Scott. "When you meet her, you will love her, Samuel, I promise," she keeps talking when I put the mobile back on my ear.

"Very well," I mumble. "It's great news."

"Fantastic..." I hung up ignoring anymore nonsense comments.

I fount Thomas and his employees as they exit what will be the new theatre room. "I can get that finished by Monday," he assures.

We enter my bedroom, and here there is just carpet and walls to be changed.

"I will take measurements. Here are the colours of carpet and walls that match with the rest," he says, giving me a few booklets. "Let's take care of the carpet ASAP, man! This is as old as my grandma," he laughs, making his entire frame shake.

In Scott's room, I request a bigger and more secure window.

We walk to the oval extension. It's the biggest in the house, with perfect light all day, and soon will be my office.

It will take at least a few weeks to be ready, but it will be worth the waiting.

Once we finish with the full tour, I head back to the kitchen to grab the picnic basket.

Thomas is calling for the materials, and employees

needed to take care of the first changes.

Saying my goodbyes to everyone, I follow Scott and Mr Wrinkles.

We just cross the road to enter the park. When I step on the green grass, my entire hair stands on end.

Wow! What was that?.

A tickle runs from my feet to my face, and there's a buzzing in my ears, but the worst is the pressure on my chest.

What is happening to me?

Shaking my head, I try to put away this weird sensation and focus on my nephew and spending time together. But as I focus, Scott is not by my side anymore.

What the fuck have I done?

"Scott!!" I release the leash and start running around like a manic. Panic is blurring my vision. It's impossible for him to have gone far. My heart is in my throat, I'm out of breath, I'm having a panic attack, and I need to focus.

Turning on the spot, I see Mr Wrinkles running towards the lake and then I see Scott. He is feeding the ducks.

He is feeding the fucking ducks?!

I run like my life depends on it, kneeling when I get closer, checking that he is fine, but he looks confused. *Why is he confused?* He is the one who disappeared.

Following the direction of his gaze, I realise he is with other kids. He is trying to make friends, and here I am, all weird and controlling, ruining his moment.

I turn and frown at them.

I've seen those kids before.

A soft hum makes me turn. I freeze when I see her, her snow skin, messy bun, and angelic face. She's here, in front of me—it feels unreal.

She is kneeling, a paper bag full of bird food resting on her lap. "Is this your son?" She asks.

She has a lovely Western accent, but she doesn't focus on me. Her gaze moves around, never stopping.

Is she looking for someone?

I glued my gaze on her, and my throat and brain empty, she looks at me.

Doesn't she recognise me?

That might be as I am wearing a black T-shirt and denim jeans, nothing like my three-piece suit from yesterday and I left my mask at home, as there was nobody to be around with, just Scott.

"He is not my dad, he is my uncle Samuel," Scott says.

I look away and cough, try to focus and find some strength to say something, not prepare for this encounter.

"Nice to meet you. I am..." I mumble. She looks at me and smiles—*gosh that's beautiful smile*—but her gaze is moving around my entire face. "Samuel, Samuel Smith," I say and melt on the spot when she look me directly on the eyes, *she sees me.*

I can't talk. Something is stuck in my throat. I can't move my eyes away from her face, and for some stupid reason, I put out my hand—way too polite, like I wasn't behaving weird already.

She takes it, her fingers brush my palm and my entire body tenses. Our hold gets stronger, our skin melts together.

She looks at our hold—I can see the shock on her face too.

"Uncle Samuel, this is Ruby, Naima and Aidan," Scott says.

She breaks our hold, pulling me back to the present moment—at the park, by the lake, with the children.

"We are out of food kids," she says, shaking her head, avoiding me. "Let's clean our hands and eat something."

When she turns, Mr Wrinkles follows her. This dog will follow anyone at the mention of food.

"Would you like to join us?" She asks, scrubbing the dog behind the ears and letting him leak her cheek. "Well, if your uncle is okay with it," she looks at me again.

"Are you sure?" I ask, but she doesn't answer.

She just guides all the kids to a picnic matt. Resting on her knees, she cleans each of their little hands and faces. Places a plate away from the matt for the dog, and she prepares the food for us.

There are veggies and fruit of many colours, mini pizzas, and lemonade.

"Come on, uncle Samuel." Scott gestures for me to get closer to them. I sit on the grass, resting my basket and the leash on my side, enjoying the fresh air while I look at her.

She is too fucking perfect to be real, the simplest most natural beauty I've ever seen, I can see her gazes travelling around every few seconds.

Are we waiting for someone else?

There is no ring on her long, delicate hands, and I will bet something that there is no man in her life, she wouldn't be looking at me this way if there was one.

"Samuel?" My eyes drop to her fleshy lips, a natural pink,

they are almost red, I lick my dry lips, and my chest contracts at the thought of brushing hers.

An electroshock that starts on my arm makes my entire body shake. When I check where that feeling came from, I see her grip on my arm. Just a gentle squeeze and my entire skin is on fire, I feel alive. Her presence makes me tremble from a distance, but her touch is a pure fire over my skin, my entire body aches.

"Yes?" I ask, moving my eyes from her lips to her eyes.

They are wide open when she moves her hand away and I see when she looks at her palm and hides it, trying to calm the burn we both felt.

"Water or lemonade?" Her sweet voice calls my attention again.

"Lemonade please." She hands it to me with a small smile, making sure our hands don't touch again. I hold it tight with my shaky hands.

"Food?" She asks, we are keeping the conversation at monosyllables, my throat is like a million knifes cutting me with every word, so I just drink and try to hide the discomfort away.

I take a mini pizza that blows me away—I'm floating on the clouds. Heaven is in front of me and an angel is serving me.

"You love mama's food, right?" Naima asks. She looks like Ruby, just a different skin tone but the same incredible blue eyes.

I just nod and smile around the next bite of mini pizza, "this is Spectacular."

Fuck she knows how to cook!

"Do you live around here?" Naima asks.

I just nod, as the paralysis mode also happens with her children.

"Naima," Ruby calls, "focus on your food."

"Do you work around here?" She continues asking.

And to hide my weirdness, I drink all my lemonade at once.

"Uncle Samuel works at a magazine," Scott answers for me.

"What type of magazine?" Naima asks.

Ruby looks away, trying to avoid the matter, that even if we can't talk or don't want to, the children will do.

"Not sure," Scott explains. "There are lots of clothes, jewellery, food, parties, that type of." He has described it perfectly.

"Are you a writer?" Naima asks me.

"No, I am..." I start.

"Mama ball please," Aidan demands means our conversation is over.

She puts the food away and stands, smiling as she runs away with the kids.

"Uncle Samuel! Come on!" Scott calls me, and without thinking it twice, I stand and join the game.

Mr Wrinkle joins us too, what make us become an even game, three against three.

Scott and Naima choose to be the goalkeepers. Aidan runs behind Mr Wrinkles and it's just me against Ruby.

She is better than I would have expected, running around me kicking the ball without mercy, slowing down as she reaches Scott.

"Can we join?" A group of six more children approach us.

"Absolutely!" Ruby exclaims.

Now the game become somewhat even, I clearly suck at this game.

I honestly haven't played in decades, our time at the park normally becomes a light picnic, some walk and back home.

Socialising has never been my strength and helps keeping new people away from me and my privacy.

With this woman I can't do that, she is like a magnet that pull me closer and closer; I believe if I try to run I wouldn't be able, and as much as it hurts, for the first time I want the pain, the agony, the discomfort, I want it all; I need more.

Naima and Scott get replaced by the other children's parents and the teams become bigger and bigger.

Ruby runs around me again, laughing every time I miss taking the ball away from her.

The next time she passes by my side, I follow her, holding her waist, trying to kick the ball away, but Scott comes on to my rescue.

She is laughing on my hold, staring at me, and for an instant the entire world pauses, her head moves back and her gaze is on my lips, mine over her perfectly beautiful face.

I am trembling, my chest is hammering, trying to keep my broken heart in place, sure that she can feel it on her back, same as I can feel her slow breath and pumping throat.

I release her, as I catch the ball passing by the side, I hold her up by the waist again, turning her the opposite way of the ball, rushing behind the kid that is like a professional football player, taking the ball from him and heading to the opposite way.

This time Naima is on my way, she is running to me, as I approach her, just when she could have took the ball away from me, she stops, paralysed, turning pale, and jump away the moment my hand casually brush her shoulder.

"Naima, are you okey?" I ask, nearly resting my palm on her shoulder, but she jumps much further, looking around confused and scared.

"Mama is here," Ruby whisper, rushing to hold her, brushing her palm around her back.

"He... he touched me," Naima whisper.

My palm aches and I understand the mistake I have made. *Why have I touched them?*

I turn to found Scott having the best time, if wasn't for that, we will walk home right now.

Avoiding what just happen, I walk back to the matt and take a seat facing the game, Mr Wrinkles by my side and I just focus on the calm water of the lake, on Scott running back and forth, while I scratch the dog behind the ears.

Ruby did the same the first time I touched her back in London. She jumped away.

I thought was what that touch created to our bodies, but now I see it was more a mechanism of self-defence.

What happen to this family?

Minutes later, they join the others. Their expression has

changed, and they are playing as if nothing has just happened.

This creature awakens to many things on me I never knew could be alive again, a part of me is hungry for more, but another wants to run away from it.

I can't let her influence me, make me week, with her I can't hold the mask everyone is used to.

CHAPTER FIVE

Ruby

Who is this guy? He shows up out of nowhere, could not put three words together, doesn't stop staring at me, and has taken any advantage possible to get any physical contact with me.

For the first time, I don't feel uncomfortable about being touched, not like the kids at least. Would that be because of Samuel? Or because my soul has healed?

A part of me knows him—I just can't remember from where.

"Mama, I'm exhausted," Aidan says, asking to be carried.

Leaving the game, I walk back to the matt, letting the kids finish the game, and placing Aidan on the grass near the matt, looking at the ducks and swans pass by.

Samuel is at the matt with the dog, his gaze burning my pale skin.

Is he not going to look away?

My hands are shaking, my heart is hitting my chest on a painful way, but I have never felt it more alive.

Advik broke me in so many ways that there were little or none feelings left after they took him away, but this man, he is playing some kind of game, one that my body might enjoy, but my brain is warning me to run away from.

I try to pack everything as quick as possible, feeling guilty of taking the kids away on such a rush, but if he isn't going, I will.

My focus is more on packing frantically, that I almost drop the lemonade jar as my hand turns into flames.

What in the hell is that?

Samuel is holding it too, he moves closer until our palms are on top of each other. The heat of his skin on mine feels like our hands are melting and becoming one.

I look up—he is staring at me, and is when my entire body turn on fire, my flesh turn pink and even if I can't see me, I am sure my cheeks are as red as a heat that is burning my entire being.

You are absolutely delicious!

Samuel move closer and I can smell him—eucalyptus and mint, hypnotizing me, I gasp when his fingertip brush my jaw, up my cheek and my head rest on his palm, closing my eyes and absolutely melting on this stranger touch again.

That feels so good!

He moves the jar away and I open my eyes, my lips are dry, and I brush my tongue over them, catching how Samuel's eyes travel all the way there, copying me and biting his full irresistible lips, I moan slightly.

I can't stop peeking at him. He is unquestionably handsome. His hair is a beautiful mess of dark waves, thick eyebrows enhance his eyes. They are bright like mine; I have a shade of gray, his are turquoise, almost green. His stubble makes him more masculine, and absolutely irresistible.

What the hell is wrong with me?

I might control my brain, but my body is dancing a different song, my hands aren't shaking much now, but I can't get my lung to breathe steady, and when I exhale sharply, I can see the corner of that delicious lips slightly rising.

I caught him smiling a lot today, a perfect white smile, but something has him tense now, making him keep those perfect lips in a straight line.

"I need to go," I whisper—at this distance he has heard me.

I stand way faster than I should, but this situation is playing a dangerous game with me, I must run away from him.

I walk back to the bike and place everything back in the carrier, unexpectedly turning, hitting my face on his hard chest.

Gosh is he made of rock?

He is so close—holding the back of my arms so I won't fall, my breath hitting his chest and his heart is beating so fast I can feel it through the material of his T-shirt.

But his fingers brush my jaw. I pull my head back and look straight at him.

He is so beautiful my eyes hurt!

His hand moves to my nape, brushing my flesh and playing with my hair with his fingertips, pulling a moan out of my raspy throat. The other hand caress my arm, down my hips until he holds me low on my back.

My hands hold his hard muscly biceps, pulling him closer, he slightly hold me higher until I rest on my tiptoes, leveling up the different on height.

Our chests rise together, my palms brush around his arms, around his shoulders until they slightly brush his stubble, his breath hit me and a scent of cinnamon make me dizzy, holding his nape for stability.

"Who are you?" I whisper, almost brushing his lips. My entire body is loose. If he wasn't holding me, I would fall. His lips part, his breath on my face, my fingers playing with his waves and the entire world pause on this beautiful man arms.

"Mama," Aidan's slow voice throws me off heaven back to reality.

Slowly resting me on the shaky legs, he steps away; I take a well-needed breath of fresh air, just brush my hair, as if something was out of place, and fix my shirt—just nervous, not knowing what to do.

He looks me straight in the eyes—he looks tense, nibbling his delicious lip, making me tremble slightly more, my body is screaming for him already.

Gosh I need to run away!

"Can we walk you home?" He asks.

My mouth wants to say no, but before I say it, I have already nodded.

God damn you Ruby!

"Mama, ready to go?" Naima asks, helping Aidan to get into the carrier, Scott is ready with his dog by the side.

I finish putting things back on the carrier and Naima announces she just wants to walk with Scott and the dog.

We walk across the park on the way to our apartment. As we approach the hill, Samuel offers to push the bike and I agree.

"How long have you been living here?" He asks.

"Six months," I say.

"Liking the neighbourhood?" he asks.

"It's a fresh start. The people are nice."

"Seems a good family neighbourhood," he agrees.

"It's safe, with excellent schools and nice green areas," I say.

"It's looks better than the city, that's for sure," he says.

He lives in the city? I stop talking for a moment. Looking back at him, exactly when my brain functions properly and I remember, he is *tour guide*! I knew I had seen him before.

"The city, the buildings, the vibe, being able to find anything—that is incredible," I say. "One day I want to hire a tour guide and do a proper visit." His eyes open wider. "Do you know any?"

He won't answer. He just looks away, avoiding my gaze.

"I know what you mean. I grow up there, but always loved the countryside more, so when my sister found this location, I didn't think twice and found a place around here too."

"Are you planning to stay?" I ask.

"I have an extensive project to finish in the city next week and my house is under renovation here. Then, I'm moving my office here and I'll be able to spend more time around Scott."

He's looking at me.

"The place I bought needs a lot of renovations," he confirms.

Before I can ask any more questions, we arrive at the

crossroads of my apartment. We always been grateful to be so close to the park until now.

"This is our place," Naima says, while she holds my hand to cross over.

"Any help with the bike?" Samuel asks, already placing it by the wall.

"We will be fine. Thanks Samuel, bye Scott," I say, helping down Aidan and taking the picnic matt and basket out of the carrier.

"Are we going to see you again?" Scott asks.

"Maybe at the park another time," I say, looking everywhere but at Samuel, I can feel his eyes burning my skin.

"Uncle Samuel will take me to the park at the same time tomorrow," Scott says.

Is he trying to set up us to meet again?

"Am I?" Asks Samuel. Scott punches his leg, and I can't help but smile. "I am!" He exclaim.

"Well, I have an order I need to work on with so many things to buy." I say. Scott's face drops. "If I get it all done on time, we might pop in for a bit."

"Mum rides to the store after the bridge, and buys as many things as we can fit on the bike," Naima says. "It will take us all day," she answers, making me feel guilty.

"You go grocery shopping on the bike with the kids?" Samuel asks, looking alarmed. I know is not the safest situation but I have no choice.

"Well, I don't have another option," I say. We don't have buses around here, and a taxi will cost a fortune.

"He will drive you!" Scott says before Samuel can even

express his opinion.

These kids are making all the decisions for us. They need to stop talking and making this situation harder.

"I could take you," he offers, looking straight at me.

Unable to tell what's going on in that beautiful head of his, I need to be logical—we met a few hours ago. My body might assume he is harmless, but my brain is working on a different level.

"We will be fine." I say looking back at him with questioning eyebrows.

Is he for real?

"I guess if you ride it will take a few days to shop; take my offer and it will be a one-day thing," he says stepping closer, my shaky legs won't hold me for longer.

Scott's hands are in a praying position, and my kids are quiet, but I can see their expressions. We are tired of the daily long, heavy shopping rides.

"I don't have car seats," I say excusing myself.

"I will figure that out," he argues back.

Come on, Ruby think!

One last look into his eyes and I am lost, unable to fight anymore, I am already in agony to think he will be gone in minutes.

"8 a.m. here." I say, pointing to the little path in front of our door.

"Done!" He says, giving a little excitement jump that makes me giggle. "Until tomorrow, kids." A full, beautiful, pure, and genuine smile builds on his already perfect face.

"Ruby," he murmurs.

That's when my legs lose the battle, and I need to hold myself on the bike. He knows what he has done, and his smile grows, reaching his eyes, they bright up and I absolutely melt on the spot.

Gosh this man!

I turn to the house and start placing everything in the kitchen, while thinking about what has just happened.

"Are you okay, mama?" I can't stop moving around. "Mama?!" Naima makes me jump out of my thoughts.

"Yes, I'm fine baby," I say. It's not a full lie, because a part of me never been better. "Why don't you wash your hands? Dinner will be ready in a few minutes."

"Samuel and Scott are nice," Naima comments, washing her hands at the kitchen sink.

I turn and serve their plates, so naïve to think I would avoid this conversation with my smart daughter.

"They are, right?" I answer, trying to sound relaxed, taking a seat at the dining table and working on my shopping list.

My hands continue shaking every time Samuel memories come to me, or I think I will see him in few hours.

The monster been keeping me awake for months, but now I have an extra reason to don't sleep—the irresistible Samuel.

It might be a small party, but Stella made it clear she had high standards.

I can't go to my regular stores. Pulling my mobile out, I find a nearby store with the best brands on the market for materials.

A quick search and I get the store where every delicatessen

patisserie purchases their ingredients.

And last, the regular grocery stores, for any extra ingredient that I might need and of course my weekly groceries.

After a quick shower, the children are in bed ready to sleep while I prepare tomorrow's clothes, way more attentive than usual about what will I wear.

May it be because Samuel will be with us?

He wakes this unknown sensation in me that calls my curiosity, but I remember what happened the last time I got curious about something.

I was a child, hidden away, begging for something I have regretted for the past decade.

But Samuel's soul is as damage as mine, he might look like has it all under control, but I've seen the emptiness in his turquoise magnetic eyes. That is something you earn when you get broken in million pieces and lose yourself.

With the time I learned how to put my mask on, how to wear this façade, one that everyone adore, a perfect contagious smile, all while I am an empty shell floating around the world, searching for my place.

If I didn't have my kids, I wouldn't be here today. They need me, a new me, someone stronger, powerful, indestructible.

And today, an over six-foot man has trembled under a simple touch. I made his heart stop only by being close.

Observing myself in the mirror, there isn't anger in me

anymore, or fright. Just a spark, a small light trying to fight the darkness that surrounds me.

Walking back to the bathroom, I place the kids towels on the rack and take a shower. I wash away the heat that the thought of Samuel builds up in me.

Grab some comfy clothes and head back to the kitchen. There are dishes to wash, a breakfast to prepare, and cookies for the local stores to get ready for Monday, as tomorrow evening I will be busy with Stella's tasting on Monday.

If I get to all the stores on time, we won't be back until late afternoon—*Gosh!* That means I will have to get dinner ready too.

By eleven I'm in bed, looking at the ceiling, but I'm only thinking about Samuel.

The first time I saw him in London, focused on the children. My head was a blur with the situation at court, but for a second the entire world stopped and I looked at him, wearing a stunning suit, looking all polished and perfect.

His expression sad when he looked at me, but I thought he'd just watched someone else passing by, but today I understood he was staring at me.

Everything changed at that instant at the traffic light. When we laughed, we touched, he pushed the world away from us.

This afternoon in the park, *gosh he is breathtaking*, it isn't because of what he wears—it is the way how he moves, the way he looks at me, how his body reacts under my touch, and the way my body reacts under his.

At 4 a.m. I am done with my shower. My clothes are on and I am finishing the croissants I started last night, as well as the lasagne for dinner.

I have fresh coffee and orange juice for the kids. I serve myself a strong mug and head to the garden, at the best time—dawn.

Just there, letting the sunlight fight between the houses until the town come back to life.

I walk back and find Aidan dancing in the bed, without music, just following Naima's laugh and claps.

Haven't seen them this relaxed and cheerful before. My heart stops and assembles pieces together before hammering back on my chest.

"Good morning," I say from the door, unable to hide my own silly smile.

"Zopppiiinnngg!" Aidan says, making me laugh this time at the horrible trouble he is having with S and Z.

Miguel says it's a transition. I love it anyway; it's his own language.

Helping them get dressed, I guide them to the kitchen, sit them by the island and serve them juice.

I check the timer. Any minute now, it will ring, and we will enjoy it before Samuel arrives. He might be in a rush.

Someone like him has better things to do on a Sunday than taking a mother and her children grocery shopping.

"Mama, you look pretty today," Naima says in between bites.

"Thanks baby," I say, readjusting my top.

"I don't mean the clothes," she assures.

Making me stop for a second, raising my gaze and understanding.

Yes, something in me has changed.

Yesterday awaken an unknown aspect I haven't experienced before.

CHAPTER SIX

Ruby
Fifteen years ago, Shepperton, TX

The phone rings while I'm on the porch brushing my riding boots. After the heavy rain last night, it was a muddy ride.

Mom is stitching my trousers. It's the third time in two weeks. *What do you expect when you keep falling?* I'm so clumsy they have to forgive me for life.

Dad calls me to let me know it is for me. Who could call?

It's Lisa, my neighbor from the farm next to us. We met months ago at the store—same age, raised in the same way, I guess is the only way around here, home schooled, with few or no friends or relationships with anyone other than our animals, and the owners of the stores we visit to stock up.

I feel my parents just want to keep me hidden, locked away from the outside world, like it will harm me, but Lisa has been out. She told me all these stories—I didn't even know we have restaurants and bars around.

"Hey Lisa," I say, cleaning up my hands with a dry cloth.

"Ruby!!" I pull the telephone away. "There's a party tonight." I move out of the kitchen where dad is reading his newspaper and having some coffee.

"You know I can't," I say. I would love to go out, but dad will never allow it.

"You will never leave if you never ask." She is right.

"I will call you back." He is in a good mood today, after Olivia, our youngest cow, gave birth last night.

I take a few deep breaths as I return to the kitchen.

"Dad, can I talk to you?" He raises his nose away from the paper and softens his face.

"Everything okay Ruby?" He asks.

I take a seat on his side, moving away the boiling coffee, just in case he gets mad and by accident drops it.

"Was Lisa, the neighbor?" I am trying to make it clear just in case he asks.

"Joseph's daughter, yes, very polite girl," he nods like he's agreeing with himself.

Dad has been multiple times to their farm over the years. They are the sellers of goat's milk, my specialty goat soap bars. I needed a hobby and an excuse to meet Lisa often. We sell each other's milk, artisan, pastries, anything.

"She would like to take me to the local bar." I nibble my bottom lip, nervous about it, and he just puts the paper away, trying to listen.

"You want to go out?" *Is he asking or affirming?*

"I've never been out, and since you know her, I thought you'll be content with it." Keep it cool Ruby.

"I don't think you'd be interested in that type of thing." *Is he serious?* The furthest I've been is Mrs. and Mr. Johnson store.

"I think it will be a good way for me to socialize." I don't want to upset him.

"You will be restless, I need you, especially now that we have a new calf." He is right, but I'd rather tired tomorrow than lose this opportunity.

"You are right," I say. He nods and smiles. He loves when I tell him that. "But I promise I will catch up on work. You won't feel any difference."

"Trust me daughter, you will feel it," he says.

He's not threating me, just warning me I am not yet aware of what is coming my way.

"Let me try once, and for ne—"

"No daughter, there is no next time. It will be enough for you to know that you aren't ready." And that is a firm statement. I better prove him wrong, enjoy the night and work hard tomorrow.

"Thank you, dad," I just smile a little. "I will call Lisa back."

I get out of the kitchen, taking the phone with me, so I can hide away from him, though it's not like he couldn't hear me.

She answers, waiting for my call back. "Tell me you are coming." She is desperate to go out.

"What time I should be ready?" She just giggles in response.

"One hour, wear something nice. There's a new band in town." What does she mean? I have no nice clothes. I'm a farm girl.

At 7 p.m., I'm walking in circles in my room, pulling down

the old flower dress Mom let me borrow, and my boots are hitting the wooden floor harder than usual.

The excitement and nerves of what will happen tonight are keeping me anxious, Lisa should be here any minute.

I listen to the rough beeping from Lisa's dad's truck and I run to the porch. She's waving her arms, calling me to get in the truck ASAP.

Walking back inside the house, I find Mom tidying up the dinner dishes. I give her a squeeze and a deep kiss on her chubby cheek.

"Te quiero mama." She just giggles and continues with her things.

Dad went to check on the animals and met me on the porch. "Have fun." He tries to smile, but he can't.

"I love you, dad." I just drop a kiss on his cheek and head to the truck.

"Are you ready for the best night of your life?" There's her mischievous laugh. She is such a naughty girl compared to me.

We drive for ten minutes before we reach a building on the side of the road. It has so many lights—you see it from miles away. The music is loud and gets louder every time someone opens the door.

Lisa parks at the entrance, and we jump out.

I feel more nervous than I should. Once I hear the music, something wakes up in me, making me feel different—alive.

This is better than I imagine. It's like the movies.

People are everywhere chatting and drinking, some people dance, especially couples.

The lady from the bar is announcing a new band. They are

all wearing cowboy clothes. The singer has a guitar, and he plays a few notes, tuning it.

Lisa finds a small table with two dark wooden chairs in front of the dance floor, at the center of the stage, so we can watch the band.

Giggling when the singer winks at her.

"Do you know him?" She has been here multiple times, so it wouldn't surprise me.

"I meet him a few weeks ago," she says and a pink blush brightens up her face. "He walked me to the truck and kissed me."

She already kissed a boy? Well, more like a man, that country boy looks at least twenty.

"He has a cute friend we want you to meet." She sighs.

"We came to hear the band, right?" I've never met a boy, never talked to one either.

"Hello Shepperton!" The singer greets everyone, nodding at the rest of the band.

He plays the guitar, a lovely melody, it makes me smile.

Everyone cheers, he sings, and when everyone is getting tune with the lyrics, he stops and says, "This is for you," looking at Lisa and winking at her.

That makes me blush too. He is into her. I hope this doesn't mean they will leave me behind, alone.

After a few songs, the band goes for a break and join us at our table. The singer sits by Lisa's side, dropping his arm over her shoulders, kissing her cheek, and saying something in her ear that makes her blush.

The keyboard guy comes in with a tray full of food, many unknown things. There's a drink called a milkshake.

Gosh! That tastes good.

Everyone chats about a tour they are preparing for the summer—they will cover the entire southeast coast.

They speak of places I've only read about in my books—my dreamy head can't help but wonder how magnificent would feel to travel, pack a bag, and leave for months—to see other people, other towns.

"Girls, join us!" The singer says, "we have space for two more." I laugh so hard everyone turns their heads to me.

It makes me feel weird, but if getting out a few hours was hard, imagine asking my dad for a full summer on the road. That is not happening.

I stand, searching for the toilet, trying to avoid explaining why I found that hilarious.

The line is long; it seems like they are taking a lifetime. Mumbling the song that someone has put on the machine. I miss the guy in front of me. He is in line as well.

"Seems like someone drinks the entire bar, right?" *He is asking me?* I just look back at him, surprised.

"Pardon?" He laughs a little and gives me a cute smile.

He is not from around here. He has a dark brown skin, light brown eyes, a beautiful white smile, and a charming attitude.

"I was saying they are taking too long." There is his cute smile again.

"Yes! They are." I feel awkward, like a lost person.

"Are you from around here?" I wonder if it will be safe to

tell him where I come from?

"You aren't, right?" Let's just turn the conversation around.

"I come from India." I look shocked.

"Wow, that's far." Another beautiful country I've read a lot about, but I'm not sure I will ever visit.

"I'm in America as a backpacker."

"Sorry, as what?"

He simper and shakes his head. Someone would find it rude—I find it cute.

"I left my country, came to America, and move around the entire country with my backpack." He is very lucky. "I sleep in my tent sometimes, other times in road motels. It's the best way to know a country and culture."

"That sounds incredible, I nev... well... you know... farm life."

"You are a cowgirl!" He sounds delighted at that. "I guess you love the animals and quiet life."

"I've never known better," I answer, raising my shoulders.

"What do you mean?" He gives me a cute frown. "You've never left Shepperton?"

"No, I never left my farm until today." He looks back at me in shock, but moves his head and softens up his expression.

"You will love what I do. It's cheap, exciting, challenging." It sounds like it, but dad will never let me go.

Avoiding his comment, I appreciate when the girl in front of me leaves the toilet, so I go in.

When I leave, he is gone. The singer and Lisa are missing. Our table is empty.

I panic and run back to the exit, just to realize her truck is also gone. Unable to believe she would have done these to me.

We are miles away from home in the middle of nowhere.

But I guess walk will be the only option to get home. Under no circumstances I will accept any stranger to take me home.

I try to replay the trip in my head, all the turns we made. We did a left first. I walk away from the pavement, but close enough to don't fall down on anything, I march home.

I got to the intersection after twenty minutes of walking.

That means now is a right turn. I am about to keep going when I see a movement between the corn. I'm not an easy to scare girl, but I've also never been alone in the middle of nowhere.

Trying to hide, I keep walking on the opposite side of the road, as fast as I can, wanting to get home as soon as possible.

But I wasn't fast enough. The corn moves closer and closer. I see someone crossing from behind as it catches up with me. I speed up, but it's way faster.

"Wait!" I run, but whoever is around me is way faster. "Hello? Please stop!"

I can't stop. I need to get out of here. Once I reach the end of the road, I'm lost. The panic doesn't let me think.

I turn left and don't stop running. After what seems like a lifetime, there they are, the lights from my farm. I can hear my cows, so as a safe choice I reach the top of the fence and jump on. I'm in my field and I know where I'm going.

"Hello?! Toilet girl???"

Gosh, is it the boy from the toilet?

"I need your help."

"You need to leave. This is a private property!" I won't get anywhere near the fence or that guy.

"Someone stole my backpack!" It might be the truth and I might have been mean to someone who needs help, but I can't risk it.

"What do you want from me?" I have nothing for him.

I could run the fields blindfolded and be fine.

"Can I borrow your mobile? I will try to get a lift somewhere."

"I don't have a mobile!" I've heard of them but never owned one.

"Someone you can call?" I will most definitely not be calling my dad to give him a lift.

"Sorry, but you have to leave." I order.

"Can I get something to eat? They took all my money, too." Gosh, he is making it harder to not help him, but something tells me I shouldn't.

"Wait away from the fence!" I get into the barn, grab some milk and bread.

I put it in a bag and walk towards the fence.

"I'm gonna leave a bag at the fence, step away. I will let you know when you can take it." If he doesn't follow my directions, there's nothing for him.

I put it around the post so he can grab it.

"You can take it now." I say, step back.

To be honest, I've just done my kindness commitment, so I step away, going back home. He should be on his way soon.

After a good six hours' sleep, I wake up before anyone else, run for a shower, and get my working clothes on as soon as possible.

I'm already in the barn by the time dad comes in with his hot cup of coffee in his hand, surprised to find me getting the next order of soaps ready for the Johnsons. I replaced the milk, and well, I guess nobody will realized about the bread.

By 6 a.m. I'm around the stables, making sure I feed Moon and Dalia, letting them free for a while and cleaning the stalls.

When I reach the last stall, I come to an abrupt stop. In the hidden corner, I see boots dirty, old, black boots.

Tiptoeing, I grab the shovel and open the stall door. Whoever is there doesn't move—I raise the shovel, but stop. I recognize the clothes, and when I check closer also the face, it's toilet guy!

I just kick his boots with my riding boots, making him shake and wake up.

"What are you doing here?" I ask, holding up the shovel.

"I found this place." He sounds tired and anxious.

CHAPTER SEVEN

Samuel

My forearms and forehead rest on the wall of the shower while I run some cold water, trying to wash away all my thoughts and sweat.

I have this pressure on my chest that won't let me breathe.

In the sink, I rest my hands. My head is low and heavy.

And when I check in the mirror, I see it. I'm nervous, scared, and excited. I'm not imagining things. She can't breathe near me either. She shakes in my presence, too.

But I can't have her, everyone around me suffers, my darkness will pull her to a place she doesn't want to be.

And by what I saw and experience yesterday, they have been through enough, the only way to protect them is to run in the opposite direction.

Scott push all of this to a hard to avoid corner, my head wasn't focus, my entire being was acting the complete opposite that it should, I will do what I promised, take them for shopping, avoid her gaze, touch, presence and never see her again.

I will have to spend the rest of the week in the city anyway, perfect excuse to avoid any encounter or after school visit to the park.

Closing the last button of my black shirt I head downstairs, ready to leave, unable to wait here any longer.

Rosita is at the bottom of the stairs, I can see a small smile on her lips, opening her arms as I approach her.

She can't be content with this?

There is nothing good coming out of this.

"Show that lady who Samuel Smith is. Open your heart, *mi hijito*. It's time," she whispers in my ear, brushing her palm over my broken heart.

At 7:30 a.m., I park at Ruby's door, so nervous I couldn't wait at home any longer.

The car seats are in place with the help of the delivery guy. I step out and start a frenetic walk back and forth on the pathway.

With a clear head, I observe the building, this is not a normal apartment building, this is council building, on one of my walk back, a shiny plate calls my attention, confirming this is a '**Women aid centre**,' she is here hiding away, and this proves it.

From what are you hiding Ruby?

Resting back on the car, I realise there are no windows at the front of her flat.

Should I knock?

A deep breath and I march with all my confidence to her door, leaving my hand suspending on the thin air when her face pops out of the door—like she knows I'm here. She gestures for me to come in, my foot glued to the ground in shock, I was so naïve, absolutely not ready to see her again.

I jog the door and a delicious scent welcomes me. It's like her—wildflowers and a bakery.

I follow her through the door on the left wall. An open space with a little dark green couch in the corner. She has covered it with a colourful blanket that makes it cosier, and a dining table sits in the opposite corner with three spots.

The kitchen is not a massive space. There are herbs everywhere, colourful bowls of fruit, and jars of every size and shape. A glass door leads to the garden.

"Good morning, Samuel," Naima and Aidan welcome me in unison.

"Breakfast?" Ruby asks, holding a plate full of croissants while her attention is over an extremely long list on her delicate fingers.

I realise how beautiful she looks today—her mane is down, beautiful wavy dark brown hair, so long it passes under her hips.

She is wearing a pretty floral off the shoulder top, a long green wrap skirt which matches the colours of her top, making her skin brighter.

Fuck me, she is gorgeous, if perfection need a human shape it will be this woman.

My chest hurts in a deeper way than the other times, it's like if my broken soul is attaching pieces, and God damn it's a sweet torture.

A soft cough gets my attention, her soft forehead covered by a sweet frown, *woman you are a fucking angel!*

"Won't say no to an espresso." I try to smile while grabbing a croissant.

When I eat it, the room spins around and my tongue melts, as my body did under her touch, "this is Spectacular"

"There you go," she says. "We are ready."

She turns around and starts playing with the pen in her fingers, whispering the list bitting the pen—*woman you better stop the torture!*—she moves her hair forward and plait it.

Naima and Aidan are eating on the kitchen island, looking good, too. She is wearing a floral top with a denim dungaree and he is with brown shorts and a yellow T-shirt—I feel overdressed with my denim jeans and black shirt.

"Just Tesco's?" I ask, finishing my coffee and leaving the mug on the sink. Ruby turns and her cheeks blush with my question—*Fuck me, she looks even more beautiful with that natural pink shade on her cheeks*—"over one store," I say, nodding while I finish my croissant.

At 8 a.m. we are leaving the apartment, Aidan rushes to hold my hand and I can see something is making him nervous, approaching the car, it becomes clearer that getting into the car is creating these feelings over him.

I turn to face him and go to my haunches—I learned with Scott that visual contact, and to explain things step by step is important.

"Do you see this car big boy?" I ask, and he nods. "It's mine. Inside there are two car seats. One is blue, and the other is pink with flowers." His head tilts. "We will help you up and drive to the store."

I try to caress his arm, but he turns to the side avoiding my touch.

"I'm sorry," I say.

My hand drops to the floor. He jumps on me and gives me the tightest hug I've ever experienced in my life.

When I search for Ruby, she looks away, avoiding my gaze. I can see tears filling her eyes, but she tries to push them away.

Naima's head is on Ruby's hip, sad, unable to look straight at us neither.

I knew someone has hurt them, but not how much. The kids are frightened of being close to anyone, to be touched, making even more clearly what happened yesterday at the game.

Saying nothing else, I rise and carry Aidan to the car. He holds me tight. Ruby follows me with Naima closely.

We sit the kids in their brand-new car seats. They are way happier than five minutes ago—I try to enjoy the situation, knowing that somehow I'm making their life somewhat better.

But that changes nothing, this is a bigger reason to push them away from my life, I realise we are four broken, hurt souls.

I start the car, making the kids giggle, nervous for what is coming. When I try to move the gear lever the back of my hand brushes Ruby's skirt, but she doesn't move.

My eyes move from our contact to her eyes. She is looking at me, her lips parted and her breath is slow, proving I was right; she feels the same way I do.

You can't react to me, you shouldn't!

We drive in silence—she checks on them every once in a while, resting her palm on my arm while she does.

I'm not sure she understands what she's doing. My entire body is on fire. I try to stay focused on the road, but it is getting difficult.

After following her directions, we arrive at a local party decoration store. The front window is full of balloons, cake stands, banners—anything you might need for a party. It's a crowded road, but I find a parking on the side road.

"Let's start the shopping," I cheer at the kids, not sure why I'm so excited, because I am not the one doing my grocery shopping. Rosita does.

Ruby gets out of the car and starts taking Naima down. I help with Aidan, placing him by my side.

"Hug," Aidan says, and his little arms keep pointing up, asking me to hold him again. "Please hug."

I hold him in my arms, and a huge smile of triumph grows on his little face.

"Aidan, you need to walk baby," Ruby says.

"I'm fine Ruby." Her cheeks turning pink, as she nibbles her bottom lip. She can't keep her eyes on mine for over two seconds.

"I think we should go," she whispers, shaking her head. She turns around and starts walking towards the store.

Minutes later I am pushing a little trolley with one hand, and the other continues holding Aidan.

There are cake stands, paper of different materials and colours, multiple balloons, table cloths and goody bags.

Ruby and Naima are holding hands while picking up new tools. I don't know where she will put all of this stuff in that small apartment.

"Almost done," she says, giving me a cheeky smile, knowing I'm out of my comfort zone.

I might want this woman out of my life for her best, but never out of my pathetic brain, pulling my mobile out I capture her angelic face, her gorgeous backside, every single angle she gives me access to.

After an hour of Ruby explaining what she needs each item for, we are done.

As we arrive at the till, I place Aidan in the kid's seat, forcing him to rest his head on his arms as he is asleep. Naima is scrubbing her eyes too.

I put everything on the counter and packed it with my shaking hands under Ruby close supervision, as she is holding Naima on the arms.

Taking Aidan back on my arms, I head back to the car, I can't breathe and I need the fresh air immediately.

Ruby places Naima in her seat and moves close to me and do the same with Aidan.

Once the kids are secure and comfortable in their seats, she joins me at the trunk where I was unloading the bags.

I sense how uncomfortable she is, taking the trolley away while I tidying the trunk—that gives me five seconds to breathe fresh air, but she return faster than I can get my trembling frame to calm.

I thought she will sit in the car, but she joins me, stepping way too close, her delicate palm resting on my forearm and pulling her head back to look into my eyes.

"Before I forget, thank you so much for this amazing day." She whispers, blushing under her words.

I push a strip of hair that has fallen out of her braid behind her ear, letting my fingertips follow all the way down her neck, over her collarbone, through her throat, drawing a fire line over her jaw and resting on her cheek, observing how she trembles under my touch—her face moves with my hand, I hold her waist with my other arm and pull her up, our noses touch, her hands resting on my biceps.

"You are more than welcome," I say, letting my breath brush her pink flesh.

What are you doing Samuel?

Her holds release my arms and brushing my shoulders, tickle my neck and I close my eyes when her nails play with my stubble, my entire body is on fire and a soft moan leave her delicious lips when her core meet my hardness—*I need to stop this, before is too late.*

One hand moves to my nape and holds my hair, while the other moves from my jaw to my lips, they are apart and my tongue lick her fingertips, my hair receive the first and most delicious pull and a deeper moan leaves her throat, resting my forehead on hers, I turn her and place her on the trunk, myself in between her thighs and I open my eyes.

Too fucking late!

I pull her closer, her groin meet my arousal and her lips

devour mines.

There is no warning, no reaction, our tongues are on a personal fight, her lips are softer and way more delicious that I could imagine, my hips roll, her back arch and my waves receive another pull.

But my entire world pause when she pulls back—*I need more!*—She looks into my eyes and I understand it's not them been pull into my darkness, it's me falling on the deepest, darkest hole, one where she will torture, enjoy me and use me to climb up, leaving me underground broken and hidden for life, but it will be the sweetest punishment.

Take me there Ruby!

Our forehead join, we caress each other, when a crazy driver honk at us. "Move the fucking car!" He shouts.

I take a deep breath, drop a soft kiss on her nose and lower her. After closing the trunk, I guide her to the passenger door and I walk to mine, ready to continue the shopping adventure.

As I start the car and change the gear, Ruby takes my hand and places them between us.

Our fingers play with each other, we both smile, she is making me behave in this unknown persona, but fuck it, never felt better, I can't remember the last time I grin to the smallest gesture as it's holding hands.

"Next exit, turn left twice," she says, her voice low, different. It's a delicious sound, one that I'm creating.

We arrive in Tesco's car park, empty on the early Sunday morning, we will have to wait at least an hour.

One hour with Ruby in the smallest space we are sharing?

My throbbing cock is screaming for freedom, *no I can't.*

I find a family parking space in a hidden spot. *Bravo Samuel, make it any easier.* As I stop the motor, Ruby moves her spare hand over my jaw, making me face her.

We are in darkness, but I can see her, her head resting on her seat, observing me.

Sick of the middle seat compartment that has been breaking our closeness for long enough, I pull her towards my seat, and place her on top of me.

I push my seat back, making sure we don't disturb the kids in the back.

My entire body is shaking, my palms are resting on her thighs and hers over my chest, playing with the fabric around the buttons, *game over Samuel!*

This might be one of the craziest things I ever done in my life, but I can't stay away from her anymore.

I push her skirt higher and hold her hips, pulling her closer and closer.

Feeling dizzy and alive, especially when her groin meets my hardness. My breath is slow, my hands hold her tighter, and she fists the back of my hair, her forehead rests on mine, biting her bottom lip when a deep moan leave her throat.

I hold her nape and pull her to my mouth, devouring her delicious lips, leaving her breathless moving to her neck, licking, biting and sucking her flesh until I meet her lobe, her entire body trembles and a deeper pull of my hair and moan on my ear answer my question.

But I need to ask, "are you sure?"

"Samuel..." she moan as my breath blow her flesh on her

sensitive flesh around her ear.

"Answer Ruby," I pressure, licking her neck and receiving another pull of my hair, I rise my hips and her head fall on my shoulder hiding a deeper moan, "you just have to answer," I order.

I pull her head up and force her to look at me, her lips are moist, her eyes glassy with lust, her breath broken and her heart nearly leaving her chest.

Without an answer I move my palms on the outside of her thighs, all the way to her knickers, brushing my fingertips over her soft, round, killing bum, her back curls and her clit brush my cock.

"I can give you more," I assure her on a cocky voice, "I just need an answer."

My tongue brush my bottom lip, desperate for some moist, for her taste.

I see how her eyes follow my tongue trace and her hips push forward again, moaning and biting her lip to keep it low, I can't resist any longer, I push myself forward, hold her nape slightly harder that I intend it, but I can see on her eyes she actually liked it, "answer the question Ruby," I murmur on her lips, pushing her bum lower and giving her a harder rotation of my hips, holding her head in place as she try to let it follow the curl of her spine.

"I want more," she whisper on my lips, I growl in acceptance and kiss her—raw, carnal, our tongues are fighting.

Our bodies rock on each other, sending me to a new level of pleasure. I want her as much as she wants me, and I'm not willing to let her go.

My hands work their way under her top, making her back arch under my touch, while her fingers work on my buttons, as she finishes, she opens it, exposing my a chest.

But she doesn't break out the kiss. Her fingers caress my chest and abdomen, continuing until she reaches the waist of my jeans.

I hold her hips harder, my entire body tenses, and our kiss speeds up, nibbling her bottom lip.

She undoes my belt, buttons, and zipper quickly. Her fingertips hold the waistband of my boxers and pull it away, exposing my hard as rock cock.

Embracing it she expands the drop of cum resting on the head around, this is the best torture I ever experienced, her long fingers curls around my throbbing erection and start working me, slow, precise, and firm.

My fingertips leave the previous game with her knickers and move under the soft fabric, pushing it aside, brushing my fingertips around her flesh and feeling how her skin becomes alive, until I reach her entrance and feel how wet she is, *perfectly ready for me.*

My heart and middle finger brush her arse, entrance and clit making her back curl, but she pushes her hips back, what gives me a better access.

I can feel how wet she is becoming just by the softest touch on her clit, getting ready for me, until a drop fall on my palm, followed by a deep moan hidden on my lips.

Spreading her wetness around her entrance, I introduce my fingers painfully slowly. Her walls squeeze and suck them, making my hardness grow.

I draw circles inside her, my thumb massaging her perineum and my index and pinky brush on her labia.

We catch each other pace, in my head I am inside her, thrusting her while she melts under me, her holds become steady and harder her walls pull me closer.

After a few more slow movements, her movements speed up, and so does mine, holding her nape I force her to look at me, dying a million times when I see her eyes.

She won't last longer and neither do I, using my spare hand to reach for some fabric I know it was by the door, placing it on top of the tip of my ready to explode erection.

I return my attention to her soft flesh, brushing her clit while my fingers push deeper, her walls squeeze frantically and she devours my lips hiding her screams, kissing each other harder to quiet our noises until it's just our breaths.

Ruby rests her head on my shoulder, her fingertips playing around my torso, my skin reacts to her touch, making me smile.

I pull my fingers away, clean them and her with another cloth and move my hands to her nape, playing with her messy hair, kissing her crown, and brushing the exposed skin.

"Ma..." Aidan whispers, bringing us back to reality, but before she run away, I give her a deep kiss.

Aidan takes a few minutes to become completely awaken, enough time for us to put clothes back in place, tidy our messy hair, and straighten our blushing faces.

I can't take my eyes away from her, knowing I'm in the

deepest trouble I have ever been.

Eager for more, willing to lose myself under this angelic creature touch again.

CHAPTER EIGHT

Ruby

"Mama?" Naima's sleepy voice makes us both look back.

"Hi babies." I can feel a change in my tone of voice. I sound calm, soft—feelings I haven't experienced in so long, and some that I never experienced before.

What are you doing Ruby?

I just broke all the self-promises, throw out of the window all the pep-talk about being enough, not needing a man, run away from any male at least for the next ten years, and here I am, losing the little part of me left on the arms of this irresistible man.

The logic part of my brain tells me I need to run away, but my entire system want me to keep him, to drag him to my darkest corner, just us, where we could hide together.

A noisy yawn bring me back to reality, when I look at him I can see I wasn't the only one miles away from here, lost in my own thoughts and punishing my wounded heart even more.

He shake his head, take a deep breath and comes back to the moment.

How did he do that?

"Ready for more shopping?" Samuel asks. "I sure am!"

Who are you Samuel Smith? How can you be the darkest soul and the brightest spirit in a matter of seconds?

I turn away, stepping out of the car and helping the children out, Aidan holds Naima hands and they start walking when I turn and realize that Samuel continue in his seat, "coming?" I ask.

His body shakes, he brush his temple and jump out of the car, just like if nothing has happened.

"Who would like a drink at Sarah's café?" I ask the kids.

She is our neighbor and works on a small café at the entrance; she waves at us as she finishes with a customer, dropping her jaw to the floor when she observe Samuel walking towards me, stopping by my side, resting his palm on my lower back and whisper his order on my ear.

"Morning Sarah." I feel my cheeks blushing.

"Morning, guys! So nice to see you here," she says.

She is a short Korean woman in her midthirties. She moved to the apartments over a year ago. Louise helped her find this job and soon her children will come to the country to be with her.

"May I have a juice?" Aidan asks, and he looks back at me. "Please Sarah," he says, sending a huge, cute smile.

"Anything for you, big boy." She is always kind to us since we meet.

"We will have two kids' juice, a Power for me and a Super

Boost for Samuel." I say as quick as possible to hide my shaky voice.

"Right away!" She says, giving me a cheeky wink.

I hand her a note, give the kids and Samuel their drinks and walk away to get a trolley.

Sarah and Samuel gaze burning my skin until I enter the store and at least I'm away from one of them.

I just had the best sexual experience in my life, *YES!*

My body is screaming for more since he pull out, *YES!*

The smartest and most mature side of my brain is telling me to run away from this Adonis, *YES!*

I take a deep breath, seat Aidan on the child's chair, hold Naima hand and follow nearly my daily stroll over the aisles, just filling up slightly more the trolley.

Samuel is walking behind me, I can feel his turquoise gaze burning my skin, stripping me in the middle of the store and killing me at the same time.

Torturing me every once in a while, by touching my arm, placing a hand on the bottom of my spine, on his way to help with anything too high on the shelves, and leaving me shaking begging for more.

God damn you Samuel Irresistible Smith!

We reach the tills sooner than expected and we join Martha's queue.

"Morning Ruby," she greets with wide eyes as she spots Samuel with us.

"Morning Martha," we all answer unloading the trolley.

"It's this week's order delivered?" She asks.

Every week, I deliver cookies to the local stores and to them some employees can add their personal ones.

"Tomorrow as usual," I confirm, loading the bags.

"I have an order, but don't worry, will text you to confirm. We have a little meet up coming up."

"Anytime," I reply grateful, finish packing the last bits.

I grab some cash out of my purse and walk away as fast as possible.

"Have a lovely Sunday kids," she says, and the children wave their goodbyes.

I help the children back into their seats and take a seat while Samuel finish unloading the groceries, looking away in the moment he opens his door.

Heading to the last destination, a patisserie farmer's market.

Over there I will get my final high-quality ingredients.

Samuel park at the assigned space and help one more time with Aidan.

As we approach the stalls, he holds my spare hand. Naima doesn't miss it, holding my other hand, drawing a new smile on her little lips, and she squeezes our hold.

Aidan just rest his head on his shoulder and Samuel drops a kiss on his little forehead.

I try to break the hold, but he tightens the fingers around me and keep it that way until I surrender and let him hold my hand as if that is the most natural thing for us to do.

The market is way busier than I have expected, but I found all the ingredients—we have some nibbles in different stalls, as sample of what Stella expects from me.

Samuel knows a lot about high-quality food, and even if I know little of him, you just have to see his clothes and car. He has money—he has lived a different lifestyle than us.

Around an hour later, we walk back to the car, with at least two bags each. Even Naima is helping, Samuel has finally given up on holding me and I walk as far from him as possible.

Getting the kids ready one more time, he waits at my door, hold it open and drops a soft kiss on my cheek.

What are you playing at Samuel?

"Before I forget," he murmurs on my ear, "thanks for the day."

Making my entire body shake, while a triumphant smile grows on his delicious lips.

Looking by the window, away from him all the way, we arrive at Miguel's shop. The children stay in the car while I drop the different type of cardboard, paper and banners I bought.

Getting back into the car, and driving home, passing by our dream castle and then the cottage, Naima doesn't miss it.

"That's going to be our house soon," she says, "*one step closer to heaven*," she sings.

Why Naima?! I mentally hide away and burn in hell.

Something change on Samuel's expression, a thick frown grows on his forehead.

"What was that?" He asks.

"Mama just bought the little cottage. I like to call it *one step closer the heaven!*" She exclaims.

"*Heaven*," he mumbles, "do you love that big castle?" He

asks. I look at him and realize the question was for me.

"When we moved to the neighborhood, the house was for sale. I saw the pictures online, way too big and over budget, but that cottage is the perfection in the world of properties." I explain.

"What do you like about that castle?" He asks.

Why is asking about the castle and not the cottage, haven't I just said that is the property I am trying to buy?

"You should see the kitchen. It is a dream come true," I exclaim, that kitchen is the size of my apartment right now.

"The master bedroom, with a full view of the park," I say pointing to the park.

"There is a room facing the little cottage. It would be an incredible room for kids—bedroom and toy room."

"Bedroom and toy room?" He asks.

"Yes, it has a lot of potential, personally I will paint it all with multiple colors around. The arch between the rooms will be a rainbow, and there will be a jack and jill toddler bathroom." I explain.

I look back at him and I can't describe what I see, have I talked too much?

"Sorry," I murmur.

Why you apologize, idiot?!

"For dreaming? For having ambitions? I admire it," he says.

The last man I trusted, and that told me I have beautiful dreams in life, turn up to be my worst nightmare.

It's 3 p.m. when we are back at the apartment, I unload all the packages with Samuel help from the car, connecting the oven and unloading the shopping.

Is he gonna leave? I need to breathe again.

"Dinner will be ready in ten," I say.

The kids run to wash their hands and play, but Samuel looks at me with a cute frown.

So fucking irresistible!

"I prepped it last night, so we could eat as soon as we were back."

"You want me to stay?" He asks.

Is he inviting himself to stay?

"Can't let you go on an empty stomach."

What in the hell are you doing Ruby?!

His frown deepens up, he nods and step closer.

"Let me help." He offers, standing by my side.

If I am doing this, I need you at least three feet away.

"Okay, wash your hands!" I point to the kitchen sink on my side while I dry my hands.

"Bossy cook," he says in a whisper, giving me a cheeky smile.

Stop looking at him Ruby!

"When you are in my kitchen," I say while he dry his hands and walks my way, "I am in charge." I whisper as we are breathing the same air.

Please step away, we can't do this.

He smiles and gets closer to me, totally aware of what he is doing.

I can feel the heat of his skin, his arm brush my hips and

rest on the counter behind me.

Please don't touch me!

His eucalyptus-minty scent hypnotize me, and I close my eyes, taking it all in, shaking as the cinnamon scent hit me too, that means he is extremely close, his lips nearly brushing mine, I inhale every exhalation that he does and my body become loose.

Please touch me!

His palm rest on my waist and hold me up on his chest, my hands land on his shoulder and my eyes open widely, completely melting every inch of my being when I meet his turquoise killing eyes.

I brush his back and rest my fingertips on his nape, pulling him and devouring his delicious lips.

He welcomes me, making me tremble. He sets me on the kitchen counter. Placing himself in between my thighs, I cross my legs on top of his ass, forcing us to stay as close as possible.

His finger plays on my back, working under my top, caressing every inch of my flesh, but before he goes any further, the timer screams, and my mobile does too. We both growl.

"Can you get the food out of the oven, please?" I jump down, grabbing my mobile.

Breath Ruby!

Louise's name flashes on the screen, but I reject it, turning around and try to act as calm as possible. Her call on a Sunday afternoon, after Friday news, is a call I don't want to have now.

"Everyone to the table," I say, turning to get everything ready. But Samuel remains, not moving, not saying a single word. "Is everything okay?"

He is on a trance again, like his mind is going a thousand miles per hour and he need a minute to hold those thoughts in correct place.

"I promised Scott I would pick him up after shopping," he says, making me remember when he mentioned visiting the park in the afternoon.

Is he going now?

"It's understandable if you have to go," I say.

He freeze again, the deep frown resting on his beautiful forehead and his gaze traveling away.

"Or you could pick him up and bring him over for dinner."

What the fuck was that Ruby?!

He looks at me and gifts me with his new heart melting irresistible smile.

"Will be right back," he sighs, dropping a soft kiss on my cheek.

He walks away and I hold myself on the counter.

What have I done?

I text Sarah for chairs and finish the dessert, my hands can't stop shaking.

"Mama, I like him." Naima says.

Please don't do this baby, don't fall deep as I already have.

"Me too, baby." I admit, I can't hide how he makes me feel.

"I want him to stay," so much sadness on her words, and I just kneel to hug her. "Please let him stay."

"Baby, we can't..."

Before we can continue with this conversation, my mobile

rings. Louise's name is on the screen again.

I walk to the bedroom, leaving the kids to take care of the table. I'm sure they should not be listening to this conversation.

"Good evening, Louise." I try to sound polite, but her call can only be bad news.

"I just received the news." She sounds nervous. "It's official. The documents will be at my desk tomorrow, and they will transfer Advik in a week."

"A week? But you said..." Panic reaches my throat and I can't breathe. I can't talk about this now.

What are we going to do?

A soft knock pull me out of this tortuous call

"Thanks for the call, but I'm busy right now."

"But Ruby, we need..." I hang up the phone before she can finish.

Before I leave the room, I do what I promise to *my protector*, the only person who will make sure Advik never hurts my kids again. The text is short and specific:

He will be out in less than a week, have everything ready.

I walk to the door, brush away a tear that I fight so hard to keep hidden and fix my messy plait.

This will be last time I see Samuel.

I take a deep breath, put the pleasant Ruby mask on, draw a beautiful smile on my face and open the door.

"Hi Scott, please come in. Dinner is ready."

"Thanks for having us Ruby," Scott says. He is the politest

little boy I've ever met.

I guide them to the dining table when another knock gets everyone's attention.

"Those are our spare chairs," I announce.

Sarah's shocked face meets my red, embarrassed one.

"*Amiga*! You better call me tomorrow."

I just give her a quick hug and kiss, closing the door with a kick.

Jumping on the spot when I see Samuel at the door frame, "sorry," he whispers.

That won't put my heart back in place.

He is observing me, his gaze moving around my entire frame and I tense.

"Is everything okay?" He asks, looking straight into my eyes.

I lower my head, avoid his gaze and try to push myself through.

Samuel take the chairs, put them aside and step closer, he isn't touching me, but my entire body can feel him, my body remembers him.

One of his hands holds my jaw up, so we can look at each other's eyes.

This close to him, I can't hide anything. I can't talk. My hands hold his hand that was caressing my cheek.

I need his touch—his comfort—and he doesn't talk, he just gets closer and closer until our lips are touching. I kiss him, holding his nape, losing myself in him, trying to transport myself away from all the trouble to somewhere where I am free.

You are in deep, crazy fucking trouble missy!

Putting me back on my feet, he place a stripe of hair behind my ear and rest his forehead on mine, taking a deep breath he guides me back to the living room, holding easily the chairs.

Samuel's gaze set on me the entire dinner, studying my every move, every expression.

Stop!

"I will get dessert," I say, trying to avoid him.

Leaving the plates at the sink, I take a few deep breaths, while his gaze burns my back.

"Are you a cook or a baker?" He asks, staring at me while his second full spoon of cake meets his mouth, and a delicious moan leave my delicious lips, he licks them and my entire body is on fire, "this is Spectacular."

I need you out of here asap!

"Baking is my passion. When I do appetizers, clients love it too, so I'm planning on offering both," I explain, helping Aidan with dessert.

A soft nod and an irresistible smile force me to look away.

I need you all over me again!

"This is Spectacular," he says, filling his mouth with another spoonful. "I wish my sister has found you. She is planning a big party in the next few weeks."

I can't take my eyes away from his lips, his tongue brushing them every time.

I am in so much fucking trouble.

"Mama, can we play?" Naima asks, bringing me back to reality.

I need this man away from me asap!

"Yes, kids play. I will take care of this." I just agreed to a dangerous and painful time around Samuel.

It's been a long day, but I need to work on Stella's tasting tomorrow.

"I should give you some privacy," he says behind me, while placing the last things left on the table by the sink.

Turning around, I want to tell him I need him, that he should stay, but I know it is wrong. I just turn away again, as I can't face him while I say what I'm about to.

"Thank you for the day."

My chin drops and I try to hide the sadness I feel, but the hair of my nape stands on end—he is getting closer.

"I want to stay," he whispers.

Oh please Samuel run away, before is too late.

He stands behind me, not touching me, but I can feel the heat of his body.

"Then stay," I declare.

What the fuck RUBY!!!

Just like that, he grabs my waist and twists me around, forcing me to hold his shoulders for stability.

CHAPTER NINE

Samuel

She trembles in my arms. I get closer and closer until our lips are almost touching.

"I won't leave you," I whisper while her hands brush my chest.

What are doing Samuel?!

Her arms hold me around my waist, pulling me closer, and she kisses me. My arms cover her, protecting her, taking her away from whatever it is I can see is troubling her.

"I need to work," she whisper on my lips, smiling when my fingertips brush her back and I cup her angelic face.

Gosh, that smile just woke up every fibre of my body and my throbbing groin confirms it.

"You are such a bad influence, Samuel."

My name sounds like angel bells on her lips, forcing me to kiss her again and again.

Walking backwards, she push me into one stool on the island.

"Sit here," she orders, giving me a soft kiss on the cheek.

You need to stop this asap Samuel.

Ruby lose up her hair from the plait, turning it into my favourite sexy messy bun, removing her sandals and mumbling some song.

Holding it in place Samuel.

I need to remember why I haven't rush away from here in the first chance I had, hearing the giggles as a reminder I just want Scott to have a nice game time.

As soon as I can take him out of here in the coolest way we will be out of their lives for good.

Knowing I won't see her again I grab the camera I took from the car when I picked up Scott.

She loves what she does, attentive to detail, I can see her preparing mixes without measuring a single mixture, baking is her safe, comfort place, as the gym is mine, and you can taste it on her food as you can see it on my figure.

Wake up Samuel! She can be the last business we been looking for.

I take out my mobile, film one short video and send it to Helena and Matteo.

Subject; I present you our special edition cover.

My mobile screams, but I silence it and move to the carpet with the kids.

We laugh, play cards and domino—but a few seconds into an extra round of the game, I have three children sleeping on the floor. I stand and walk back to the kitchen to let Ruby know.

It's time to say my goodbyes and get out of her life for good.

As I reach the kitchen, I see the most delicious picture. She is all messy, so focused, her tongue brushes her lip, while her hands are kneading some dough.

"Come here," she whispers, and so I do, standing behind her, smelling her. She smells delicious, like a bakery first thing in the morning.

Fuck off woman! You are putting a delicious spell on me.

Unable to resist it any longer I hug her, one of my arms around the waist and the other playing around her chest, brushing the top of her breast, making her giggle.

My face hides in her neck, and for the first time in decades I feel at home.

I rest my forehead on her shoulder and breath through the pain of my broken soul assemble more pieces together.

Why are you doing this to me Ruby?

She stops working and turns around, forcing me away from my new favourite place.

"This needs to rest in the fridge," she says.

Being taller than her and been on a small space, gives me multiple privileges.

I open the fridge, take the bowl with the dough, and put it in without moving from my spot.

As I shut it, my hands rest on her perfect face, her eyes close and her head rest on my hold.

"Open your eyes Ruby," I whisper and she does, making me tremble, while her fingers brush my chest, stopping at my heart and leaving it there a lifetime, suddenly replacing it with her ear.

My heart bombard my chest and I know she can feel it, her head moves with the rise of my chest and her entire body calms under the drums of my broken heart.

"Home," she whispers so low, but I hear it.

I need to run! Hide and forget her!

"The kids are sleeping on the floor," I say, my voice back to the regular rough way. If I want her to go, I need to show her my worst side, one that she definitely will not like around her children.

She pushes me away and rush to the other room, taking Aidan in her arms.

"I need to take Scott home." I miserably fail this time to keep it on a hard tone.

She doesn't answer, just nods and leaves, but I can see a change in her expression.

Please hate me, send me away.

For an unknown and stupid reason I wait for her to return to pick up Naima, now wearing a big T-shirt that could be called a dress, making her look even sexier than before.

Gosh, this woman is tempting me.

"I could be back," I say, biting my bottom lip.

What the fuck are you doing SAMUEL?! I thought we were running away!

"That would be nice," she whispers and my entire being is back alive.

I can't run, she has trapped me.

"See you in twenty." I say rushing out of the apartment

with Scott is in my arms.

I can't wait to be back.

Scott is in Naima's car seat. He doesn't need one anymore, but he is sleeping, and I want to make sure he is secure and comfortable.

I drive faster than usual back to Stella's. She opens the door as I park, ready to take her boy.

"In a rush?" She looks surprised and is using her mum voice on me.

Please, give me a break.

"Have a lovely week Stella." I say sharply, with her I can easily use my nasty tone.

"Samuel?!" She shouts through her teeth.

I turn and jump on my car, she can't talk to me like that, she knows and it will never happen again.

Minutes later, I am at her door; she opens and walks away.

I take a seat on the stool, repositioning my hard cock.

Fuck me that T-shirt!

It's a thin white material and I can see every inch of her body.

She finishes and places another bowl in the fridge, and walks straight to me—there is no more time to lose, so I turn on the stool, ready for her.

Let's do it, baby!

She just jumps in my arms, her thighs around my waist, her hands directly to my buttons and mine under her T-shirt. She's not wearing anything under it.

I am going to lose myself on you, woman.

Our gazes glued, our breaths broken, and we kiss in a more

possessive way. There is hunger and need.

Her palms brush my bare chest and pushes my shirt away, my entire body trembles when her fingertips brush my skin.

From my hands, up to my shoulders and down my torso, awakening every inch on my body, my hands harder around her waist and my hip rise creating a delicious moan.

So fucking perfect!

Her hands move to my belt, and flashbacks of the car come to me. I won't be able to take off my trousers while I'm seated, I stand and leave her on the island; she helps to pull my trousers off, brushing my arse, while I kick my shoes aside. Here I am, exposed, in front of this angel.

Not willing to miss any inch of her skin, I step back and take care of her T-shirt. She raises the arms and I waste no time, brushing all the trace from her thighs, her torso, her arms until our hands meet.

My eyes glued on hers, ready to lose myself.

Gosh! Isn't she the most beautiful creature I ever seen.

I brush the trace back until I reach her hips, moving to her round bum and pushing her to the edge.

She moans at her clit brush the head of my hard as rock cock.

Take it easy Samuel, she matters.

We are a mix of sharp breaths, groans, and mumbles.

Pulling her face up, I kiss her while I get myself ready, letting my cock fall into place, then rolling forward, finding her wet opening, holding her hips slightly harder trying to control myself.

I go in, trembling, welcomed, and satisfied. Her hands fist my hair and she kisses me, quieting our moans.

Our bodies are melting, we are both sweating, trying to get our connection even closer, I pull her closer to the edge, pushing forward and growling as I reach the deepest of her core.

Her back keeps arching with every thrust, with every rotation and her chest raise, giving me access to her perfect breast, I hold one and brush my thumb over the nipple, feeling how it becomes harder under my touch, while my tongue gives the same attention to the other.

A low scream leaves her throat and her chest trembles, making me smile around her nipple.

Her walls squeeze my cock, and her legs push me closer, I let go of her now pointing breast and observe her.

Fucking perfection!

Her gaze is glued on mine while I brush my fingertips at the centre of her torso until I reach a small section of pubic hair, play with it while her body trembles, her back arch and her walls pull me deeper, placing my thumb on her clit and applying some pressure and drawing circles

She is close—so am I.

I harden my thumb pressure and I thrust her faster, deeper, her nails land on my shoulder and I growl.

"Samuel..." she cries.

"I know..." I murmur, pushing her to my lips and devouring her moans, "not yet."

My hips rotate even faster, pushing us to the limit of our pleasure.

My scalp would kill me if it was not the reason, I'm reaching my climax. She is pulling harder, letting me know how close she is.

Holding her arse harder, I rotate faster and deeper, my thumb is wet and numb, but I don't let go.

Fuck, this is getting too much, too delicious, and I'm reaching a further stage of pleasure.

"Samuel…" she says, biting my bottom lip and licking it.

"Cum for me Ruby." I think she's been holding it for way too long. We are both ready to reach the limit, so we do.

We stop kissing, but our mouths stay connected, hiding our moans and screams.

After what seems a lifetime of lovemaking, we stop giving each other small kisses and caressing each other's sweaty bodies. She just looks into my eyes a breathtaking smile grows on her perfect face.

"Hungry?" She asks.

Well, I just devoured her, so I'm okay on that sense for now, but a lion roaring in my stomach answers for me.

"Give me two minutes," she says, pulling away and jumping away from the island.

Sadness and cold cover my entire body as she moves away, putting her oversize T-shirt back on, grabbing some pans from the cupboard and then ingredients from the fridge.

I'm observing her every move, all are synchronise, like if she is dancing around.

What have you done to me?

While something gets ready on the pan, she is transferring

trays from the fridge to the oven.

I grab my boxers from the floor and walk closer.

"Working?" I ask.

Her cheeks flash pink and my heart jumps into my throat. She is the cutest, more special person I've ever known.

"I have a sample tasting tomorrow," she says, but seems nervous.

"Is it a big deal?"

"They want me to do the entire party," she pauses, sounding anxious. "I'm trying to get organized but am a little overwhelmed."

"What can I help you with?" I ask.

She just observes me from the corner of her eyes and laughs at me in boxers.

Guiding me to the corner near the fridge, where the entire pile of trays is ready to be washed.

Me? Washing dishes?

I look back at her and my arrogance flies away; she needs help, and I genuinely want to help her.

Rolling my imaginary sleeves up, I wash everything and hang it where different side metal rungs are screwed into the wall.

I turn to the rest of the kitchen and start clearing away more bowls and tools. I just hold them up and receive a quiet nod, confirming they are ready to be washed.

Ruby is busy cutting different cake sponges. They are all shades of yellow—the smell is making me even hungrier.

On one of my rounds for dirty dishes, I realise there's two plates covered, waiting for us. I hadn't seen she was done and was just waiting for me to finish.

"Done with the cleaning," I say, while drying my hands. "What else?" I ask, as she is putting another tray of mini cakes in the fridge.

We are millimetres away from each other. She turns to face me, resting her palms on my bare chest, moving them to my neck and face.

"Let's eat." She smiles, but it doesn't reach her eyes. Something is happening.

I drop my hands from her back to her arse and under it, pulling her up, keeping her close, not able to run away.

"Whatever it is," my voice shakes, she cups my face, "I will always be here for the three of you."

How can you promise that, sir?

Her bottom lip wobbles. She nibbles it, trying to hide it, and fails, so she kisses me.

I sit her on a stool and place myself by her side, removing the plates covers and revealing a delicious sandwich.

"Ruby, what would you think of being part of my next edition?" I ask giving a small bite.

"For the magazine you work?" She asks.

"I own the company," I say, chewing.

"Wow! What is your magazine about?" she asks.

"Big and small brands, the party or events of the season, interviews, fashion, beauty, food, a little bit of everything."

"Why me?" She asks, surprise. "I'm not a celebrity."

"Not only celebrities can be in our magazine. This one is the 100th edition." She looks at me. "We want to promote new entrepreneurs."

"Am I an entrepreneur?" She asks.

"Well, you are starting a business from home. You do all the jobs that make this work with kids, so I could think of you as more of a mompreneur, but yes you are."

"What do you need me to do?" She asks.

"To be honest, just one more picture as I spent the entire day creating all the content needed."

"You don't need me to do a big photoshoot, interview, or stuff like that?" She looks surprise and disappointed.

"I want this edition to be natural—serious, boring stuff will come later on, believe me." A part of me is relieved. "Is that a, yes?"

I pull her stool even closer, turning my body to face her, spreading her legs, and positioning myself in between them. She is the most gorgeous and perfect creature I have ever had in front of me.

"What happens Ruby?" I ask when sadness covers her face again.

"Do it, take your last picture," she says.

"Put on your best clothes and get ready, as it's the cover."

"I will be back in a moment," she says, tiptoeing away.

I prepare the camera and move the files to the laptop, glad I took everything with me, giving her a few minutes to get ready.

"You look gorgeous," I say when she walks back wearing a tight, white and blue flowered dress, with off the shoulder straps.

I can see into her eyes—see her pain. She tries to hide it from the camera, but she won't be able to hide it from me.

"Just be you. Continue cooking," I say. "Look at me," I order, so she does.

After over fifty shots, we are done. I let her continue with work while I sit on the laptop, ready to upload everything.

I email all the teams at the office, making sure everyone has the information and images needed for tomorrow.

She finishes wiping all the counters after she puts all the tools and ingredients away, walking back to me, but I am admiring her pictures, unable to take the smile off my face.

Before she can sit, Aidan's voice brings us back to reality. We aren't alone. She just walks away without saying a word.

Taking that as my sign to leave, I pack everything and drop a quick note on the counter.

I will see you tomorrow x

Sitting in the car by her front door, I check my mobile. There are over twenty calls from Helena and Matteo.

I made a quick group video call.

"Samuel Smith!!!!" Helena screams.

"*Hermano*, she is an angel." Matteo is as delighted as I am. "Helena, don't be jealous. She is perfect."

"I just need you to be focused with your beautiful brain and head on top of shoulders." She argues.

In the office she will always be polite and nice to me, but out of it she has always felt free to talk to me as she pleased.

"She is perfect. Everyone will love her food and her personality when they meet her." I assure them.

"Are we doing a press release?" Helena asks, taking notes.

We might have a friendly conversation, but she doesn't rest for a second. Or so I thought until Natasha appears in the background.

"Hi boys!" She calls, we just wave to her. "If you don't mind, I will take this beauty to bed."

Matteo laughs. I need to cover my mouth as I do it, too.

"Please do. I will see everyone tomorrow morning at 8 a.m. sharp!" I say.

Everyone disconnects, and I head home.

Rosita walks out of the kitchen as I close the front door.

"Don't have to say anything," I say sharply.

I don't like to talk to her this way, but whatever she wants to say, I already know.

But I won't regret anything of what I did today.

I walk upstairs, and she follows me.

Resting her short frame at the door, "I heard the news." I look at her removing my watch and taking everything out of my pockets. "You found the cover entrepreneur *hijito*," she says.

"Just followed your advice." I assure.

"For once," she says, I can hear the sarcasm on her tone, but I ignore it.

"*Buenas noches*," I say, kissing her cheek.

"*Dios te bendiga mi hijito*," she answers, drawing the cross over my forehead and chest.

Closing the door behind her and throwing myself in bed, Ruby is now on my head and soul, any hope of taking her out of my life, has just flew out of the window.

CHAPTER TEN

Ruby

The small old clock on my night table hits 5 a.m., I'm wide awake—I doubt I will ever be able to sleep again, knowing Advik will be out in a week.

However, seeing how quickly things have changed in the past few days, I can't help but be petrified knowing Advik could be out any minute now.

Getting out of bed, I head straight to the shower, sad to wash away Samuel's touch and kisses, but my anger and sadness need to be washed away too.

By 5:30 a.m. I'm in the kitchen, a fresh coffee in my hand, while I go through today.

Last night I prepared a few samples of cake, dough, and cupcakes. I just need to add the filling that been resting overnight in the fridge.

Playing some soft music, I place my mane in a messy bun, and let go of any thoughts.

At around 9 a.m., the kids are playing after a heavy

breakfast—samples of cake. It's the best way to have over one opinion.

The kitchen is spotless—on the island is the full presentation. I cross each item off my list while I place it there:

- 4x types of yellow sponge.
- Green and brown buttercream, with different shades.
- Dinosaur shaped and round cookies.
- Green and brown cupcakes with lemon flavor.
- Flat fondant dinosaurs.
- A miniature of the 3D T-Rex.

I text Miguel reminding him to drop the samples I brough yesterday, he will help to print the banner and small decorations.

They need a special paper and a cut that I can't do manually. He replies and promises to drop them off any time now.

I decide to take a well-deserved break and sit down to play, chat, laugh, and cuddle my little babies.

A soft knock stops our card play. I walk to the door and find Miguel with an enormous box with the work on his arms.

"*Buen día* Ruby. Where you want me to keep all this?" He asks. His big natural smile just makes me smile, too.

"Please follow me," I say, so he does not able to grab the box from him. He carefully places it at the dining table.

"Something has come up, and I'm sure you will be interested," he says.

"What is that?" I ask, and he hands me a leaflet.

Summer Fair

In collaboration with Three Angles Church, The Children's Shelter, and Blue Valley Council.
Join us for our famous Summer Fair, enjoy the kids' games and activities, try our best local business food, and help us raise money for the children in need.

Tuesday 5th of July, from 10 a.m. to 6 p.m.
At Bluebell Park, near the recreation area.

"This is incredible, Miguel." I'm up for anything that can help children in need, and he knows.

"I knew you would be interested in taking part," he says and nods.

What?!

"Take part? I was thinking you want me to assist. How could I be ready for two events on such a short notice?" I ask irritated.

"Ruby, you need to promote your business, and it's for the children," he says, determined to convince me.

"I have the birthday party, the store orders. How can I organize everything? That's madness," I say, panic in my voice.

"They don't need nothing fancy, anyway you need to prepare the store's orders, so just create a bigger bunch and *listo!*" he says.

"Why I always let you trap me into everything?"

"I will let them know you agree," he says, "do you need help to deliver this?" he asks pointing to the store orders.

"We could go after the tasting," I say.

"None sense, I can easily do it with the car, bye niños!" He exclaims carrying the boxes and waving his goodbyes.

A few hours later, we are in the garden. Stella's tasting was perfect, and now she has to choose everything.

We have agreed on all the sweets and I will drop an appetizer tray by her house at the end of the week so she can give her approval for that too.

The sun is burning my over creamy skin, forcing me to open the umbrella and hide under it.

I enjoy the kids' games, the quick lunch I prepared and even the extra cookies I got from the store orders.

But I panic when the front doorbell rings. I check and find a short lady accompanied by a tall, good-looking gentleman.

"Samuel sent us, please open the door," he says, from outside, like he knows I am there.

I open the door, but my entire body relaxes when I meet two smiley faces.

"Afternoon Ruby," she says.

"Please, this way," I say, walking to the kitchen.

"Nice apartment," she says.

"Would y'all like some ice coffee or maybe lemonade?" I ask.

"Matteo will appreciate an espresso and I," she pauses,

pointing at herself, "Rosita will be glad to have some lemonade."

The kids have stayed in the garden, and Matteo joins them when I give him the coffee.

"You might wonder what we are doing here," Rosita says.

I just turn around and face her while we both enjoy the fresh drink.

"This is delicious. Samuel will be stuck in the city for the rest of the week," she says and I try to look cool.

He is running away, good, is for the best, why is she here then?

"You don't have to come and talk for him. I think he... he is..."

She cuts me off, "You never exchanged numbers, and he had to leave—"

"He could have added it to this," I accuse holding up his late-night note.

"Ruby, I can see your life. Your situation is delicate, complicated even, but Samuel does not know what he is doing."

He seems perfectly fine last night.

"You don't have to justify him."

"I am not sure how much he has shared, but this is all new for him," she says, pointing at me, kids, house, everywhere.

"He has shared nothing," I say, hurting my broken heart even more.

He is hiding things.

"I can't do this. We have enough on our plates," I say.

Turning away and pushing away a thick tear that was fighting the way out.

"Samuel lost everyone except me and his sister at a young age—that broke him into millions of pieces," she says. Her voice is shaking. "I've been picking all up for over twenty years. It has been exhausting—I'm not complaining, just explaining."

I turn and nod offering some cookies to accompany the heavy conversation.

"Then you appear in his life," she says. She looks at the cookie she just bit and smiles. "For an instant, I thought all my hard work would be crushed again. But Ruby, in two days, you have put more pieces together than I could in over a decade."

What does she mean?

I look away, her gaze fixed on mine and something warm inside me grows, something that I haven't felt before, or at least something that with the years my body has forgotten.

"He is walking on dangerous path here."

He? What about me?

"The only thing we need from you is to be patient and prepared," she says.

Patient? Prepared for what?

How can a man like Samuel need anyone to be gentle with him? He looks invincible, like he owns the entire world.

"When Samuel loves you, the world becomes colourful. It keeps spinning so fast you can't focus much, but then he holds you and everything gets better."

Exactly how I felt for the past 48h

She has been with him for what I'm understanding is a lifetime.

"I saw that boy born," she says. She clears her throat and wipes away a tear. "Since the day I held him for the first time I could feel how special he was. I was there the day he disappeared, leaving us heartbroken, and I was there the day he returned, the day he broke, and all has been dark since then."

"Mama, can we play paint with Matteo?" Naima asks, taking me away from the huge amount of information I'm trying to process.

"Of course, just show him where to find everything," I say, refilling Rosita's lemonade, and we take a seat at the dining table. "Samuel broke?" I repeat her last comment.

"He disappeared for over two years. My heart was in pieces wondering where he was, but when he came back, it was too late." She pauses, as if that is all the information she can give me.

Why is she telling me all of this?

"You might not understand it right now, but you are the light in his darkness. I just need to know he is your safe place too, otherwise we need to stop this now," she says.

Please help me stop it!

"Rosita, things aren't that easy with us," I say.

"*Mi hijita*, I can see your apartment, your approach to strangers, the darkness in your eyes. I can smell a broken soul miles away," she says, defining me in two minutes. "You want each other. Which is the correct and healthy choice, but communication is too."

Well, we have physically learned a lot, but not much words has happen between us.

After a few hours, a jar of lemonade, a few coffees, and a large box of biscuits later, Rosita and Matteo head back home.

I gave her my number as Samuel requested. The hours have passed by without him calling, but I guess he is busy.

Stop it Ruby! It's for the best, let him go.

While I finish washing the dinner dishes and the entire kitchen, my phone screams. It's an unknown number.

"Ruby Sweet Dreams, Ruby speaking, how can I help you?"

"Hi," his raspy voice make my entire body tremble.

"Hi," I softly answer.

"How was your day?" He casually ask.

What the hell is this?

 "Productive, yours?"

"Spectacular! I've worked all day editing a gorgeous angel pictures, How was your tasting?"

"Spectacular! She loved it all," I answer mimicking his tone.

"Kids?" He asks.

"In bed, you?"

"I can't go home as the builders have invade every single room," he explains.

"I'm sure you have many other houses," he is wealthy, not sure how rich, but he can pay a hotel easily too.

"Yeah, but they are too far from where I want to be," he says casually.

"And where that will be?" I ask.

Please stop Samuel Irresistible Smith!

A soft knock brings me out of my madness conversation

with this man.

My body is playing weird tricks with me, but I can't be around him anymore, I need to avoid any contact or better touch from this Adonis.

If I let him trap me one more time, there will be no way back.

"Someone is at the door," I say.

"Don't hung up." He orders and I frown.

Why he thinks he can give me orders?

Muting the call, I head to the door, open slightly and for a second the entire room spins around until my back hits the wall and I am pull back to reality.

Samuel shows in front of me when he pulls away my mane that just flew away with the rush push.

"Hi," he whisper near my lips.

"I didn't invite you," I argue back.

God damn you Samuel!

"Haven't you miss me?" He ask, inspecting my face, brushing his fingertips over my cheeks, to my lips, who part and a triumph grin grows on his delicious lips, "I missed you too."

My feet leave the ground and I curl my legs around his waist, hiding my face in his neck, breathing him in, while he closes the door and walks us into the living room.

"Gosh it's smells like heaven and I have a goddess in my arms," he murmurs in my ear, giving me a little bite.

Walking until the couch and taking a seat, resting me in place, his strong muscly arms squeeze me in a safe, protective way. I can't wait any longer and I move my face away from his delicious neck.

At this distance, it hurts to look at him. I can't stop touching and inspecting every inch of his face.

I am in big trouble!

"I missed you so much all day." He speaks so low—I melt in his arms.

Holding his jaw, I get closer until our lips are touching, my hands move to his nape and I fist his hair, pulling him closer until I lose myself in him.

I moan into his mouth. He tastes like heaven. I can't get enough of him. But the way he holds me, his hands touching my entire body, proves me right.

My groin meets the hardness under his trousers, making my entire body tremble. My hands move everywhere—my fingers work on every button of his black shirt, making sure I enjoy the entire process.

Once I'm done, he moves forward and I remove his shirt, exposing his arms, chest, and back.

Breaking our kiss, he takes my dress away too, and I'm not wearing anything under it.

"You are so beautiful it hurts," he whispers, holding my ass again, pulling me even closer.

I work on his fly, making his hands hold me tighter. His breath is slow, and I know with a simple move I can turn this perfect creature on, have him under my not-so-experienced control.

"You are so delicious it hurts," I confess, and he smiles.

I can hear his shoes hitting the floor and then raise me, he grabs some pillows and the blanket while I'm still in his arms, kissing his neck, breathing him. He prepares everything on the floor, placing me on top of it.

Resting on his knees, taking care of his trousers, rising and taking them away.

Fuck me! He isn't hot, this is raw, pure, dangerous fire.

Resting back on his knees, I jump on top of him, curling my legs around his waist again and devour him.

I can't do slow, painfully delicious Samuel today, I might want to deny it, but I've been begging for this all day.

His big palms brush my thighs, scratching, squeezing, and caressing my flesh. My entire system is alert—shaking, alive, and on fire, his palms move until my ass and he pull me open exactly when the head of his delicious throbbing dick brush my lips.

My hips rotate and he holds me in place, brushing his wet head from my clit to my perineum while I desperately scream on his lips.

Pulling his head away, I look into his eyes, my expression should scream out low as on one of his trips back from backside he thrust in, my nail dive on his flesh and my head fall on his forehead, biting my bottom lip to reduce the scream of pleasure that my entire body has just felt.

"Fuck... Ruby..." He mumbles, short of breath.

I know Samuel! I am dying too.

Closing his eyes I know he is trying to control himself like yesterday, but today I need him, how he really is, rough, merciless.

I can take it Samuel!

"Open your eyes Samuel," I order with a raspy voice.

He does and I lower myself bringing him to the deepest of my core.

We both scream, I leave his shoulder and move to his nape, brushing his waves, moving to his handsome face, scratching his stubble, raising my hips up and brushing his delicious lips when I hardly lower myself again.

He bites my fingers, and I giggle.

You aren't the only one with power here, sir!

His big palms hold my ass and squeeze harder and harder every time my hips drop.

As I relax and stop worrying about anything else, my walls melt around him.

"Fuck! Ruby!" He screams when I lower myself again and this time he touches my cervix, my back curls and his mouth fall into my little round breasts.

Squeezing, biting and caressing my breast, licking my collarbone until he reach my ear and he bite my lobe.

"You are fucking killing me!" He growls.

You are killing me in the most spectacular way.

The pressure on my core increase and Samuel dick reach the hardest stage possible, nearly exploding, ready to release this orgasm I know it will be *Spectacular*.

Holding his shoulder for support I look into his eyes like reading my mind, his palms move to my hips, holding me tight and in place exactly when my hips rise and lower on a faster speed, I do not control them anymore, but it will be the only way we can reach the highest level of pleasure.

His nails dive on my flesh, my palms hold his stronger shoulders and I pull his mouth to mine letting go, screaming of his mouth just as I feel his warm cum inside me, my hips keep rolling in a slower pace, my walls squeeze every drop held inside him.

Rather than break our contact, Samuel moves back and rests his head on a pile of pillows, dropping a blanket on top of us.

I rest my head on his chest and his breath and heart beats give me a peace I didn't have on a long time.

If I ever thought I could run away from this man, now is too late.

"Samuel, I know you won't talk about certain things," I say, and he stops my hand that was brushing his torso.

"Would you talk about anything with me Ruby?"

Touché!

"Something been bothering you since I left for Scott," my body tense and he nods, "Whatever it is, I will understand it. I will protect you and the children."

"You can't," I say sharply. His big palm rests on my cheek, making me rest my head on it, in need of comfort. "This isn't your battle to fight."

"Anything that concerns you and those beautiful kids, is my battle, too."

Is he for real?

"Why don't we enjoy the time we have?" I move away from him, standing and heading to the kitchen.

He tries to hold my arm, but I was faster that he expected, he rush behind me and catch me in the kitchen.

"Ruby, talk to me," he is pleading.

Samuel pleading? This man is nothing of what I thought he was.
"Baby, I beg you."
Am I hearing correct? Why he need to know it?!
"I need to know!" He is getting anxious, but his voice is always low. "I deserve to know!" he screams between his teeth and I just spin, a move he wasn't expecting.
What the fuck he thinks he deserves? Just because we fucked twice?

CHAPTER ELEVEN

Samuel

My heart stops for a split second. Her eyes are glassy, she is in pain—afraid, and I don't even know what is happening.

Let me help you Ruby! Don't push me away.

"Please..." she can't hold it anymore, covering her face. She sobs, her shoulders keep rising; her entire body is shaking. The best thing I can do is hold her as close as possible. "Don't... leave," she sobs.

I'm here baby.

I pull her chin up, moving her hands away from her perfect face, now red, with a purple line under her beautiful eyes that makes them look way darker.

"I won't leave Ruby." I assure her. "I'm always one call away."

Why is she afraid of being alone?

Her lips tremble, and thick tears pour down her red cheeks.

"Ruby, do you need me to stay here?" A small nod is her

answer.

What the hell is going on?

Closing the little space between us, she just hides her face in my neck, breathing me in, holding me tight, and I can't help but hold her tight, too.

She continues shaking. If me sleeping on her couch or floor will make her feel safer, so be it.

I carry her to the stools and walk back to take the snack she was preparing.

Sit by her side, turning her to face me, and feed her little bites of the toast.

We don't say another word. She let me feed her, clear her mouth and take full care of her.

A few minutes later, I hold her in my arms and take her to the bathroom, finding a facecloth on the sink's side. Rinsing it with warm water, I wash away her tears, making sure her swollen eyes won't be worse in the morning.

"Time for bed," I say, carrying her to the bedroom, but she shakes her head. I move to the living room and she asks to be put down.

She moves to the couch and opens it, it's a huge spare bed, big enough to hold my entire length. I won't have to sleep on the floor, *thank goodness*.

Placing the blankets and pillows from the floor, I help her to one side of the new bed. She hides herself under me when I lay on her side, which makes me understand she needs protection.

Never slept with a woman—it was always just sex and I left.

No woman has even been in my bedroom, and here I am—in the woman of my dreams' house, with her in my arms.

This feels scarily good.

For the first time feeling I am where I meant to be, like I found my purpose and place in the world, I am not lost anymore.

I'm still drowsy, can't open my eyes yet and it's cold, search for the blanket but realise it's on me already.

The coldness is because Ruby isn't here. That makes me jump off of the bed and before I can panic and search for her, I smell her.

There's a delicious scent coming out of the kitchen. It smells like fresh coffee and baked cookies.

When I walk closer, I see her. Her wet mane is in my favourite high messy bun, wearing an oversized T-shirt with denim shorts, mumbling some song and unaware that I'm right behind her.

"Good morning, Samuel," she sings.

Or so I thought. It's like she can smell me, or maybe she can feel me as I can feel her.

"Good morning baby," I say, as a huge smile draws on my face.

"One or two shots of espresso this morning?"

I have slept little, so I need caffeine.

"Two shots please," I say.

Getting closer, I can see she is busy and focused on a mixing bowl. Her hands are kneading dough.

"Is this for the birthday?" I ask, resting my chin on her

shoulder.

I can't wait to see the result.

"Nope," she sounds cheerful, "They are for the local stores."

Turning her face to me, she kisses my cheek and places a biscuit on my lips. Excited open my mouth and take a bite. It's the most delicious biscuits I've ever tried.

"Like it?" She doesn't have to ask. She knows. "Rosita bought you a large box of them."

"This is Spectacular," I mumble.

I look at her confused for a second, but then I realise I sent Rosita here, and of course Ruby invited her in.

She wipes her hands and turns around, devours me with her eyes, making me look down and realise I'm just wearing my boxers.

"The kids are about to wake up," she chews her bottom lip, "was thinking maybe you could go home, change clothes, and come back here," she says.

"That sounds like such a great idea." I step closer while I pull my trousers up. "We don't want these cuties to find out what gets cooked here in the nights," I wink and she giggles.

She holds herself at the counter, and without touching her, I let my lips brush hers.

You are so fucking beautiful!

"I will see you in..." I say, "about an hour?"

She just nod and I smile, having a better idea for the day, but I will let her know when I am back.

Grab my shoes and shirt and put them on while I head to

the front door.

Back in the car, I send a quick message to Matteo. He should be with the boys at *Little Castle.*

Be at Ruby's front door until I return, ASAP.

Ruby might not have asked for, but after what she told me and what I understood, she isn't comfortable been alone or feeling safe.

As I open the front door, Rosita appears from the kitchen.

"Did you taste them?" She asks me.

I pause for a second, questioning her comment, but she doesn't give me time to think much.

"Those are your mother's biscuits!" She exclaims.

My mother was an excellent cook, but better on the sweet side. She made all the desserts and treats we used to eat.

But sadness covers my clear of trouble mind. I haven't tasted her food for over two decades.

"I am so sorry," Rosita whisper understanding what she just did. We made a promise. We don't talk about them for a reason.

"Get things ready. We are going to spend a few days in the city," I answer in my disgusting, harsh voice.

She just nod, and step back into the kitchen.

"Boss!" Logan and Calvin walk in from their room at the back of the house.

"Morning," I greet.

"Are we going anywhere?" Calvin asks.

"We will spend the rest of the week in Belgravia. Logan, I

need you in Stella's 24/7, she might seem right, but I need someone monitoring her," I order.

"Yes boss," they answer in unison.

I am packing a few documents and clothes when Rosita appears by the front door.

"I will take care of that," she says, grabbing a pile of T-shirts I was putting on top of the mattress. "informal trip, I like that," she mumble trying to hold a smile.

"Will see you in the city," I answer, dropping a kiss on her chubby cheek.

There're a few bags packed by the front door when I leave. Everyone as efficient as usual, getting ready for a little getaway trip.

This will be the best way to give Thomas the time he needs for the renovation. Take Ruby and the children from whatever they are concern off and for me to keep up with the century edition.

Yesterday's meeting didn't went as expected, but I don't need the investors' or executives' approval or money anymore.

Ruby will be the cover, and the other businesses will have the spot they deserve, the online magazine will be launched and few corporate changes will happen.

Grandpa used to run the company from a distance, and everything was as smooth as butter. My father did his part, but I think they were big shoes too filled, and I won't make the same mistakes.

SaStel is my legacy, my empire, and it's my responsibility

and priority to keep it as one of the most important magazine in the world.

I reach Ruby's door, spotting Matteo at a bench in the road at the front of the apartments building, reading a newspaper and drinking some take away coffee.

Without a word, he gives me a nod. Understanding is time to leave, dropping away the paper and coffee and walking away through the park.

Ruby opens with a wide new smile, her eyes are glassy and I can hear the children screaming in the background.

She just jump on my arms and I close the door with a kick.

"Is everything okay?" I ask. She is screaming and laughing at the same time on my neck.

"I did it," she says,

"What was that?" I ask, pulling her out of my neck our noses are touching.

Her hands are holding my face, and I get lost in her blue bright eyes.

Gosh you are gorgeous!

"I... I did it, Samuel," she whispers.

"Mama, you told him?" Naima asks. She is screaming and running around the entire house, with Aidan following her.

We all just start laughing. I put her down and cup my hands around her perfect face.

"What you did?" I ask, dropping a small kiss on her lips.

"They say all the documents are getting ready," she talks way faster than I can understand, "they need me to be there in an hour," she continue, jumping from one foot to another like a nervous child, "I know we plan to spend some time...." I can't stop smiling, "well, I can drop the cookies first, well you come with us of course, we can drop the cookies, stop by the agency and then well, doing something nice, it's gonna be a nice weather, you know, yeah that should be a good plan,..." she stops as her mobile buzz on the back pocket of her shorts.

Pulling it out, her skin becomes even paler, her lips tremble and become white too, I see it, but she just shakes her head, reject whoever was calling and put it back on the pocket.

"You were saying?" I ask, trying to take her away from that little momentum and back to happiness.

"We are the new owner of the little cottage!" She exclaims, jumping around and laughing.

But the buzz comes back. She looks at the screen, rolls her eyes and walks away, avoiding the possibility of me making questions.

I meet her in the kitchen. Everything is spotless now, and XXL size brown cardboard boxes are resting on the island.

"The store orders?" I ask, pointing at the boxes.

"Yeah, they pick them up for the further stores, and I just drop a couple of them," she explains, looking anywhere but me.

Whoever was calling has made her uncomfortable. The best time for my getaway trip.

"I was thinking, as you are done with orders for the week, the meeting is done, and I want to spend more time with you," I murmur walking closer and closer, "why don't you and the kids spend the rest of the week with me at the city?"

"What? Us?" She asks shocked.

"Of course you say yes. I want to take three of you around. I can be your *tour guide*," I declare, bringing back the spark to her eyes and a smile to her beautiful lips.

"I will love that," she replies, tiptoeing and kissing me. "Give me a few minutes."

I nod and she walks away, leaving me lost in my thoughts, looking away through the glass door to her small garden, trying to call that little voice questioning why she has become pale and off the call multiple times.

"Samuel," Naima calls, and I jump back to reality.

"Yes, baby?" I ask.

"Would you like to join us?" She asks, pointing to the spread toys around the grass, and some paint is ready at the garden table. I nod and we step outside.

Aidan is on some type of expedition, mumbling and experimenting with dinosaurs and trucks.

I sit with Naima—we are at the table, painting anything and everything, mixing colours, creating new beautiful and ugly ones.

"Thanks Samuel," she whispers. When she looks into my eyes, I can see pain. This poor child has been through so much in such a brief life.

"You are more than welcome baby." She doesn't have to explain herself. I saw it in Ruby's eyes and now in hers.

"Mama won't tell me, but I think there's something going on," she says, looking over her shoulder at Aidan and behind me to Ruby, now she is at the kitchen packing some stuff, but Naima wants to make sure nobody is listening. "There's something going on with Advik."

My frown in question, but her body shakes, making me understand she can't talk about him—he must be the bastard that harmed them.

"Will protect you." I place my hand over hers. "No matter what," nodding, giving her a small smile.

She just nods and carries on with the drawing.

I can't help but check over my shoulder to Ruby.

She is floating around the room when her mobile rings again. This time she answers, making the little colour on her face fade away—she holds herself on the counter, but her legs aren't fast enough. I jump out of the chair and grab her exactly before she hits the floor.

The kids run behind me. She is unconscious in my arms. I can hear someone on the phone, holding it in my ear, I hear.

"I'm so sorry, Ruby. The judge won't listen to us. His safety has become a priority over yours," the woman at the other end says.

Everything makes sense now. I hang up, and raise Ruby in my arms, bring her to her bedroom and place her on the bed. I rush to the bathroom to get a cold towel and some water.

As the cold cloth touches her forehead she comes back, "Baby, it's me," I whisper.

When her eyes open, they are red as fire; I can't see the blue in them. Her skin is pale, but all makes sense. This is what petrified her. They aren't just coming on a getaway. I can't let them come back here.

This is a council apartment, but does that person know where they are? I won't be waiting to find out.

She jumps in my arms and holds me tight, shaking in a way I never experienced before.

"We are leaving," I assure her, breaking our hold. She looks into my eyes, questioning what am I talking about.

"Mama?" Naima's voice is pure panic.

"Everything is fine, kids," I say, caressing Ruby's cheek. "I will call my team and get everything ready, take anything that you need, empty this apartment if you need to, but you are not returning here." I assure.

After what I heard on the phone, no measure is enough to protect them, but *Little Castle* is not ready for them. Belgravia will be good while I get Hammersmith's house ready, or better Surrey, and nobody will get to them there.

I drop a soft kiss on her lips and bend to Naima.

"Help Mama with anything that she needs. I have a few calls to make."

She just nods and runs to grab the suitcases under the bed.

I look at Ruby from the door. She can't talk, but she moves as I give her a nod, knowing there's no time to lose.

CHAPTER TWELVE

Ruby

Fifteen years ago, Shepperton, TX

It's dark outside when I walk back to make sure I fed all the animals, and they are warm and secure.

I don't want to run behind cows in the darkness ever again in my life.

Coming to a halt when I hear a noise in the stables. I just was there, covered them, cuddled them and I'm sure Moon and Dalia were down for the night.

The noise increases and I grab the rake. It might be anything, a cat, a rat, a fucking snake. *Oh gosh, why me?!*

It's not an animal, it's *toilet boy.*

Why hasn't he left already? I think I was way too clear about it.

"Upsy," he says, drawing a cheeky smile to his shocking face.

"What is wrong with you?" I whisper, "If I were my father, you would be underground by now!"

"But the universe sends you." That smile again. "Right?" he whispers, getting closer.

"Stop right there!" I raise the rake, and God help me, I will use it on this crazy man.

He just keeps his smiling, raising his hand in a pleading motion.

"I just need a place to stay until I find a way out."

A part of me feels sorry for him, but dad will be crazy about it.

"I understand, but this isn't the correct place."

I can't trust him, even if a part of me, the curiosity of the unknown tells me to keep him close.

"Are you offering a better place?" He smiles, I smile, and hate myself for it.

"No!" I answer way too loud. His smile grows, probably reading my inside battle with the absurd situation and the visible signs of blush on my pale cheeks.

"Listen..." he gets closer, this time taking the rake from my shaking hands and tossing it aside.

"Ruby," I whisper, holding my breath. He is way too close, but I don't move away, just hold still.

"Listen Ruby, I know this is a difficult, way too weird situation." He comes closer, "But you are a smart, sweet girl," his fingers brush some hair away from my face, "and wouldn't be pleased to let me be out there." His face is so close I can smell him, breathe his air. He raises a questioning eyebrow and I just nod.

What is happening to me? I've never been this close to a man before, and here I am, with a complete stranger, trembling, sweating, and wanting to be even closer to him.

He is like a magnet, a mysterious, sweet magnet.

"Why don't you be an angel," he is studying my face, one of his hands brushing my cheeks, the other holding my hand, locking our fingers, "get me something to eat, and…" he gets so close to my ear, "some water to wash up."

Dropping a small kiss that makes me shake and throw away all the air, I didn't know I was holding in a loud exhale.

His nose is touching mine. He brushes them together—I close my eyes, and he kisses me, slowly, delicately.

My arms curl around his shoulder, and he pulls me closer by the waist. Our kiss becomes deeper, our breath broken, faster—I can feel our hearts hitting each other.

He walks backwards. I can't see, but I know where I'm going. Instantly I confirm it, when my back rests on the thatch. He treats me so gently, keeping our kiss while unbuttoning my overall. I tense and he moves his hand in between my thighs— I tense more, but when he moves his palm around, his fingers playing around my groin, I relax, enjoying the moment, moaning in his mouth. To what he smiles and keeps it that way. My breath becomes broken, a nice but painful unknown feeling grows in my lower tummy. His hand hardens and works faster, making me fist his hair.

The stable is spinning around me. This is too good, and I let go. His fingers continue working slowly, the kiss becomes more like small kisses. I'm trying to catch my breath, and when I open my eyes, I see him, smiling, with a new spark in his dark eyes.

"I better take something for you." He just smiles and nods.

I run back to the house. When I open the front door, everything is quiet. Dad is sleeping on his armchair, mum is in her bedroom, applying some cream to her hands and fixing the bow of her nightcap.

"Mama, you need to tell dad to move to bed."

He loves to fall asleep in there, gets grumpy for needing to move, but we know it's hard for him to rest and sleep first in bed.

"You know him *hija*," she gifts me with one of her special smiles. I kiss her cheek and wish her goodnight.

I have a quick shower, change my clothes, while I hear how mama walks to dad and gently wakes him.

He is trying but can hardly wake up, my mum step on the kitchen and I run to their room for some clothes. Back in my room, I look at what I have accomplished. I have the clothes, some food, and toilet stuff.

A few minutes later, I can hear my dad snoring again, this time in bed and mama's sleepy breath. She covers her ears at night as it's hard to sleep with dad.

By nine, I'm back in the stables. He steps out and looks at me, smiling brightly, offering a sunflower. I respond with a small smile.

"You can get warm and cold water from here." I point to the faucet and a clean spare bucket hanging on the wall. "And stop taking my mom's sunflowers or she will kill someone."

He just nods, then I nod and walk away.

"Can you stay?" He is whispering, but I hear him clearly.

"I will be back in the morning."

It's for the best. He nods sadly and I walk away.

CHAPTER THIRTEEN

Ruby

I jump off of the bed. Naima is throwing a lot of our clothes in the luggage and taking all the toilet products we might need, but my priority is the kitchen.

Samuel is in the garden, having a call. He seems agitated, and I can't blame him.

Louise's call was like an ice cold water bucket dropped over my head. Advik is out.

But that isn't the worst. He has escaped from the social centre they assigned him to and it's nowhere to be found.

I knew he wouldn't give up. He has a mission since the day he met me, and he won't stop until he fulfils it.

Putting away what I don't need, I place the most important items on the island.

My mobile ringing makes me freeze. It's on the counter near the glass door.

I grab it and see it's Martha, the cashier at the supermarket. That's the text she mentioned on Sunday, an order of one hundred cookies—she needs them for her crocheting group on Thursday morning at the library.

It makes me remember to take all the materials and ingredients I'll need. I can make it at Samuel's house, and I pack for the stores' orders too, not sure how long I will be there.

"Mama," Naima comes to me while I finish putting everything away. "Can we talk?" She sounds serious, way too serious for a child.

"Of course, baby." I sit her on the island and I lower myself on the stool, ready to listen to what she has to say.

"Was that about,... Advik?" She spit his name like poison. I just nod. "Do you love him?" She asks, tilting herself towards the garden, where Samuel is walking around, pulling his waves and at his phone.

"It's hard to explain baby." I look away, but she touches my cheek, getting my attention.

"I love him." Her eyes are glassy. "The way he looks at you, the way he talks, the way he loves you."

"He isn't..."

"He loves you, mama, in a way I've never seen in..." she pauses. It's hard for her to mention him again, so I just hold her hands and kiss them. "Please, if you love him, let him stay forever," she pauses, "here, in the new house, wherever we live, let's be together."

"Are you sure?" I ask. This is not a straightforward decision, and my feeling for Samuel isn't enough to drag everyone with me.

"Mama, you deserve it," she says, dropping a kiss on my cheek.

"When have you grown so much?" She might be five, but she speaks better than many grown-ups I know.

"The day I thought we would lose you, that it would just have been Aidan and me," she says.

"I'm not going anywhere." I kiss her hands again. "No matter what happens, I will always fight back."

"Mama, let Samuel know. Let him protect us."

"That might scare him away," I confess. He knows something is happening, but he might not like the full story.

"You always talk about honesty. You are not being honest this time." She just taught me a powerful lesson.

My ring tone announces a new message. Naima jumps down from the island and continues taking anything she knows we will need.

It's Grace, everything okay?

Shit! I forgot the appointment, and the doorbell confirms I am running extremely late.

When I open Sarah is there, "you didn't drop the order," she says. We agree I will drop the boxes, so I will be on time for the agency appointment. That way, if the delivery guy was late—he is, I wouldn't miss the collection.

"We are going," I spit.

"What?!" She exclaims.

"He is out on the run," I explain. She knows the full story, so no more information is need it.

"I will help you," she says, pushing herself inside the house, but immediately returning with the deliveries, "I will take care of this first," she walk away and come back after I see her handing the boxes to the delivery guy, "And I will drop the rest on the way to work."

Stepping inside the house again, she walks straight to the kitchen. I am just a few steps behind, but I step back when she comes to a halt.

"Morning!" She sings, catching Samuel on the kitchen island.

"Sarah," he nods and tries to fake a smile.

"Don't sweat it, I know everything," she says..

"I will check everything is packed," I say to them both. "Sarah, can you just finish here?"

"Done *amiga*."

I take my mobile, texting Grace back with a quick update of the situation. She replies—I will handle all. So I rush to the bedroom and bathroom, checking we have all that we need. In the kitchen, Sarah and Samuel are almost finished. Multiple boxes are near the front door, and I just give him a nod.

The kids are waiting by the door, ready to leave and start this new temporary adventure. Aidan just nods and holds Naima's hand.

When I open the door Matteo, another good-looking tall guy and Rosita are there, the men get hold of everything and fill up a black, window tinted van.

After a good half an hour, the kids are in the same car we

use for shopping on their car seats. I'm fastening my seat belt. Samuel is joining the other cars driving away from Blue Valley.

We reach London an hour later. The roads were busier than usual and I recognize where we are—Belgravia.

Samuel turn on a mews, followed by the van and park inside a private parking. We are exactly on the same road I saw him for the first time, weeks ago.

Getting the children out of the seats, we walk out of the garage and into an over the top posh apartment. Everything is black and white here, slightly bore for my taste, but that match Samuel perfectly.

The hallway floor is a marble shiny floor, the front door is almost the size of the wall at my little apartment, I follow Samuel's steps into a family room, white soft velvet couches set by the front wall, under a window that bright the entire room, a chimney by the side in front of the door and a little tea table in the center, the other walls are fill with paints, they look as posh as the place, and there is a second door, Rosita get into it, letting me have a pick to a kitchen.

The children and I take a seat at the biggest couch and for the first time in the past few hours I relax, taking a well-needed breath.

"I will make sure they arrange all," he says, dropping a kiss on my cheek and stepping away.

Rosita comes back with a tray, there are biscuits and juices, the children take them and seat back at the couch.

I see one guy passing by with my boxes and I stand, ready to take care of it.

"Mama, will help put our things away, enjoy the biscuits," I say, walking behind him and entering the kitchen.

It's another massive room, white marble counters, and at least three times the size of my island in the center and the dining table in the corner, at least ten people can seat in it.

"Where would you like this, Ruby?" Rosita asks.

"Where will I have space?" I ask, pointing at the shiny black cupboards and drawers.

Rosita steps closer to one of them and opens it, it's absolutely empty, and then another, and another.

Why is this house empty?

"We spend little time here, just when Samuel has to work at the office here," she assures. That makes sense.

Few minutes later, all my boxes are empty and folded away, the cupboards and drawers are full, and Samuel appears by the door.

"I can see already here too," he says, walking closer and resting his arm over my shoulder, "I have a little surprise," he whispers, dropping a small kiss on my cheek, getting hold of my hand and pulling me away.

The children are not anymore on the couch—they are by the door.

"What is going on?" I ask curiously.

"We all need a nice day off," he says, gifting me with his gorgeous smile and a wink.

I look back at the kids and I just see smiles, giving everyone a nod and walking out of the house.

Matteo is waiting outside, opening the van side door for us

and we all just get in, the car seat are now here, and it's a way more luxury space than I thought, nothing to do with the regular transport or delivery vans I see before.

Samuel is sitting by my side, the children behind us, he place out his hand and I hold it, let it hang in there while we drive away, joining the busy London roads.

I look out of the window, but my mind is in another place, in a peaceful, safe place.

The van stops and Matteo gets out, sliding the door open and Samuel standing to helping the kids out.

"Ruby?" He whispers, calling me out of my thoughts.

I shake my head and turn to find everyone out waiting for me.

"Sorry," I say, stepping out.

Suddenly shocked when I realized where we are, it's Buckingham Palace, and I know why we are here.

It's not Samuel trying to give me a full tour, it's the sexy *tour guide* I met in a hot dark suit few days ago, the crazy man I found running behind his nephew at the park, the kind man that was concerned about us and spent the day shopping with us.

The second man I was with on my life, but the first I ever loved, the one that stop and bring to life my broken heart, the one that brings a smile to my face with a simple gesture, the one I've dreamed off as a child and I been looking for all my life.

Walking closer to him, I curl my arms around his waist, rest my head in his heart and listen to the most beautiful sound, the heart of the man I love beating for us.

Dropping a kiss on my crown, Samuel holds me by the shoulder and rests his arm there, bend to take Aidan on the arms and Naima holds my hand, but I tense when I see Matteo driving away.

"Some of my men are around, but I just need you to be natural," he whispers in my ear.

We have no clue where Advik is, how much information he has or even if he is looking for me, well, the last one I am sure of it.

Walking through St James Park, until we reach the Big Ben, over here there is more people that we see at the Palace, but Samuel safely put Naima between us and take us to the other side of the bridge, the second I see London Eye, I have a million heart attacks thinking Samuel was planning to take us there, but he says the surprise is way better.

At the other side of the river, we walk down beautiful stone steps and even we are marching in the highest attraction in London's direction. Samuel stops by the Sea Life, London Aquarium.

"An aquarium?" We all ask him in unison.

"Have you been before?" He asks, but it's over our expression, no we haven't.

This is the first time we have ever visited the city. The first time I came here was months ago for the first court hearing and then a few days ago, never in the mood for a tour.

We accidentally met here days ago. I was lost searching for a shortcut to Hyde Park.

We join the fast track queue. After a few seconds of

stepping inside the building, everything is like a bunker, drawings of pipelines, little circle windows, and machinery.

But as we turn, there is no more floor, just a long piece of glass with SHARKS! Under us! Samuel can't hold it and start laughing, pulling his mobile away and recording us, Naima is the first brave to cross it, Aidan cutely cover his eyes and run as Samuel instructed, but I stand at the edge, looking up to who is waiting for me, the three humans I love the most, *for God shake Ruby! Get it together!*

I stroll. It might sound silly, but I am not actually scared of the sharks. I am of the water, always been. Could that be because the first time I was at the beach it was my first episode with Advik with my head ending under the water?

Shaking my thoughts away, I give one step after another, fighting my demons and giving myself the power over me again.

Absolutely delighted with the entire place, but my favorite, the under the water tunnel and wall size glass with sculptures inside, for the children definitely the penguins.

Samuel's mobile rings as we reach the store on the way to the exit and he holds my forearm.

"Yes?" He asks, "perfect."

Without another word he hold back my hand and take us to the street, walking back to the stone staircase and then I can see Matteo and the van are waiting for us, we securely seat the children and drive away, but this time I rest my head to Samuel direction, enjoying the view, examining every inch of his perfection.

But he is away, pensative, distracted, tense, can't blame

him.

After an hour at the apartment, Rosita continues moaning and apologizing for how messy everything is. For me it is spotless, and okay they have an empty fridge but it's something easy to fix.

"Why don't we change to something more comfortable?" Samuel ask, "we will get some groceries," Rosita gasp in disbelieve.

Samuel ignores her and guides everyone upstairs. We were here this morning, but we haven't seen around. I have no clue where our things are.

"Ruby, you go through that door, Naima you come with me, Aidan you go there," he keep pointing to close doors and we just open the door, but I don't step in yet.

"Do I have room just for me?'" Naima asks surprised.

"The princess of the house, deserve her own place," he answers and opens the door, "I know it doesn't look perfect, but we can decorate it as you like."

I step behind them, compare with our regular bedroom. This is a queen-size, perfect for Naima. Everything is beige and baby pink.

"It's perfect Samuel, thanks," Naima says, holding his hand.

Samuel goes down on one knee and looks into her beautiful eyes.

"You are more than welcome," giving her a small smile. "Now, get changed and out in 5 okey?" She just nod and start opening drawers, found all her things are now placed there.

We walk to Aidan's room. He is by a corner playing already with all the books and toys he found.

"Having fun big boy?" Samuel asks from the door. He nods and gets back to it.

"I will help him," Rosita says behind us, but I tense. He won't let her get closed, "let me try," she whisper resting a soft hand on my arm.

"Go, I will be here just in case. I will meet you in a minute," Samuel says, dropping a kiss on my cheek.

I walk back to the bedroom he point out before and head to the shower, I really need it.

My clothes hit the floor and I step in it, standing under the big panel waterfall, regulating no temperature I just close my eyes and open the water.

Call me crazy, I'm a believer that people we have learned what real pain is, the one that kill bit by bit parts of who you are, don't feel pain in regular things, like cutting, burning, cold water, because we already know how much it can hurt, those are tickles under our thick skin.

CHAPTER FOURTEEN

Samuel

While I remove my clothes she comes out, I hang her a bathrobe and let her get changed. The evening is too long to be distracted now—we have two hungry kids to feed.

Everyone is waiting downstairs and we leave immediately, Aidan in my arms as usual and Naima between us, holding our hands.

I take them through the roads until we meet the village shopping street. It has multiple small businesses where you can find anything you can imagine, but from my apartment we have to cross a dark narrow road.

We are in Belgravia. Nothing harmful ever happens on these roads.

What a dark mews will do to us?

While we cross the mews, all the hair on my body stands. I look back, and I will swear on my life I saw a male figure observing us and walking away.

I am not the only one that feels it when Naima holds my

arm, not my hand.

Without thinking, I bend and hold her in my arms too, just to realise Ruby is a statue, freeze looking to where I know I saw someone.

Once in the store we are all tense, looking over my shoulder, Naima can't stop looking around either, confirming I might not be the only one feeling this, I hold her tighter and whisper on her ear, "everything is going to be okey," to what she just hold my neck tighter, hide away and breath several times.

I won't let anything happen to you.

After a few minutes at the store, the child's multiple questions about any new ingredient that they found and a few giggles. The ambience seems to be calmer, back to normal.

It's a tiny, but packed with everything we need in store. I take care of filling each of our bags.

The kids don't want to be in the arms anymore, so they can help better with the bags I fill up with insignificant items. We step out, to the fresh summer evening streets, Naima come to a halt, her gaze if focus, her skin is pale as Ruby's, her body is shaking, I try to look in her direction but I just see darkness, Ruby entire body tense and become cold.

"We need to leave," I just say, grabbing both of the kids and walking as fast as I can while carry them, looking for any shortcut, but we can't go through the small dark road anymore.

I never been afraid of anything, but now? I am petrified of anything or anyone harming them.

If it was just me seen things, feeling things, I could call it paranoia, but see Naima and Ruby's reactions confirm my worst nightmare, the one I tried to figure it out all these days, someone is looking for them.

When I can see the apartment in the distance, I run a bit to reach the door as quick as possible and lock us all in. Ruby rests her back to the door.

I try to catch my breath, to focus, but Naima's hold on my nape is waking every fibre in my body. She is terrified.

Rosita appears in the hallway, alert when she sees the situation, Ruby on the floor, both of the kids curled in my arms, and I am a frozen mess.

"Give me that," she murmurs, taking the bags away from the children and myself and walking away.

I step closer, kneeling in front of Ruby, spreading my legs around her and pushing the three of us closer.

I am here guys!

We just stay there forever, comforting each other, calming each other, loving each other, protecting each other.

Soft steps approach us. I can't see her, but I know is Rosita.

"*Mis hijitos,* dinner is ready," she says softly, "you need to eat something," she explains, and her small palm caress my hair.

I stand and take the kids back with me, but Naima shakes, asking to be put down. There is a fire inside her I have never seen before.

"It was him, right?" She asks, her eyes are glassy.

Ruby steps closer, kissing her face. Unable to say a word,

she walks through the same door Rosita did.

Naima isn't finished with this conversation, and she rushes behind her. I am on her heels in no time.

All the shopping is now presented in a delicious meal, and everyone is waiting for us at the table.

"Our captor was on the small dark road," Naima declares.

Captor?

"I can't do this," Ruby says low, standing, placing her napkin near the empty plates, "if you will excuse me," she says, walking away.

Wow! You can't run from this one lady!

"Enough!!!" Naima screams, "you can't run anymore!"

"Naima, please," Ruby begs.

"Please what, mother?" She asks, her little fist on her sides, "I won't run anymore. I'm not scared anymore."

"You don't know what you are saying. I will never stop running to protect you and Aidan."

My throat and heart blocked. She can't possibly be planning to run, not when I have felt and seen the danger on our backs.

"And lose all of this?" She asks pointing at everyone at the table, "is he really worth that much?"

"Running has away kept us alive," Ruby fight back, tears run down her cheeks.

"He will find you, he always does, and this time will be game over mama!"

I step closer, hold their hands, and pull them to my arms, they fist my shirt and hide their faces away, until a soft cough brings us back and we all seat at the table.

This has been the hardest evenings since I lost my parents. Listen, feel, see the anger and fright inside Naima was shocking.

She is too young and went through so much. Who could blame her?

But what they went through has them in an alert mode for life, Matteo was pissed off, he wanted to follow us, keep us safe, but I refuse it, if he was there, he could have monitor who it was following, but Naima told us clearly *her captor.*

They refused to be apart—they refuse to sleep—they refuse to speak anymore, and they forbid me to leave the bedroom.

But now they are sleeping. I roll out of bed and head downstairs. Matteo has called the entire security team. Rosita is serving coffees.

"Evening gentlemen," I say. "I wish we didn't have to come to this point, but we aren't sure who we are dealing with. Only Ruby and the kids know his actual appearance." We need a plan.

"Espera mi hijito," Rosita interrupts me, "there's someone that knows him too, the lady on the phone."

"Calvin, I need you to find her. Rosita, get me Ruby mobile please," she just nod and walk to find Ruby purse.

By midnight, I'm back in the bedroom. They continue as I left them, hugging, sleeping peacefully, unaware of the plans, the concerns, nothing, and that will be the best.

I can't remember when finally my eyes gave up and close away, but when I start drowsily try to move, I feel Aidan is sleeping on top of me, Naima is extremely close to my ribs and Ruby is hugging both on top of me, breathing so close I can feel it on my shoulder.

Maybe in another moment I would have missed my space, but right now, after all what has happened, I can't blame them, and a part of me knows this is what I've been needing for many years.

A soft knock calls my attention. Is Rosita with a breakfast tray. I can smell the toasts, coffee, and homemade jam.

She knows they might not want to be around anyone yet, but we need to take care of them, same as I force them to sleep last night. I will do it now to eat.

Holding Aidan tight to my chest, I stand, he found a comfortable place and continue sleeping on my arms—I walk to the table and prepare a latte for Ruby, espresso for me, pour some fresh orange juice for the kids and slowly walk back to the bed, bringing one by one.

Once I'm done, I seat, resting my back on the headboard, caressing the hair of three of them, whispering their names, Naima is the first one in heavily stand her head, smiling to the juice, she seat on my side, placing my arm around her and drink her juice, enjoying the peaceful moment.

Aidan doesn't take long to join Naima and me on the bed drink party, but Ruby needs to rest. Her eyelids are purple, her cheeks continue red after how much she cries last night.

"Some toast?" I whisper, asking the kids.

They both shake their head, well at least they drink all the juice.

"Would you like to join me in the gym?" they immediately

nod. "Let's go!" I whisper.

I jot a note to Ruby. We will be at the gym, but to please wait here.

This is a one of the smallest properties, but she doesn't know the way around, and we don't need her having another anxious moment.

Inside the gym, I follow my ritual, nice morning music, one that actually make them giggle and dance around, I will normally start on the spinning bike, but I change it for the recumbent one, because as I knew, Aidan is the first one jump up with me.

Not looking for burn anything away, well maybe yes, clear my head, kill the time.

This wasn't the plan I have for today. I planned to take them all day to the park, go for a ride, take them to a pleasant terrace for lunch, visit the city slightly more.

But now, everything has change, looking it on the bright side, I have them, we might to have to spend all day in doors, but why we don't make the best out of it?

Holding that thought, I stand off the bike. Aidan is on my arms, quietly approaching Naima that is watching and dancing, holding her up and make her giggle and scream at the same time.

That is the best music I choose to hear. I never want to stop hear it, and if I cause it, let so be it.

When I open the kitchen door I regret it, but instantly the kitchen is empty again. I knew nobody left last night, but waiting in the kitchen for anything to happen was not a good idea.

"They have everything they need in the guest house," Rosita casually says while she finish tiding up the breakfast all the guys have eaten.

"Can we make sure they stay away from the house for the time been?" I ask Matteo, who is finishing the coffee on the island.

He just nods back at me, so I place the kids there too, turning around and grabbing anything I can to feed them. They refuse any food before, but not now. The gym has changed the mood for everyone.

"You finish this, and I will check on mama okey?" Rosita steps closer and hugs Naima. She is sensitive after last night.

When I enter the bedroom, the most beautiful view is in front of me. Ruby's mane is spread around the pillow, her lips slightly open, and somehow this few extra hour of sleep has helped with the eyes swollen.

Dropping a soft kiss on her less red cheek, I walk to the shower, standing under the waterfall and letting the water regulate by itself.

The steam surround me—I rest my forearms on the wall and close my eyes, no matter how warm the water it is, my body reacts before her fingertips brush my skin, her arms curl around my waist and her cheek rest on my back.

My heart hammering in her ear, her breath slow and calm, and I smile. This is the Ruby I fall in love with.

Turning around me, I smile brightly when I get a full view of her beauty. The water falling on my nape splashes her, and she closes her eyes, holding herself on my waist.

Without a word, I stand and let all the water fall on her. I take my shampoo from the shelf and start massaging her scalp, cleaning her gorgeous mane. She slightly moans in satisfaction.

Once I rinse it, I take the soap and sponge and start scrubbing her body, kneeling to reach her legs.

There is nothing sexual in this shower, it's pure love and the sense of care for her.

I love this woman more than I could imagine loving anyone.

Rising, I make sure her entire body gets rinsed and quickly washes over mine, stepping out of the shower, covering her first and then me.

Walking back to the bedroom I take a what it look like a comfy dress for Ruby, some knee length denim for me and a t-shirt.

Help her get dress and seat her by my desk, walk to take her comb and start taking care of her mane while she looks away by the window.

"I love you," she murmurs while I nearly finish.

I have heard it perfectly. It's not me imagine things, just humming as I finish with what I was doing. Turning around her and kneeling, I hold her hands on mine and rest them on my chest, over my heart.

"I love you too," I whisper, letting a thick tear drop.

Her soft small palm cover my cheek, brushing the tears away, the last time I said those words was to my mother, the last day I saw her, and since then I've feared saying it again, of the possibility to lose whoever I say it again.

CHAPTER FIFTEEN

Ruby

After a nutritious breakfast, I rest on the dining table, watching by the glass door heading to the rear garden. The sun is high and everything seems peaceful.

"I want to go out," I mumble to Samuel who was playing outside with the children.

"Ruby..." He calls.

"I will not hide anymore," I say. He found us, but that proves that there is not a way to hide away.

If we lock ourselves here, we are giving him the power back, the answer he needs, that he creates some kind of effect over us.

"Just for lunch!" Samuel assure, and I nod.

We are in the van again. At least three more cars are following us, but I can see it in Naima's face. We will fight back; we won't hide again and not giving up this second chance.

Matteo drive pass Piccadilly Circus, the panels are amazing, brightening up the entire area, the roads are packed with people, some are tourist, but other are speeding in between them to go somewhere else.

After a few more minutes we stop, the following cars move forwards, I tense, but see they are entering a parking nearby, just as the driver stays in the car, and the rest walk away, well aware of the direction we will take.

Rosita helps with the kids and Samuel holds them both. We cross over and I spot a minor road decorated with Chinese lanterns. *We are in China Town.*

A smile grows on our faces and I let Rosita hold her arm around me—we walk in.

There are grocery stores with spices and ingredients I've never seen in my life, medicine clinics for any type of sickness, hair salons with funny hair styles, buffets that spread a delicious scent on the streets, bakeries with things I never tasted before, and by the time we reach the restaurant Samuel was looking for, our tummies are half full of bread, bubble waffles and snacks, discreetly Samuel has gave our shopping to one of his security team members, that way is just us we have to worry for.

Naima asks me to buy ingredients to copy the cake we tried, I will try my best, seen how calm and content she is, if the taste of that cake other day will bring her back to this moment, I will do it every day.

We enter a restaurant that welcome us with a little bridge, there is a river under it with fish of any color you could imagine, we spend few minutes there, but the reservation give us a quick entry to our table, is a simple place, but is decorate it with Chinese sculptures, paints, lights, I guess is like travel to

Asia but in the roads of London.

I've never tried this type of food and neither of them, so we follow the waiter suggestions and get various plates, we all enjoy sharing, laugh at new flavors, Rosita can't stop laughing telling how pikie Samuel has always been with food, how much she struggled all her life cooking for him.

It's a really warm afternoon, forcing me to put my hair up in a messy bun, absolutely forgetting how low my dress is at the back, freezing when Samuel gasp.

I turn, it's in Naima face too, my scars, I forgot them for a split second, but seen their expression make the old wounds burn as fire over my healed flesh, so I let the mane down again, none of them change the expression, I just shake my head, making them aware this is not a conversation we will have.

The sun is low over China Town buildings when we get into the van, it's been few hours since they see my skin, but Samuel expression hasn't changed, I have been naked in front of him, but he has only seen my torso, and I was thankful for that.

We enter the apartment again, walking straight to the stairs, looking over my shoulder at Samuel.

"I will need to shower first," I whisper when the children walk into the kitchen with Rosita, "I feel really... dirty." I mumble, walking upstairs.

He gave me a narrow look and an extremely hot smile, one that warm the last inches of my body that weren't already in flames.

"I could help you wash up," he says, licking his bottom lip.

"That would be... nice." I say from the top of the stairs.

He jumps the last steps that were between us, grabbing me by the back of my thighs and pulling me over his shoulder.

My entire mane is on my face, but I get a delicious view. His hard as rock ass, fighting with his waistband and introducing my hand, his skin comes to life and his muscles tight up.

Without warning, he let go of me, and I land on the mattress. He pulls my dress up and uses it to hold my wrist away.

"It's that okey?" He asks in a whisper, to what I just nod.

This is gonna be another painfully delicious Samuel!

With a satisfaction reflecting on his face, he takes off his shirt, kneels between my thighs, resting one fist on the side of my head and brushes my lips with the other. I open them, lick, suck, and moist them.

Once he is satisfied with it, they brush away, from my lips to my breast, he first cup it, draw a circle around it until it becomes harder and then slightly pinching it, my back arch and I get even more wet that I already was, after taking care of the other breast, he play around my tummy, suddenly stopping when his fingertip reach my small pubic hair area, playing around, giving me a mixture of tickles and irresistible pleasure, I can't take my eyes away from him and regret approving the wrist tied up.

I can see his muscle contracting and expanding with every movement, his skin reacting as he touches me, feeling the same fire as I do.

In an extremely painfully, delicious way, his fingers brush

my clit over the knickers, easily pulling them away, brushing his palm over my calf, drawing circles on my thighs and without warning into my wet entry, making me releasing a moan that was holding on my throat all this time.

"Silence," he murmurs, bringing his fingers to his lips, licking my wetness. "Would I have to gag you?" He asks close to my lips, I lift my head and kiss him, tasting my wetness from his delicious lips, "would I?" He asks again, to what I surprisedly nod, nibbling my bottom lip, a spark grow on his eyes and he stands away from the bed, walking to the drawer, returning with two ties.

"Open," he orders. "Bite," I obey when he places a soft material tie between my lips. He drops a kiss on my lips, brushing his tongue over them, and gives me a wink.

I trust him—I desire and love him, so for the first time I am happily ready to be at the mercy of this God.

Holding my hips he spins me around, resting slightly over me, "we can stop at any time," he whispers on my ear, making my bum raise and meet his hard cock, "that will have to wait," he murmurs again.

Tying the tie at the corner metal of the bedframe, removing the dress away from my wrist and replacing it with the tie, the material is so soft, I can't feel the hold that much.

His palms caress my skin from my forearms to my shoulders, moving my mane away, my body tense at the exposure of my back, he lowers and drop a kiss in every single wound, somehow taking the memories and pain away from them, just becoming part of my thick skin, of my shell.

His palms rest on my hips now and my bum rise, he follows the trace of kisses he has started, now dropping soft bites on my flesh, until he reaches my pussy, licking my lips while the tip of his nose pusses over my perineum, sending me to an unknown level of pleasure, his tongue pushes in, my entire body trembles, my hips rotate and that gives him a deeper access.

I bite the tie, hide my face on the bedsheets, but it doesn't feel enough to hide away my moans. The hold on my hips becomes tighter and so do my walls, sucking his tongue deeper inside me.

Everything become blur, his movements become faster until I can feel my inside exploding and melting around his lips, that now are sucking my full climax and kissing my swollen lips.

I melt in the wet sheet, while I hear his zip, buttons and the elastic of the boxer, his hold on the headboard and remove his clothes, brushing the head of hard arousal over my bum, down my entries until my clit, making me automatically rise my hips ready for it, placing the head on my entry I push back, pulling the hold of my wrist and sending a burn over my entire body.

Taking him in without warning, he growls and my hips rotate, rising slightly more, giving him a deeper penetration that pushes me forward, but I instantly pull back, way deeper inside.

Samuel pulls out slightly but thrust back harder and deeper. I bite the tie, pull the one on my wrist and my neck curl up, looking at the ceiling.

His hands leave my hips, cupping my breast, kneeling

closer until I seat over him with every rotation, desperate for holding him. He read my mind and releases my wrist, brushing his fingertips over them, but I want to touch him.

I curl my arm over his nape, turning to face him, melting when I meet his gaze. They are brighter, clear, deep.

His fingertips brush my lips and remove the tie. I gesticulate, nibbling my lips to hold the moans when I rise and drop again, letting him reach the deepest part.

Holding his nape, I push him closer and lose myself on his lips—he tastes different, delicious, a mixture of us and our love.

Gosh, I love this man!

Curling his arm around my hips, that helps me to raise steadily, brushing the best orgasm I could ever imagine it exists.

"Ruby..." He whispers on my ear, sending me to heaven, I can't feel my body anymore, everything around us it's gone, his breath on my ear, one hand over my breast, stimulating my nipple until the limit it should hurt, but pain doesn't exist when you are on this level of pleasure.

My walls get tighter, I can feel my climax growing, forcing me to move even faster. I bite my bottom lip, tasting the metallic taste of blood.

The entire room's spines around and I let go, Samuel met my shoulder, biting slightly, hiding a deep growl away.

Once I had extracted every single drop out of him, I raise, pull him away and turn, sitting on his lap, cupping his face with my hands, brushing with my fingers his now thick beard.

"I can trim it," he says.

"No, I love it," I say, following the full trace. A new beautiful smile grows on his delicious lips. "I love this too," to what he smiles more.

"I love this time with you, but we have two beautiful children waiting downstairs," he says, and I just nod, dropping a soft kiss on the tip of his nose and moving away.

We share a quick shower, get comfy clothes on, and walk out of the bedroom. I can smell dinner from the top of the stairs.

Rosita is finishing setting up the table when we enter the kitchen. Naima and Aidan are at the island drawing on the new books we bought them this afternoon.

"That looks fantastic," I murmur in Naima's ear, getting a beautiful giggle back.

"Logan helped me with the small parts," she explains, making me look at him and give him a thankful smile.

"*Hijitos*, dinner is ready," Rosita calls everyone.

We enjoy a full feast. The entire security team is with us too, making me understand how protected we are, and that Rosita is used to the big meal prep.

They are all at least a head taller than me. Samuel has muscles, but some of them are like if it has blown up. I guess it goes with the job.

Few minutes later, and a great teamwork, the kitchen is spotless, nobody could say we have been over twelve people just having a feast here.

Rosita hand them some drinks, a bowl full of fruit and

everyone move to the guest house. Samuel and I bring the kids upstairs and put them to be way more tired than usual, but warm and settled on their new beds.

Samuel meets me in the corridor, and we walk back to the kitchen. Rosita has prepared some coffee and the cookies that I extra baked from the store's orders.

But I have Martha order to take care of.

"How can we help Ruby?" Rosita asks.

"It's fine, honestly," I say shyly.

"We are four grown-ups, we can't just seat here and see you working," she explains and I just nod.

"I need the metal bowls," Matteo stand and found it, "ingredients now, flour, baking powder..." as I mentioned them, Samuel and Matteo keep grabbing them.

"What is the temperature you need?" Rosita asks, walking to the oven on the wall.

"180° for ten minutes and down to 120° for another five minutes." Rosita nods, opening the door. "Wow, that's a big oven," I say.

Everyone laugh at my comment. I guess they are used to big spaces, big furniture, big everything, but that's not my case.

"Is that something good?" Samuel asks, hugging me while I pour all the ingredients in the mixing bowl, resting his chin on my shoulder.

"That is the best news. It means I will probably just need to do one batch of cookies. That will do for Martha's order."

"We have two ovens," he whispers, and I look shocked.

"Thanks," I murmur, and he kisses my cheek deeply.

We seat at the big island. Rosita is sharing stories of Samuel and Matteo when were younger, about Samuel's childhood. All while we finish with the dough, this is the part where nobody can help me.

"I know you might all feel it's unnecessary," my gaze on the bowl, incapable of looking at them in the eyes, "but I really appreciate all of this. Nobody has done much for us in a while."

"Where are you exactly from Ruby?" Rosita asks, and Samuel cough in disapproval.

"My mom is Spanish, my dad is from Texas," I say. "That's where I was born, in a little town call Shepperton." I smile, remembering home, my parents, my animals. "you wouldn't be able to see anyone for miles. It was peaceful, but I was really busy taking care of the animals all day."

My heart hurts!

That is all I can remember since I have memory, running around the wheat fields, feeding animals, cleaning stables, riding, having an amazing life that I appreciated little as a teenager.

"When did you come here?" Rosita asks.

I look at Samuel, who raises the shoulders and gives an apologetic smile.

"My hus... we..." I can't look at them.

I don't think I am ready to talk about all of this.

"Your parents might miss the kids a lot," Matteo says, focused on his cookie, but entire body freeze, my heart explodes and a thick tear runs down my cheek.

"They..." I look away, trying to hide my eyes filled up with tears. "They don't..." a knot on my throat blocks the words and

I can't talk.

"Know the kids exist," Matteo finished for me. "Holy shit... that's bad." We all look at him and I stand to prepare the oven tray, "I mean for him to do that to you, and to those sweet children," he sounds nervous, "they deserve a family, they all deserve to enjoy each other."

"It's too late for that," I whisper, dropping my chin to my chest.

Rosita stands by my side and curl me by the shoulder.

"It's never late to start over. We all deserve a second chance," she says.

"But I don't know how to find them," I whisper, just as my tears drop at a none stop pace.

"You left just a few years ago," Matteo says, assuming I left before Naima was born, but that wasn't the case.

"I left fifteen years ago," I whisper, and the room become silence, I can listen to their hearts humming on their chests.

"Holy shit!" Matteo spit, nearly choking.

My eyes are glassy, my chest hurts, and I can't believe I just confessed to the worst decision I could ever do.

"I'm sorry," Samuel says, there's pain in his voice.

I look back at Rosita, and she is cleaning away some tears.

Turning around, I just hide my face on his chest, embarrassed.

"We all have a past," he whisper holding my face away, cleaning away my tears, "I made horrible mistakes too," Rosita stops breathing, "they still hurt, me and everyone around me," he confess and I can hear the sobbing Rosita is trying to hide away.

I just keep going with the baking. Samuel and Matteo take a seat at the dining table with Calvin, he brough a pile of documents and they are each on one laptop. Rosita is helping rolling cookies and a few minutes later taking them out.

As usual, I baked some extra for the children, this time slightly bigger batch as we are more mouths to feed.

Walking back to Samuel, I notice they all get slightly nervous as I approach. He even closes his laptop.

Taking a seat on his lap and placing a cookie on his lips.

"Nice cookie?" I ask, making him smile brightly.

"It's spectacular," he assure making me smile back.

"Ruby," Matteo calls, making us all focus on him. "I can't imagine what you have been through since you were a kid," he says slowly. "I'm sorry for my comments, and I swear I will protect you and the children."

"I really appreciate that and I understand it's hard to understand what I did many years ago," I say, playing with the edge of my shirt. "I was fifteen, naïve, in love, and didn't know better. It was the best opportunity to have a what I thought will be a better life. Yes, it didn't turn out as I planned, but thanks to that mistake I have two incredible children. I live in the city of my dreams. I'm recovering, alive," I whisper, looking at Samuel.

A thick tear rolls down his cheek. I caress his cheek, and he closes his eyes under my touch.

"That mistake has taken me to this very moment." I look around and smile. "I own *our step closer to heaven*. Before I had my freedom, I dreamed of it." A sad smile covers my lips.

"That I will be in it, with my children, safe, loved, by the side of the man of my dreams," I say, brushing his perfect thick waves. He is the perfection incarnated. "Yes, I dreamed of you before I even knew you existed," I sigh. "Yes, I was a bad daughter, I've paid for it every single day since I left, but I promised myself to always fight for my life, to never give up, and I think I haven't done so bad," I explain, letting some tears drop.

"We all sacrifice a part of us in life," Rosita says, holding Matteo's shoulder by my side. "I can't imagine what you went through, but I know you are a survivor," she tries to smile. "Those children, that's what matter, they will understand everything when they grow older, as we do mothers. So, let's all take a good rest." Rosita drop a kiss on Matteo's head and tap his shoulder. "I will take care of the last bits. Everyone out now!"

Like obedient children, we head out of the kitchen and to the stairs.

Samuel rests his arm on my shoulders and guides me back to the bedroom.

Then into the bathroom, where he gives me a brand-new toothbrush and toothpaste.

"I brought my own," I assure.

"You can just keep this one here," he replies casually.

He is in seated, resting his back on the headboard by the time I finish in the bathroom—I join him, resting my head on his chest.

"Where have you been all this time?" I ask, looking up to

face him. Locking our gaze, he lowers his head to level with mine. Our noses are touching.

"Waiting for you baby," he whispers, pushing us down in the mattress and playing with my mane while my eyes become drowsy, his heart my lullaby.

CHAPTER SIXTEEN

Ruby
Fifteen years ago, Shepperton, TX

It's been a week since Advik walk into our farm. Now I know his name.

We have three meals a day together. Work has increased as there are many things to be prepared before the storm arrive.

I enjoy his company, his stories, his dreams, and they make me dream too.

He has promised he will take me around the world with him, and that just builds hope in me.

And at night, every night, I enjoy his kisses, his whispers on my neck, his touch.

I felt safe and comfortable masturbating him—it was a weird first experience, but when I saw what my touch creates in him, the same pleasure as mine, I actually enjoy it, and definitely so does he.

I wake up on a gray day. It's the storm we've been waiting

on for a month, all the animals are secure in a new closed barn, and so is Advik.

Dropping him some breakfast, I explain the plan again if things get ugly. But they shouldn't, as dad and I have spent many hours making sure the barn is safe and warm for everyone.

"Ruby, I need to leave," he says. There's sadness in his voice.

"You can't leave now!" I panic to think he will leave me here—that he will leave during this storm, one that might last days.

"Come with me Ruby," he gets closer, holding my face, looking into my eyes. I can't answer. "Nothing will happen to you. I will take care of you."

I'm scare. I shake my head and he softly kisses me. "Please," he begs, "let's go, you and me, forever."

Tears fall in between us. I can't stop them.

Moving my head back, I can see his face. He is scared too, *of what? Losing me?*

"But my parents..." I whisper.

"They will understand," he cuts me off before I can finish. "We will contact them as soon as we are safe."

I fear a life without my parents, but I want the life I deserve to be, and they won't let that happen while I'm here.

"Let's go Ruby!" He insists. "It will be you and me forever." He kisses me again, this time deeper, and I just surrender.

CHAPTER SEVENTEEN

Samuel

It's the middle of the night and I can't sleep. Dropping a soft kiss on her cheek and leaving a note, I walk downstairs to the kitchen.

I locked us in the apartment for two days. After what Calvin found out, I can let them leave again, not until we get everything under control.

He found the bastard, but he doesn't have a fix location.

When I enter Matteo, Calvin and Jackson are at the island, they aren't pleased, but we have no choice that leave for some shopping.

Tomorrow is the annual gala, and this year will be together with the launch of the century edition. Ruby will need an appropriate gown for the occasion, and I need to make sure everything is under control at the office.

"What do we have?" I ask them.

"His image has been share over all the teams, Lorna has it too, if that bastard step closer to any of you the entire London police department will be on him in seconds," Jackson explain, sharing with Matteo that his ex-girlfriend is now involve on family matters.

"It's unnecessary, but I need everyone aware that we don't need a tribe of security gorillas walking around us," I explain, raising an eyebrow at Jackson. He loves to do that.

"What about the children?" Matteo asks.

"They will stay here. Once we finish, we are moving back to *Little Castle,*" I answer.

"Back to Blue Valley?" He asks worried.

"We can't hide forever, and besides, that fucking place is a fortress. No way something happening in there," I confirm.

"I will be at the gym," I say.

Messaging everyone at the office on my way, explaining the recent changes and the urge to have everyone at my office first thing in the morning.

But the room isn't empty. Some of my guys are working out too, stopping the moment I step in.

"Please don't stop for me, this room is big enough," I assure.

After who knows how long, my entire body dripping I leave the room, leaving my team working those blown up muscles they wear nowadays.

Ruby is sleeping when I return, so slowly I step into the bathroom and have a quick shower, changing quickly and silently.

Before we can do any shopping, I will need to pop into the office, but I first choose her clothes, leaving them by the end of the bed.

Can't wait to see her wearing them. She will be hot as hell.

I walk downstairs, grab my keys in the kitchen, and inform every one of the plans. I will be back as soon as she is awake.

The streets are empty when I leave the garage and drive easily to the office. There is barely nobody at the office, it's 5 a.m., but we have a big team working on the organisation of tomorrow's event.

By eight, Helena is at the door with all the illustration teams. "Welcome everyone, please find a seat." I say.

"Samuel, this is what we have come up with on such a short notice," Isaiah, the head of the team says, handing me the tablet with the virtual prototype.

"I like it, but it's too old-fashioned. I need everyone to imagine from now on, our new readers are twenty to forty years old. We need more colours, more energy—the magazine needs to make people smile, at the first second they hold it."

"Are we keeping Ms Ruby's picture in black and white?" Iris, Isaiah's assistant asks.

"Yes, we are," I say, and everyone nods. "But as you can see, in the online magazine they can see straight away the next page, that's where all the vibrant colours need to pop out, fewer words, more colour," there are more nods.

"Thanks everyone," Helena says, inviting everyone to leave us. Closing the door, she gives us some privacy before she jumps on me like a lioness. "Are you out of your fucking mind?" She asks.

"I will appreciate you watch your tone."

"Fuck you, Samuel!" She screams. "You message me at 2

a.m., then at 4 a.m., and then send us a ridiculous email changing everything after what happened at the Monday meeting?"

"I changed my mind and I don't need anyone else's approval but mine," I say, typing on my computer, ignoring her angry gaze.

"Samuel, talk to me," she begs in a much lower tone. "Not today," I warn her.

"I know what happens," she is talking about Ruby.

"Nothing to worry about," I assure her.

"Avoiding situations doesn't make them any easier."

"They found him! Everything is under fucking control," I assure.

"Found him? One person couldn't do that!" She exclaims, and I stop typing.

"What the fuck are you talking about?" I ask harshly.

Her perfect eyebrow rise and I know there is something missing.

"I am talking about Edinburg," she says, confused.

"What the fuck happens to Edinburg? You know I haven't been there in decades," this conversation made me realise the date, but I shake my head dismissing those dark thoughts, "They are gone, everything is gone, there is nothing to talk about anymore, he doesn't deserve my time," I say, trying to leave the conversation to rest.

"Samuel, he loved you, more that you could imagine."

"He was a selfish arsehole that didn't deserve the life and family he had."

"You didn't know him, Samuel." She is trying to defend

him, make him look like a saint.

"He didn't know me either. He didn't care about us, just the fame and fortune," I say, looking into her eyes this time. They are glassy.

"You are so wrong that the moment you know what happened that day, you will be the arsehole in the room," she assures.

Not letting me fight back, she just turns around and leaves me and my anger in there.

We have tried to have this conversation for many years. She was my father's second assistant—she worked with him while I was gone, but that doesn't give her the right to talk like that.

He never cared about us, always too busy playing the perfect family elsewhere.

Turning on my chair I look at Hyde Park, letting my mind travel in time, far away, to the time in Edinburg, the time while grandpa was with us.

My ringtone pulls me out of my thoughts. It's Matteo, Ruby and the children are awake and ready to leave.

Without another word, I step out of my office and head to the garage, Helena didn't even turn her face to me and for once I didn't care, she has no rights to step on my family issues, especially after this many years.

Stepping into the kitchen, I can hear the children having breakfast and Rosita preparing some more coffee.

'Good morning, everyone' I sound better than I feel, but honestly now that I am home, I feel even better than before.

Holding a toast in my hand, I seat on the dining table, realising how all the boys that were at the table stand and walk away, reminding me of Helena's comment.

Am I missing something?

But before I can investigate Ruby walks in wearing the outfit that I choose, I got Helena to pick it, gosh that women know how to cut my breath with a piece of fabric, is a two pieces, flowerily cropped cami top, followed by a high waist, extremely tight skirt, that ends under her knees.

You can see every curve on this goddess body, making me aware we are both enjoying the outfit.

"Mama! You look gorgeous," Naima claim, while Ruby kisses her head and Aidan cheek.

"Be ready in half an hour," I order, standing and leaving her taking care of the children.

I walk downstairs after having the look at the last changes of the magazine. It's perfect and everyone is ready for tomorrow evening.

Ruby is by the door waiting. Grabbing her hand, I pull her outside and into my car.

A few minutes after, a uniformed gentleman opens the heavy crystal door that leads our way inside Harrods.

I know where I am going, so I don't stop holding Ruby and forcing her to keep up with my pace. I can't wait for this any longer.

We arrive in the woman's section, make a few more turns and we meet the most incredible gowns.

"Ms Ruby, welcome, I'm Leticia, your consultant today."

There is no response from any of us. We just follow her to a private room. There's a red velvet couch and a pedestal in front of it. I take a seat and wait for her to stand on in front of me.

My elbows are resting on the back of the couch, and one leg on the knee of the other.

I look at her in the mirror, sexy, powerful, feminine, in a way I haven't seen her before.

She runs her fingertips around her figure, letting me enjoying every curve.

My body feels on fire, one that grows when I catch her gaze in the mirror. She is doing it on purpose, looking at me, and enjoying the game.

I stand exactly when Leticia comes inside holding multiple gowns.

There's every type of colour and fabric you could imagine.

"Ms Ruby, we weren't sure what your style preference will be. Mr Smith just mentioned your love for colour and flower prints."

"We will keep all the pastels, light grey, and white gowns," I answer, "you can take the others away while," I try to keep it calm, "Ms Ruby tries them." A mischievous smile grows on me.

I take a seat back on the couch, ready to enjoy the best part—*Ruby naked,* she pulls the skirt down her thighs, pushing her ass out, all of it while looking straight at me in the mirror. I try to keep my eyes on her, but it's hard.

Once the skirt falls at her feet, she steps out, placing her palms under the ribs and pushing the tiny top over her head, exposing her braless breasts.

She stops me when I was about to jump over her.

"I need you to wait outside," she says, with a firm tone I wasn't aware she could have to me.

A soft nod and I step as close as possible without touching her, enjoying how her skin turns pink, the shade I create every time I am this close.

"Choose the sexiest, the one you would never wear," I say, looking at her in the mirror from behind.

"I understand, but can you make sure everything is ready, I don't think it will be hard to do, even you are working from home." Helena is in the other side, sick and of course she won't be at the gala. "I think it's unnecessary to remind you how important this gala is." there's only silence on the other side, but I can hear her breath, trying to calm herself.

"Everything will be as it should," she says. "Just make sure you are there in time, too."

Without another word, I hang up, inspecting the documents Calvin gave me last night. Some related to the gala and some to Ruby and her ex-husband.

I don't want to be a paranoid, but from tomorrow I won't be able to hide her anymore. The entire country, worst the entire world, will know who she is.

It wouldn't be a surprise if her parents find her through the news or the magazine, even on the other side of the world.

After waiting what seems like a lifetime, I see Ruby stepping out of the changing room, having a few words with Leticia and walking towards me.

"Time to go," I say, holding her hand again and walking her away.

When we exit Harrods, I guide her towards my office building. She knows where we are when the SaStel sign welcomes us, but she doesn't say a word, just keep walking.

Stepping inside the lift, I press my floor button, letting go of her arm, resting my back on the back wall, enjoying her back, her sexy curves, my body shakes, I fix my groin, knowing she is feeling the same, when she is incapable of stay still, slightly moving from one side to another, the bell of the lift announce we have arrived.

The office is full. Everyone is turning their heads toward us, but I don't have time for them. They can't miss the stunning goddess in front of me.

I walk forward holding her hand, Helena is home, so there's nobody around us anymore when we pass the conference room, we reach my office door and open it—I let go of Ruby hold and she walks to my desk and rest her palms on the edge.

I close the door behind me—she turn and face me, lifting her skirt slightly and sitting on top of my desk, my back is resting on the door, shaking in desire for this woman, but I push myself away, when her thighs open slightly, inviting me in.

Walking extremely slowly, she stretches her back and raises her neck to adjust to my height.

I can breathe her, my breath brush her skin, the delicious skin that starts turning pink under the slightest proximity, the softest touch.

My fist rest on the side of her in the table, making our closeness even smaller, she smiles and I don't hold it anymore, without touching her, my lips devour hers, her tongue fights mine, her lips melt with mine, making both moans.

My palms rest on her bum and I squeeze it, pushing her forward, but we don't meet each other because her skirt is on the way, so I quickly move my fingertips to her thighs, painfully slowly pushing the fabric away, I could keep it there, but I want her naked in my arms, so I pull it up and remove it together with the top, exposing her breast, leaving her with the little thong she has chosen today.

Her hands land on my T-shirt, working fast to remove it, slowly meeting my belt, opening it, and taking boxers and jeans down together.

Keeping me naked in front of her, my cock meets her tummy, desperate to have her, but there's something else on the way, resting her palms on the table, she raises her bum, giving me access to remove the thong down her thighs.

I spread her legs wider, pushing herself closer to the edge, and without soft movements I thrust myself inside her, making her back arch, her head fall back, and I fall forward, her walls are squeezing the life out of me, shocked of the way I came in, and burning for more.

My hips have their own purpose. Thrusting repeatedly, hers are rolling and pushing closer with her heels.

Her neck is expose and I don't hesitate on devouring it, kissing and biting her everywhere, fisting her mane, that today she has kept loose, making her head move even more back, giving me a better access, kissing every moan, every cut of breath, every exhale that pass through her throat.

We are getting closer and closer, my hips are uncontrollable, her hands are holding herself on my shoulders, and mine are holding her hips, I can feel how her walls pull me higher and higher, touching in the deepest, building a climax that the entire building might hear.

Her nails sink in my shoulder, making my hold harden and my hips to move even faster, the only way to control what is coming is by kissing her, so I pull her neck up and loose myself in her lips, licking, biting, tangling our tongues, catching every moan that comes out of her, every growl that comes out of me, and suddenly her screams, her heels pull me deeper and send me to hell and heaven at once, but our hips keep rolling at unison until we feel we are absolutely empty and full at the same time.

Hiding her face on my neck, I lift her and place us both on the couch at the other side of my office—I cuddle her, brushing her hair with one palm and her flesh with the other, her hands rest on my torso, playing around, drawing small circles.

We dress back up. She won't be able to find her thong, but she doesn't even bother to search around. Maybe aware I kept it for myself. I want to remember this moment every time I'm at this table.

Once we check each other, making sure everything is in place, we walk out of my office, but this time, my arm is around her shoulders, her face resting nearly on my shoulder, those sandals make her be way taller that what I am used to.

CHAPTER EIGHTEEN

Ruby

I woke up to the noise of the shower. Samuel must be done with the gym.

While I stretch my body, his magnificent figure exits the bathroom dripping water everywhere, but he pauses, turning to me and sitting by my side.

"Good morning gorgeous," he murmurs softly.

I hold his perfect face and drop a deep kiss on his delicious lips—he pushes me and spreads his frame over me when a knock interrupts us.

"What the fuck?!" He growls, opening the door just in towel.

Rosita and Matteo are there, horror on their faces. Without a word, Samuel gets into the closet, grabs some joggers and walks away.

"We need you to get dress *hijita*," she says. I can sense the worry in her words.

I grab a dress and rush downstairs. When I enter, the

kitchen is full of the security team, but my entire world stops when I hear a deep, raw scream in the garden.

Rushing outside, I found Samuel on his knees, his forearms and forehead on the grass.

Rosita approaches him and kneels by his side, pulling his shoulders up and resting his head on her lap.

"There is so much you don't understand *hijito*," she says, brushing his waves. "I fight all my life to protect you, but the past is catching up with me at a fast speed. I can't keep up."

I can feel the pain in her words, and I can feel it on half of these guys, they have been with Samuel for a long time, making me realize I don't know Samuel's age, but he is way older than me, he been suffering for longer, struggling for longer, and something is going extremely wrong right now.

Matteo rushes outdoors as I try to step out. "Samuel, we need to go!" he screams.

Samuel rises, turns into the house, not understanding what might have happened anymore. They throw him a T-shirt and some trainers on the way to the front door.

I stand there, not understanding anything.

"Cover yourself," Samuel order as I catch up with him at the door. I see Logan and Calvin carrying the children downstairs and head outside.

"What is happening?" I ask, panicking.

Rosita approaches me, holds my arm, and guides me out.

Everyone is in the car, rushing away from the city. Samuel is in the van in front of us, with Matteo and Rosita, Logan, Calvin, the children and I right behind them.

They drive as if we are rushing away from the end of the

world, over the speed limit, but everything stops when we approach a house. There are at least three police cars and one ambulance when Matteo tries to park.

Samuel run out of the van, and Scott was in his arms in no time.

"Mom needs to go to the hospital," he cries as I step out of the van, realizing we are in Blue Valley.

"Everything will be fine, I swear," Samuel says in his little ear.

"Uncle Samuel, take me away," he begs, pulling his face away from Samuel.

"I will take care of this. Go to *Little Castle*. Ruby will be with you." He just nods and rushes to me. I hold him up immediately.

Samuel doesn't say a word or turn away, he just walk away and enters the house followed by Rosita.

"We will take you to Samuel's," Matteo explains, approaching the van and giving some instructions to the guys.

I step inside the van and seat Scott on my lap. He won't stop sobbing, so I just hold him, brushing my palm on his back and dropping soft kisses on his head.

We cross to the other side of the park and our future house comes into view on the horizon.

"We will soon move to that house, the cottage with the orange door," I say casually.

"Pardon?" they look at each other, surprised at what I just said and so do I when Calvin drives to the house next door, my dream house.

"It's this Samuel's house?" I ask with a frown.

"Mama, is this Samuel's house?" Naima asks, now awake.

But they don't answer, just park and open the side door so I can get out. Scott continues on my arms and the boys help my children out.

I shyly head to the front door. It's like the steps are on fire because I find it hard to step on them. This is too much.

Paralysed, I look around me. I'm about to enter my dream house, the house that the man of my dreams owns.

"Come on, mama!" Naima pulls me and I come back to life.

I step into the foyer. It looks even more impressive than in the pictures.

"Apologies, but the refurbishment has started just a few days ago." Logan says, walking around the house.

I can't look at him. My eyes are moving around the huge open space, taking in the beautiful stairs and the big white doors heading to different rooms, hungry to explore it all.

I go through the door that the boys have been. It's the kitchen, bigger than the one in Belgravia, all in broken white, really old-fashioned, but extremely beautiful.

An island on the center matching the cupboards and at the end, behind a little arch, is the dining area with an over ten people table, matching the with the rest of the kitchen.

Scott way more relaxed stand on his feet, asking Naima and Aidan to join him in the garden. What gives me the opportunity to have a look around.

I exit the kitchen, there are two double door in the opposite wall, I choose the left first, is a theatre room, there is a screen as big as the entire wall, but it doesn't have the regular seats I saw on the movies, it has was seems like posh comfy couches.

Moving to the next door, I found an office/library, one wall is full with books. They aren't new; they are antiques.

A dark brown thick wood desk rest in the center of the room, with a matching color leather chair at the other side, but what calls my attention is, despite how tidy the table and bookshelf looks, the floor behind the desk is a mess.

It's a corner they have used to drop junk or old stuff.

My curious side can't help it and have a look at what is all of that. There are some old documents, you can tell how much of an antique they are by the type of paper used.

There are some contracts, bills, but as I move around the documents, I come to find some personal letters. They have beautiful handwriting. I take a seat on the leather chair and amused by the treasure I found, the first from 1956.

Dear Scott,

This will be the last letter I will send as a free woman.

News might have reached you of my marriage.

Father has arranged it all with the Murray family.

It will take place next Sunday.

I wish you all the best. Never forget how much I loved you.

Yours forever,

Catherine Thomas

Samuel's grandfather was in love with a lady and let her go?

If Scott senior was something like Samuel, I would not understand what could happen.

I have a look at the next letter. This one it's from 1952.

Dear Catherine,

I inform you of the death of my lovely parents on their journey back from London.

This will mean my immediate departure from Edinburg into the great city of London, where I should finish my studies and take the control over SaStel. I will hard work to honour the loyal, love, and hardworking legacy they left me with.

Please wait for me, I will soon return and you will be my wife.

I am the heir. There is nobody else above me to impose on me any ladies from any wealthy families around this empty castle that I sadly leave now.

Remember me and my love in these months.

Forever yours,

Scott Smith

The company was founded by the great-grandfather, not by Scott senior, but if my maths isn't wrong, they have all passed at a young age.

What reminds me of the other old documents I found. I rush to check them. There are birth certificates, marriage, but I can only find Scott's senior death certificate.

Where are the parents one?

These documents are way more important that I could ever imagine. Wanting me to find more and more information, I separate them by date and decade.

After a few hours, I step out of the office and walk to the kitchen. I need something to drink and maybe eat, something to process everything that I've just learned.

The children are in the garden. There is Logan with them and a tray of drinks and remain sandwiches are resting by his side.

I've been so submerge on Samuel's past that I have neglected the children.

"They are fine," Calvin says, while his gaze continues to focus on the laptop.

"Coffee?" I ask, and he just nod.

I step closer to drop it, when today's newspaper calls my attention, well more the headline.

Smith's family house robbed.

On the 20th anniversary of the loss of Sebastian and Samantha Smith, a group of unknown burglars broke into the family property in Edinburgh.

Samuel

One of their largest properties, where it is known all the family treasures, trophies, and most valuable items were preserved from the late Samuel Smith. The family members have given no declarations, but…

I stop, understanding what has happened today. Samuel was screaming at this, at the anniversary of his parents, and the disrespect of someone breaking at his property, the reason his sister did God knows what.

"We can't talk about it," Calvin warm me when I rise my head away from the paper. This family holds way more secrets that I suspected, but worst, nobody may say a word without the master's permission.

"It's not like if I care," I say, walking around the island behind Calvin having a million heart attacks.

I am on the screen, but so do Advik, the children. Some images are of years ago. I step closer to the pile of documents I saw him hiding as I enter the kitchen and found my passport, my past spread around.

"What the fuck is this?" I scream at his face.

"I can't talk about it," he sighs, lowering his head.

"It's my fucking life!" I argue back.

"I am just doing my job," he replies.

"And your job is spy on my entire life? Learn everything about me?" I ask disgusted.

I thought I could trust them, but this is a disrespect. I have shared what I was comfortable with, what I want it to. Samuel has no rights to do this.

He will not give me the answers that I need, so I step into the garden. They are the only people that matter.

Fuck Samuel and his stupid past!

While we play ball, Jackson approach me.

"The office sent this for you," he says, walking away once I take the thick brown envelope.

"What is that, mama?" Naima asks.

Suddenly the game stops, all eyes on me.

Turning the envelope, I twist the cord that closes it, it's big and heavy, rather than peek inside, I pull it out and have a billion heart attacks in one. I see me, my face, my name—it's the 100th edition he talked about. My hand rests on my heart trying to keep it in place. I don't check the entire magazine, just searching for what matters the most. My part. When I open it, my breath catches. There's a full four pages of me, shopping, cooking, laughing, tasting, a Ruby I never seen before, but the one that shocks me the most, the one I was completely aware he took of me, staring at me is pure and completely breathtaking.

I turn it and show Naima. She cries, laughs and screams in joy.

"Please read it!" She orders. I haven't stopped myself in that little detail.

Ruby Sweet Dreams

For many months, the entire team of SaStel was searching for the perfect business to be the headline, the most important part of this 100th edition.

They gave up, but one day, the incredible owner of this magazine, Mr Samuel Smith, was around London when Ms Rao walked by him. From that instant, he knew she would change his life forever, but wasn't just the special connection that grew in that moment that give her this first place in England's best small businesses. It was when he met her again and got the privilege of tasting her food, and I quote, *"That bite was a piece of heaven, served by an angel."*

Who isn't already looking forward to trying her food? I sure am.

She is an American Mum of two, who came to this country pursuing a dream and so far, is getting the entire fairy tale.

She impressed the SaStel team with her hard work, genuine passion, and love for food, which set her as an example.

When you want something, work hard, follow your dreams, and enjoy life.

This might be the first time you've heard Ruby Sweet Dreams' name, but believe us it won't be the last.

This writer has a sweet tooth, and I know many of our readers do too.

I'm in shock by the brief resume of my business. There's a lot more text, especially around the pictures, explaining where I was, what I was doing, how he felt around me in that moment.

He hasn't only put my brand out there—he has put his entire soul.

But why he has me on an inspection process with his team? What is so important from my past that he can't let it rest, or at least ask directly?

I thought he respected me, my work—he wanted me to grow, to share my talent with the world, but now seems like he just want to control me and everything around me, *to give me my fairy tale?* I can create my fairy tale without his power and money.

CHAPTER NINETEEN

Samuel

Rosita is at my side in no time. We have experienced this multiple times, but Scott has never been the one calling. Stella would have called before making the stupid decision.

We are at my friend William office, in St Marcus hospital waiting for any updates while this morning images torture me repeatedly.

Two paramedics surrounding her body on the kitchen floor, the lifeless body of Stella resting on the ground.

A pool of blood covers the light brown wood floor.

Rosita sobbing the life out of her. My blood is boiling.

She has tried to take her life multiple times—she stopped when she found Donnie, tried again when he passed, and well, this makes sense now, the changes in mood, the urge to be alone.

William walks inside the office and I jump out of those horrible memories.

"She called me a few weeks ago. Feeling unwell," he

explains, brushing his hair. "She filled the house with medication, the type only people in big trouble should have."

"How could she gain access to that type of medication?" I ask.

William and his father have been our only contact with health care since I can remember.

"Samuel, I would never prescribe her that type of medication, or worse, hide it from you," he is telling the truth, and that scares me the most.

"Lock her up, clean her. She can't be around Scott like this." I order.

"We can't lock her up for overmedicating herself or for what she's done this morning." William says.

"How do you expect her to be around us, alone with her child? She could harm him." Rosita says alarmed.

"Scott knows more than you think." William assures.

"This is too much," I say, pulling my waves away and resting my elbows on my thighs. "Scott won't see her until she is clean."

"She will stay here for the weekend. I have a friend in psychiatric and I will make sure she visits on Monday," William assure.

I just nod, letting Rosita brush her hand on my back.

After a few minutes composing ourselves, we walk back to the car, trying to keep all of this natural and calm when everyone in the hospital turns their faces to us.

"Stella's house has to be cleaned up. Grab all Scott's belongings and move them to *Little Castle*. Make sure everything is ready in Belgravia for tonight," I request Logan over the phone.

As we arrive in Little Castle, everything seems quiet. I walk into the office and take a seat on the leather chair, resting my head on the table and letting go of everything.

The door opens unannounced—I rise my head and Ruby is there, holding the magazine in one hand and slapping the door with the other.

Too hard for my taste. She seems frustrated, angry at the same time. *Welcome to the club baby.*

A few days ago, it was just us—I was just focused on taking care of her, giving her the world, but now everything is a nightmare.

Her gaze is burning my skin, but I can't take my eyes away from her.

I stand, walk towards her—she doesn't move, so I can breathe her in, her delicious skin that starts turning pink at the slightest proximity. I don't bend so she can't be at my eye level.

Pulling her up on my waist by her arse, pushing her to the door and devouring her neck.

The magazine hits the floor, and her hands are on my shoulders.

"Samuel, stop..." she murmurs, pushing my shoulders away, but I don't listen.

My hands hold her tighter under her dress, her hips push into me too.

"SAMUEL!" She screams, and I let go.

She holds herself in the door as I wasn't gentle putting her down.

"What is the matter with you?!" She asks.

"I am not having this conversation," I warn her.

"Oh no! You bloody are!" She screams.

She bends and gets a hold of the magazine.

"Yesterday you treat me like a whore you dress and control."

"Watch your mouth and tone," I warn her.

"What are you going to do? Punish me?"

I look at her in horror. *What is she talking about?*

"Welcome to the club mister, the difference is that this time I won't consent to a single moment of disrespect from you or anybody else."

I can feel the anger and pain in her voice. I will never harm her.

"You might have power over all of them, but guess what, nobody has power over me anymore."

"I doubt that!" I scream, knowing how close her ex is to her.

"I am done with you! Here is your fucking magazine," she says, throwing it to me.

"I did it for you!" I argue back.

"I didn't ask for it! I did the fucking favor to you, arsehole!" She shouts in my face now.

She turns and leaves me there without another word.

I follow her. Now everyone is in the foyer. They might have heard the screams—I haven't spoken to someone like this since my last conversation with my father.

And that was a way worst argument. My knuckles still

remember when they hit the wood wall, trying to avoid hitting his face.

Ruby rushes into the kitchen, and I follow her.

"You aren't leaving Ruby," I say.

"Watch me," she argues back, holding Naima's and Aidan's hands.

"There is a contract you must follow. There is an event to attend tonight."

"I am not going anywhere with you. I signed nothing. I don't give a shit about you and your business. Call one of your whores to pretend to love you."

"Ruby!" I growl through my teeth.

She abruptly stops, turning and gives me the coldest gaze I thought she would ever give me.

"You deserve every single bit of what you had, you didn't deserve us."

"You can't leave," I threat back.

She doesn't answer, just walks away from me and rushes outside.

This time I don't follow her. I can't do this anymore. I just sit on the stool, observing the wall, but Rosita won't let this slip.

"What have you done?" She asks.

"I am not having this conversation."

"Samuel, you aren't hiding from me."

"There is nothing to talk about. It's just too much. She isn't satisfied. Let her go!" I scream, facing the door.

"You don't want her gone. First, understand she isn't responsible for your parents, Edinburg, Stella or your work."

"Why don't you join her?" I ask, sick of listening to

everyone judging me.

"You don't mean what you are saying."

"Maybe I do. Maybe I am tired of poor Rosita always saving the day and letting everyone know how much we took her life away from her."

"You don't mean what you are saying."

"Maybe I do! Because I think we gave you everything someone could ask for!"

"You do not know what you are talking about."

"Your past, my parents' past, even fucking lunatic Stella's past—I don't care!" I scream into her face, "I am sick of all of you and your bullshit!"

"Samuel, you need to..."

"You need to leave right now! Go! And take everyone with you!" I scream, making her leave the kitchen.

Suddenly, the entire house is quiet. I stay there until my body becomes numb.

I walk upstairs and into the bathroom I take a cold shower, trying to wake up something that was just alive while Ruby was around, but now is dead again.

After a few minutes in the bathroom, I put on my tuxedo and walk downstairs. Nobody is here.

Walking to the office I grab the keys for one of my smallest cars. It will be just me attending the gala, so there's no need for anything bigger.

I stop in the kitchen to grab some water and stop when I find the boys there. Logan, Matteo, and Calvin are sitting on the island, having some coffee, waiting for me.

I head to the fridge, trying to pretend they aren't there.

"Samuel, would you like us to follow her?" Matteo asks.

I turn to him and give him a tired look.

"What about Edinburgh?" he asks.

"What about?" There's nothing I can do.

Someone was looking for something and I will never know if they found it, because I haven't been there in nearly twenty years.

"Don't you find it very convenient that they did it the same day your parents disappeared?" He doesn't have to remind me of all of this.

"If I show them I'm curious, bothered, or concerned, it will be worse." Keeping calm will let me focus.

Before he can continue bothering me with this conversation, I walk away from the kitchen and head to the garage. I find the car I was looking for and jump in it, driving away before any of them can join me.

All of Knightsbridge is closed for the event. Only holders of invitations may enter the road.

Yes, it might be a big inconvenience for multiple residents and tourists, but some of the most important people in the country and even the world are here.

As I get closer to the building, following the car queue, the enormous picture of Ruby hanging on the wall of the building becomes clearer, promoting what will happen in the next few hours.

Everyone will know who she is wherever she goes.

I exit the car and hand the keys to a valet.

As I enter the building, the entire atmosphere is heavy,

every head turns towards me.

"This way, Samuel," Natasha is by my side, guiding me.

Like it or not, I will have to do a speech, and introduce the special guests. All of this is the reason I'm here today.

"Helena has prepared this for you." She hands me a piece of paper with Helena's perfect handwriting.

On my way to the stage, a few clients, celebrities, and reporters approach me. I put my business mask on in the car, so it should cover me until the end of this event.

Standing in front of everyone, I try to look calm, avoid any judging gazes, any questioning. I'm here to do a job and once I'm done, I will hide away for good.

Something stops my heart, my breath, and brings me back to life at the same time.

She is there, in the back, standing with the stunning pink floral dress she tried on yesterday. All her hair is up in a stunning updo. She is wearing more makeup than usual and she is holding Rosita's arm.

I've never seen Rosita this elegant, wearing a simple light blue pencil dress. Her hair pin up too and some soft make up enhance her beautiful face.

All the heads have turned to them, flashes bright around, taking multiple pictures of the star of the night. She isn't Ruby the mum and baker anymore. She is the number one small business in all of England, and once the launch happens, of the entire world.

I mouth her. *I am so sorry baby*, she just nods and smiles, making me smile back, knowing that even in my worst moments she won't leave me.

"Welcome to our annual gala..." there's a knot on my throat, "we are not just celebrating the number of editions we have reached, but the appreciation for all the readers that have been here since my great-grandfather print the first edition."

I'm sure Helena has calculated that when I finish my speech, it will take place.

"This time, we wanted to focus on the future of our country—the best new small businesses."

They all join me on the stage. Everyone looks amazing.

"Tonight, we will launch a step into the future, with our online magazine available worldwide."

That's the end of the speech. Everyone applauds, but they stop when the white screen behind me comes to life.

I turn to find it's a video showing old photographs from when my great-grandfather started SaStel.

Printing the first magazine, my grandfather taking the control over the company, another with my father as a child walking into the printer room, my father with his first magazine.

A knot grows in my chest, appreciating to be giving that back to everyone else.

But Ruby is by my side, holding my hand tight, and I lose it.

There are pictures of the three of us in the office. My father holds me smiling, making me laugh, a part of him I never experienced.

Just then, I realise I never knew him. There was love and care for me, but down the road he stopped showing that to me.

Who were you, father? What happened to you?

A thick tear drops when I see myself alone. That picture was taken a week after I returned, finding they had passed away. There is pain and sadness on my face. That day the cold, heartless Samuel was born, unable to let anyone get too close, or myself too involved.

But here I am, in love with this incredible woman, as broken and hurt as me.

Then she appears on the screen, beautiful and sad in the pictures I took, me working on this edition, even pictures taken tonight, until you can just see us on the screen on live.

I compose myself and turn around. "Thank you, everyone, for joining us tonight. Enjoy the rest of the evening and let's get the 100th edition launched."

The screen changes to the front of the magazine and the real number of purchases and visits to our website.

I greet everyone, congratulate them, hold Ruby and step away to where Rosita was waiting.

"Ready to go home?" I ask the most important women in my life.

They say nothing, just nods and we walk away.

Matteo and Calvin are covering us in no time.

People try to approach us, but we are on a mission to leave this place before I regret anything someone asks me.

Once we are outside, the crowd surrounds us, but Matteo rushes to open the door. Ruby doesn't think twice, and jumps as quickly as possible. Regardless of her gown, Rosita joins her and I close the door behind me.

The rest of the team is surrounding our van, opening a path, and taking us away from the crowd.

I pull Ruby closer and cover her with my arms, setting her on my lap and hiding my face in her neck. But she pulls me out of my safe place, making sure I look straight at her.

"I understand you are in pain," she says, "but we all are. I am here for you." She caresses my skin. "We all are."

"Baby, I am so sorry for everything," I say low, "a lot of things have happened, things I can't control anymore. I am scared," I confess.

She just hugs me and brushes my waves, dropping soft kisses on my hair.

"I promise I will express myself in a healthier way," I say.

"We are here for you," she says.

I turn on my seat and face Rosita, the most loyal person I ever had.

"I can't handle any more of this," I say. My throat is blocked.

She holds my hand and turns to face me. There isn't anger in her, or disappointment, as she has always done.

"*Mi hijito*, you need to learn how to express your thoughts, emotions, and feelings," she says, brushing away my tears. "There is a limit on how much you can hold here," she points at my head, "and here," she says, pointing to my heart.

"I thought I could do it, be cold, no attachments, no emotions, but everything is breaking down around me," I say, lowering my head on Ruby's shoulder. "I hated him all my life, never understood what I did wrong, and I just saw a father proud, loving his son. Why I couldn't experience that, Rosita?

Why did I need to have his cruelty? His anger all the time."

"Because the same pattern cut Scott senior, Mr Sebastian and you, each of you found in each other things you despised in your own selves."

"He loved me?" I ask.

"Oh boy! He was the proudest father in the entire world, never missed a moment in anything that you did in life, but always giving you space and freedom, your sister and you never understood him. He was like..."

She stopped, coughing and moving away, as if she was about to say something she shouldn't.

Matteo it's at the phone and turns around, pale as I ever seen him.

"*Bro*!" He exclaim stepping out of the van, "we need to go! Rosita and Ruby are going to *Little Castle*," he orders to Calvin.

I just follow him, removing my blazer and bowtie on the way out.

"What the hell is happening?" I ask, taking the passenger seat as my boys step out.

"Stella has escaped from the hospital and so did an exorbitant number of drugs," Matteo says, turning away from the traffic.

I am going to kill her. No drug in the world will do it for me.

CHAPTER TWENTY

Ruby

We enter *Little Castle*, and everything is quiet. Sarah comes out of the kitchen. I called her to take care of the kids while we went to the gala.

My children know her and Scott it's such a sweet soul, that didn't mind it.

"They were exhausted, sleeping before I finished the first sentence of the book," she explains putting the cord of her handbag around her neck, "amiga, that bedrooms are amazing!" She exclaims, making me remember I haven't been around the top floor yet.

We hug each other at the front door and Rosita guide me to the staircase.

"Your bedroom is the double doors on the left," she says. "I will prepare some tea," I nod and walk away.

Sad of removing this incredible gown, but looking forward to some comfy clothes.

At the end of the stairs there is a corridor that seems

endless, remembering the photographs on the internet, I know where some of the doors lead, the one on the right is the main one, where Rosita has told me to go, and at the end is the extension I'd love to explore around, but for now Samuel's room will have to be enough.

I stand in front of white double doors, when I open the right one something grows in my belly, I take off my sandals and play with my feet around the carpet, you can tell that it is new because of how soft it feels, matching the color of the walls, a shade of broken white.

The furnitures are light colour, I couldn't say what colour, since the only light that illuminates me is from the street, a door to the right, the bathroom, another to the left, a dressing room, and an extremely large bed in the center of the room, the four of us could easily sleep here.

I walk over to the window, setting my bag down on a desk on the left, my heart stops for a second, and I hold my breath as the full view unfolds before me.

From here it is as if the village rests under my feet, and I am on top of the tower of this enchanted castle, waiting for the love of my life to wrap me in his arms, strong as metal armor.

Walking down stairs while my finger play with my messy mane, now unpinned, and way more comfortable.

I enter the kitchen and stop as I realized who is in there with Rosita, screaming on top of her lungs.

"Who the hell are you and what are you doing here?!" Stella screams, pointing at me.

What is Stella doing here? And what happens to her?

"I asked you a question!" She screams.

"Stella... what...?"

For an instant, I don't understand. It's like she doesn't recognize me, like she doesn't even know where she is.

"Where is he?!" She shouts again.

Rosita approaches her, trying to talk some sense into her, but she pushes her away and step towards me.

"You are the whore that has kept him so distracted," she says, mumbling.

This close, I can see there is something not right with her.

"If you mean Samuel he is on the way. Something important happened at the last minute..."

"I should be his priority! He promised..." she says, mumbling something else I can't understand.

"Stella, why don't you have a tea with us while you wait," I say.

"You aren't more than a street rat I can get rid of as soon as I want," she says in my face. "I fire you from my son's birthday."

Something in her awakens when she mentions Scott. Seeing her intentions, I block the door, but she pushes me away, so I hold her forearm to stop her. I can't let her get to him and take him away under these circumstances.

"Stella, please understand he is resting," I say, holding her tighter.

Looking at the hold I have on her, she looks up into my eyes and my entire cheek is on fire.

She scratches and slaps me but I don't move. I hold my

head up and prove to her she won't break me.

I follow Stella to the hallway and block her way towards the staircase. I can feel blood dripping out of my cheek, but it's not the first time. Nothing hurts or bothers me anymore.

"You won't get to him," I say, holding my position, ready to fight for Scott's safety as if he was my child.

She jumps over me, but I push her away before she hits me again. Her small body falls on the floor and she cries in pain for a second before she tries to jump on me again.

"What the hell is going on?!" Samuel shouts when he steps into the hallway.

Stella must look like a lunatic in a hospital gown and slippers.

Rosita is at the doorframe, having a panic attack, unable to stop sobbing.

Samuel rushed to me and brushes my bleeding cheek.

"I will take care of this," he says and I just nod.

I taking a seat on the last step and I let myself breathe again.

"Are you for real big brother?!" she screams at him.

"Stella, for the love of God, let me help you," he tries to speak calmly. He steps closer to her and holds her by the arms, pulling her closer to his chest where she cries and sobs in pain.

"I can't do this any longer," she says.

Samuel tries to hold his position, but I can see a thick tear leave his eyes. He is in pain too, but none of them has ever learned how to understand, learn from, love, and share their emotions.

"I don't want to be alone anymore," she says, holding his nape and resting their foreheads together. "That old lady and that whore need to get out of our lives."

"In my house we talk to each other with respect."

"You cannot see!" She cries, pushing him away, messing her hair even more. "She is after our money, our name, our everything!"

She is talking about me, who got into this family without knowing they were siblings.

"If you are going to speak out of ignorance, please shut the fuck up!" I say, screaming and walk towards her, but Matteo seizes me and pulls me back.

I'm done. There are not soft words that can make this mad woman understand anything.

Samuel pulls his mobile out and calls Dr. William. He must be the one taking care of this lunatic.

"She needs to be with you until Saturday at least. I will work on her treatment for later on," he says.

As Stella hears that, she tries to run away, but Logan stops her, making sure she doesn't harm anyone else or herself. But then I see something that calls everyone's attention.

She is hugging him, not being held. He caresses her hair, her cheeks, whispers something in her ear and Stella melts in his hold.

Is there something happening between these two?

I pull myself away from Matteo's hold, making him understand I just need to leave.

Walking to the front door, I think about it—leave the house, or hide away in the office.

For a heavy reason, I choose Samuel's family past over anything else happening right now.

I take a seat on the leather chair and catch up on what I was doing a few hours ago. It seems like a lifetime, but it's been only hours.

The advantage is that now I know what I am facing— information, answers that not even Samuel knows.

Maybe this way I will understand why they are like this, why they had everything in life and they are the most damaged souls I have ever met.

"Ruby," Samuel says at the door. He walks in, offering a cold towel for my wounded cheek.

I place it on my flesh to keep the blood from flowing any longer.

"What have you done with my office?" He asks, surprised.

"Found incredible treasures," I say.

"Treasures?" He asks, making me realize he didn't even know the documents that were in his possession.

"This house belonged to your grandfather," I explain, meeting two surprised turquoise eyes, "but he didn't live here, his secret lover and her husband did." I try to resume.

"What are you talking about?" He asks in disbelieve.

I just hand him the documents. He takes a seat at the table and reads it, and I can hear and feel how his heart hammers in his chest again.

"I heard of the Murray's, but nobody ever articulated about them. It was a family secret."

"Don't you find it fascinating that your dream house was a

family house?"

He continues reading, looking at the wall, just like a question he's had forever and has just given him an answer.

"Catherine was my grandmother," he murmurs, making me jump on his lap.

"Holly shit! Yes! I knew it." I suspected it when I read the letter, building a property, and giving it to her? They never ended their affair.

"My father was Catherine's son, Gosh! Everything makes sense now." I need to know more.

"What makes sense?" He is searching on the entire pile. "Samuel?"

"There has to be a portrait. I need to see her." There is excitement and anxiety in his voice.

"Why?" *What would that change?*

"Don't you understand? Look at my hair, my skin. I come from a ginger-headed, white grandfather, a blonde, pale as snow mother, but look at my father, Stella, and me. Who was my grandmother? There must be dark hair, olive skin somewhere down the line, otherwise..." his thoughts are screaming so loud I can't hear mine.

"That's why they broke into Edinburg? Someone suspects you are not the rightful heir!" My gosh, this is bigger than I thought. This isn't an interesting romance—this is a big drama.

"I need Rosita, I need to..." His hands are shaking, searching every folder and document.

"ROSITA!!!" He screams, forcing me to cover my ears.

Has he forgotten it's the middle of the night?

She arrives in no time, alarmed by the screams.

"Yes, Samuel?" Her voice is tired and low.

"Who was Catherine Thomas?" Just at the mention of her name, the blood leaves her face.

"Samuel, *hijo*..." she can't talk, her eyes are filled with tears.

"Samuel, I think this isn't the moment." We have all been through so much in the past few days, and by her reaction I can see it will not be a simple story to tell.

CHAPTER TWENTY-ONE

Samuel

I wake up before the sun, tiptoe out of bed, grab some shorts, and close the door.

I nearly have a heart attack when I see Aidan scrubbing his sleepy eyes, moving his messy hair back and giving me a nice morning smile.

"Gym?" he asks. I nod.

Holding him in my arms, I carry him downstairs, his little head resting on my shoulder. This has become our daily routine, I can't understand how he knows when I will come out of the room, when to wake up, but he enjoys so much the new toddler little gym I designed, a way to prove to Ruby it was necessary.

After a good gym session, we head back to the bedroom.

"Morning, my boys," Ruby murmurs, stretching her body in bed. The sheets cover her, but I know she is naked under them, which forces me to rush into the shower.

Under the cold water, I can hear the giggles, that now have got louder, all the kids are here.

It's Tuesday. Matteo and I need to be at the office, and

Ruby has the Summer fair.

Trying to follow my old routine, I take my time with my hair, face, picking my clothes, and share my mood when there's not a single perfect suit.

The kids aren't in the room anymore.

"If it's the jacket, I can help you iron it," Ruby says behind me, wearing my T-shirt from last night.

"They all have been at the dry cleaner, hanged with care, separated from each other." Holding my hands, she steps closer, keeping enough distance to make sure she doesn't touch the clothes.

"Don't you dare after your little meltdown," she tempts me.

So, I hold her arse and place her in my favourite place, around my waist.

"I will change the suit," I confirm.

"I don't want you to do it," she whispers.

"I can't wear a crumpled suit."

"I will iron it, but you will wear our scent." Now I get it, and a big smile draws on my face.

"Ruby, I love you so much," I murmur to her perfect lips.

I push her to the wall next to the door, make sure it's locked, opening my belt and trousers, letting my hard cock free, brushing her naked groin with the head—and thrusting inside her without warning.

She is ready as usual. I'm getting used to this unannounced, fast, stress-relieving sex.

With every thrust, her moans grow louder, so I hold my

palm on her mouth, devouring her neck, thrusting faster and harder. Her walls are squeezing me, my lips on hers, hiding both our moans. Reaching the pick of our climax, my hips keep rolling until I feel we are empty, that our breath is normal.

"I will iron the shirt," she giggles, unbuttoning it, dropping a kiss on my heart, and walking out of the room.

She wants to play fine with me. I just take my mobile and jacket and walk away with a bare chest. I'm aware of where she is, but her game is to make everyone know the mess she made.

"Samuel Smith, get dressed this instant," Rosita orders when I step into the kitchen.

"I can't!" I raise my shoulders, dropping my jacket on the island so she can see the crumples and sit on the stool, waiting for Ruby to come find me.

"All done!" She announces, blushing when she finds everyone is in the kitchen looking at her sleepy, messy, sexy as hell figure.

"Ruby!" Rosita cries.

We all just giggle. Ruby doesn't even bother to change. She places all her hair up and starts checking on the kids' breakfast, preparing herself coffee and checking all the fair stuff.

As per usual, I know she has everything under control, especially after Thomas' help with the storage and a new walk-in fridge-freezer where the cookies are resting for this afternoon.

Rosita grabs my jacket, walks out of the kitchen, and is back before I can say my goodbyes to everyone.

"I will be back for lunch." There isn't much to do at the

office. And since we worked all night on tidying up the one here, I will work here while she drives me mad. "I will see you at the fair," I say, kissing her delicious lips.

"Matteo," I say. He is by my side in no time, and we drive away.

Helena is at her desk as usual when I walk by, chasing me. "Have you seen the media?" She asks.

"Are you aware of all what we been..." I stop when I see a bouquet of sunflowers wrapped in pink paper over my desk.

"They are for Ruby," she mentions.

I walk to them and find a note;

I missed you little girl.

A x

"I need to leave," I announce, holding the flowers and spinning out of the office, grabbing my mobile and dialling Matteo. "At the entrance now!" I shout, hanging up and dialling Logan. "None leaves the house!." I shout hanging up.

He is tempting his luck, provoking me, and irritating Ruby. God knows if he finds our location in Blue Valley she is done.

"This was on my fucking desk!" I shout to Matteo when I jump in the car.

"How they end up there?" he asks, making me realise I am rushing again, not asking Helena questions, so I dial her.

"Who brought them?" I ask as soon as I know the call is connected.

"I wasn't here. The cleaning lady mentioned an Indian-looking male." *He was at the office.* Matteo hears it too.

"Go into my office, in the little drawer under the desk, the hidden one. What can you see?" I have multiple important documents, my properties' spare keys and Ruby's thong.

"It's empty Samuel." I can sense the panic in her voice. She was aware there was important stuff there.

"Fuck!" I shout, punching the glove compartment.

I hang up and try to breathe. He was at my office, has access to all my properties and knows where to find her.

We are stuck in traffic when my mobile rings again, Logan's name come up.

"Logan," I can't help but sound irritated.

"Samuel, I need you here. Ruby has received some flowers. Naima is freaking out, screaming and she hide on her bedroom," he says, worried and nervous.

"I'm in a fucking block in central. I will be there ASAP. Someone needs to be at the fair right now." I shout.

Matteo signals and starts driving at a faster speed, around every car is on our way, horning and making everyone moving out the way.

Before the engine is off, I rush inside the house. "Naima!" I shout, running upstairs, taking them two or even three at a time.

When I open the bedroom door, I find her in the corner near the window—her face hidden on her knees. Rosita is on the floor too, trying to talk to her.

"When did the flowers arrive?" I ask.

"Shortly after you left, Miguel picked up Ruby, and I was

in the garden with the kids." Rosita explains.

"Leave us," I order.

When I hear the door close, Naima faces me, panic, fear, and pain covering her face. I can see the red mark inside her swollen eyes.

I try to get close to her, but she closes her invisible shell to me. That is a wall I haven't been able to trespass on yet, and I'm unsure if she will ever let me.

Siting by her side, I give her distance.

"You are safe here," I assure her, "but now I need to check on your mom." She looks at me and nods.

Rosita enters as I leave. "I will be back. Nobody gets out until I return."

I arrive at the park in no time. Everything seems calm, all the stalls are in place and Ruby seems unaware of anything.

She looks gorgeous in her new dress. It matches the banner that she has behind her with her name, smiling when she sees me.

I step closer and she frowns.

"I thought you were in the city," she says, hanging a package to one customer.

"Everything was under control," I say, nervously rearranging her business cards.

"Hello Ruby, good day Mr Smith, so glad you have the time to visit us," the Mayor says, giving me a bright smile.

I try to compose myself, put on my mask, and behave as if nothing is happening.

Ruby has worked so hard for this event, I can't let anything ruined it.

"I saw this colourful stall and I couldn't resist it," I smile back at her and she giggles.

"Ruby is the best! I was grateful to hear she joined us," she says, gifting us with a soft smile and walking away, checking other stalls and chatting with more people that enjoys the event.

"The boys are here," I whisper, "I will check on the kids and come back to pick you up," I inform her, for what she just nod and start talking with another customer that has just been tasting her spectacular cookies.

I have a walk around the entire fair, buying few things, chatting with anyone and everyone that gets close to me, smiling at everyone, and being a good, polite neighbour.

When I get back home, everything seems calmer. Naima is in the kitchen with the others, having some lunch, and gives me a small smile when I take a seat at the table.

"Mama is doing amazing and I will pick her up later," I say, making everyone understand we have nothing to worry about.

After lunch, I take them to the theatre room, play one of Scott's movies, everything about adventures, dinosaurs, relaxing slightly while I enjoy them eating popcorn and laughing at the screen.

The fair should be over soon, so I step out back to the kitchen and grab my mobile to check on Ruby. There is a message from her.

Miguel will help with all the setup. I see you home. Love u x.

Knowing that she is not alone, I try to keep myself calm and be back with the kids.

Rosita is getting dinner ready and we should all have a nice feast to celebrate what I know has been a successful day for Ruby.

I walk into the room and finally get out of my suit, taking a fresh shower to calm my nerves, she knows nothing—she was joyful and the last thing we need is her coming back to a war zone, bringing her back to that dark place where she was a few days ago.

Back in the theatre room the movies are now over, the kids are jumping around the couches and I hate to be the fun breaker, so I take a seat and enjoy the moment, just as Rosita enters.

"Everyone, please head upstairs, wash hands, and come to the kitchen. Dinner is ready," she orders softly.

"I thought we were waiting for mama," Naima says.

"She will be here soon. That's why we should be ready for her. She must be exhausted," she says.

All the kids nod and do as they were told.

"That was also for you mister," she says, making me laugh at her tone.

I rise, walk to the door, and drop my arm around her shoulders.

"When are you going to stop treating me as a child?" I ask, giggling as she rolls her eyes.

"Never!" She exclaim and we enter the kitchen, where a delicious scent hit my nostrils and a roar as a lion makes me aware I haven't eaten all day.

CHAPTER TWENTY-TWO

Ruby

At nearly 7 p.m., Miguel and I are taking the stall down. They extended the closing time as more people were passing by as the sun went down.

There are no cookies or boxes to pack and a few more orders scheduled, but they should be quick to take care of, as they were actually looking for a bigger batch of cookies.

"That is everything for now *hijita*," Miguel says, helping with the last bits into the bike. Glad I brought it so he wouldn't have to come back to *Little Castle.*

I give him a brief hug and a big kiss on his cheek.

"Take care *señor* Miguel." I smile.

I put the remains of my stock on the bike and ride away. I can see the house in the distance, nearly there, but I pause.

My entire body is stiff with terrifying goosebumps. My entire system and body are in panic mode. I look around and see nothing.

The lake is calm in the nearly darkness. Around the trees

is quiet too, but when I turn to my right again, in between the trees I can see someone. Can it be the boys checking on me?

I try to focus my vision on the distance. Whoever it is, they're getting closer and closer and closer.

Jumping back on the seat, I ride away. He is getting closer to the path, and when I look back, there he is—Advik, a bouquet of sunflowers on his hands.

He could be a figment of my imagination, or real. I don't care, I won't stop to find it out.

A few seconds later, I arrive at *Little Castle* doorway. I hit the door hysterically. Rosita opens the door and I fly in, banging on the door behind me.

Samuel appears from the kitchen, wiping his hands on a dry cloth. They must see the panic on my face as Rosita runs back to the kitchen, probably to keep the kids from seeing me like this.

Samuel doesn't say a word, he just rushes to me and hugs me. I hide my face in his chest and scream all my fear away. His hold gets tighter. He could suffocate me if my lungs had any air at all inside them.

A soft knock makes us both jump, and I run away from Samuel's arms.

I need to get out of here—I need my children, so I head to the kitchen to take them.

They're clearing up the table. I hold Aidan in my arms and hold Naima's hand, throwing away the cutlery she was putting away.

She can see it on my face. *He found us again.* No matter how many men were trying to protect me, he got close enough.

When we leave the kitchen Rosita rushed behind me, but I do not stop. Samuel and Matteo aren't there, so I open the front door, drop the kids in the carrier, leaving all my belongings from the fair on the floor, but the tablecloth, jump on my seat and ride away.

I'm running for my life. The children need to be hidden. I always had a secret escape plan, one that was once made and never spoke of again, one that was a life-or-death decision.

Grabbing my mobile out I send the quickest message.

On the way.

I am riding as fast as I can. The kids are hiding in their carrier, covered. They don't know what happened, but they know there's no time to ask questions.

I cross the bridge as fast as possible and turn left. The second house on the right is my safe place. I know where the spare key is—I take it and open the backyard, hide the bike, and grab the children, knock five times. I wait, all the lights go off in the entire house. That's the secret code.

When the candle lights up in the kitchen, I open the door and go in. There is my angel, my protector—Miguel.

"Let me show you the kids' bedroom," he whispers.

I follow him upstairs while he carries the heavy candle in his hands. This is the best way to be invisible. We will only be here for a few hours, but we need to make sure nobody sees us.

Once upstairs, we turn right. Entering the master

bedroom, I place the kids in bed and let them rest.

"We will just get everything ready," I assure, making them aware we will leave soon.

I leave a fake candle on the night table, cover them and walk downstairs with Miguel.

When I head downstairs, Miguel is sitting on the small kitchen table. The kettle goes off, and he stands to pour the water.

"Should I ask?" He isn't nervous, angry, or panicking. It's the opposite—he sounds normal, relaxed.

"I was leaving the park—I could feel him. He was there when I turned," I whispered. I won't cry about this anymore. He doesn't deserve me, or my pain.

"You are safe here," he says.

Nobody knows he lives here. Months ago he bought it new, putting it in his late daughter's name. Don't tell me how he did it, but I saw the paperwork. She passed away a couple of years ago in service, fighting for this country. But that was before he moved to this neighborhood and a secret he knew one day he could use in his favor.

"The bike is hidden. It will remain like that until we make sure all is right," he assures.

"I need to make a phone call and then we will leave." I step away from the kitchen.

My screen shows over a hundred miss calls from Samuel and Matteo, multiple messages, and voicemails. He might be worried, but I can't let him know where I am or worst, where I am going.

I dial someone else, Louise.

"He fucking found me!" I'm trying not to scream, speaking through my teeth. "What the hell is wrong with you?!"

"I didn't know..."

"It's your fucking job!"

"I'm sorry... deeply sorry."

"You're fucking sorry? That won't save my life, or my children."

"I will work on..."

"No! You will find me a new social worker and get the fuck out of our lives." I just hung up, fisting my hand around the mobile. I could break it with the anger that is running through my veins.

I get back to the kitchen, Miguel is finishing my tea, and I sit at the table.

"I will need my materials. I need to work," I say. He looks cautious. "I have orders from today, and they canceled the tasting, but not the party on Saturday."

Stella is at the clinic. I'm on a runaway, but I don't think Samuel will cancel the party.

Scott doesn't deserve it.

"Where are your materials?" he asks.

I realize just then everything is in Samuel's house back in Belgravia. Maybe they brought them here when we move, otherwise in the old apartment.

"We can't go back to Samuel's," he says and I just nod.

"I can take them to the apartment. He might not know I used to live there," I say.

He knew Samuel—he knew how to follow him and found

us, but not where we used to be weeks ago.

"I will go straight away—you have a bath and change." He finishes his tea, takes his car keys, and leaves.

When I reach the bathroom, I run a bath, my mobile rolling around my fingers.

I can't call, at least not until I am in our safe place, but I go through all the messages.

All are basically the same, asking where I am, with who, if was Advik, if we are safe. My chest aches, my eyes burn, but I need to let him go.

We both knew this wouldn't last forever.

My dream man, my dream life, my dream love. I bury my face in my palms and cry while the water warm my broken soul.

I step out of the bath once the water feels cold, walk to the bed to find some of my old clothes. Miguel is back and had to make sure we have what we need.

Walking downstairs a few minutes later, placing my hair in a messy bun, I am smiling when I find all my old baking tools and ingredients spread around the entire kitchen.

Miguel is packing a few bags and placing them at the front door.

"I have prepared a few sandwiches. Not as good as yours, but is a long ride. I want to make sure we are all fed," he says not stopping packing.

Stepping into the kitchen, I prepare all my tools and ingredients and placing them with the other boxes.

Few hours later, the car is full—the children are laying at the back of the car, covered with a thick blanket and Miguel drive.

The village is dark and quiet, but a person like me knows the silence isn't safe, and it's not as quiet as other perceive it.

Advik is out there, and if Samuel loves us, as he said, he will be out there. Even the security team might be there, who knows.

We leave the city and join the trucks on the highway. The low lights, the movement, the noise give me peace, let me relax, and at some point I fall asleep.

"*Mi hijita*, we have to arrive," Miguel whispers.

I scrub my eyes and seat straight. Everything looks dark around us, but I can see the lighthouse on the right, giving light to the ocean and on the left, at the distance small lights. That must be the town.

"I will open the door," Miguel says, stepping out of the car.

The children continue sleeping, so I step out. The smell of the ocean involves me. I close the eyes and let go of everything.

Advik can't find me here, Samuel can't find me here, my past can't find me here.

At the same time that I know Advik is gone for good, I can't pull away the pain the distance from Samuel creates on me.

I want him—I want our future—I want my forever.

Pulling the mobile out of my shorts pocket, I dial him.

"Ruby!" he whispers, trying to keep to himself that I have called. "Where are you baby?"

I don't talk, but he knows I'm here, he can hear my breath and for sure the water hitting the cliff.

"I need to know you are safe!" he growls between his teeth.

"We can't see each other again, Samuel." I can't stop the tears. "We aren't safe together anymore. Forget us, we loved you."

"No!" He is not whispering anymore, "YOU FUCKING LOVE ME! You belong in my side!" I do, with all my heart. "And I love you, baby come back to me, please," he begs.

"Bye Samuel." I don't let him talk—I just hang up.

Miguel comes back and guides me through the house. It's all on one floor, but it's way bigger than I expected.

No time to tour inspection, especially because each of us is caring on child. We turn left, and he opens a beautiful twin bedroom. One bed is pink and the other blue.

There are some toys in the corner, and some books on each bedside table.

He has been preparing this for months, since the first time he found me on the street, lost and in a panic.

"I will be in the kitchen, tea?" I just nod and he closes the door.

Gently changing the kids into their pj's, there is sadness on their sleeping faces, and that breaks my heart.

We only practiced this situation once, and Naima was on alert mode. As she knew, she would have to do it alone with Aidan.

Never traveled until here, but aware that the house at the village was momentary accommodation until we move here.

"I love you so much." I kiss each of their foreheads and make sure they are cozy in the bed before I leave the room, switching on the night light on the cupboard near the door.

Walking outside, I follow the sound of the kettle. Miguel has two mugs resting on the side and quickly pours the water and milk.

I take a seat at the table, head low, mind blur, emotionally exhausted. How I was before my handsome Adonis came into my life.

"I will be back in Blue Valley in the morning," Miguel explains.

"Can you drop my orders?" I ask.

If he didn't know me, I am sure he will be shocked, but he knows I am a workaholic, especially when I have people waiting for them.

"Just label everything. I won't like to mess them up," he says giggling, dropping a kiss on my temple and walking away.

A few minutes later, I'm mixing, baking, packing, and writing a note for Miguel to understand where each is going.

This kitchen is spectacular, it's all brand new, and I can appreciate Miguel has made sure I can continue working from here.

The sun is brushing the horizon when I finish all the orders, clear up the kitchen, prepare breakfast and coffee. I would not let Miguel leave on an empty stomach after all.

"*Buenos dias mi hijita,*" he greets me, his expression concern as he realize I haven't slept yet.

"I can't," I murmur, raising my shoulders.

How can I sleep after everything?

"Nobody can find you here, nobody knows you here," he assures, and I try to take it.

After a quick coffee and once the car is full with all the orders placed at the trunk and back seats, he leaves.

I take a seat on the porch rocking chair and look at the ocean, letting the ocean waves be my lullaby and the early morning sun be my blanket.

CHAPTER TWENTY-THREE

Samuel

"Are you sure?!" I shout to Matteo while I run to the front door.

"Samuel!" Rosita runs out of the kitchen. "Where are you going?"

Is she seriously asking?

Rolling my eyes, I confront her.

"Haven't you heard them? Didn't you see her face?" I ask shouting at them, "Was it the bastard?" I ask Matteo again.

"As the sky is blue *hermano*, Calvin said an Indian-looking guy was following her, and she saw him—that confirms it." Matteo says, typing on his mobile.

"Did you hear it? I need to find her. Before he does, I must find her." I scream, my vision is blur, my chest is heavy.

"It's been hours *hijo,* you checked the entire village. She is gone." She murmurs.

Pulling my waves slightly more, I sigh, turn around and leave her there.

I get in the car—Matteo jumps in when I was about to leave the path and we drive away.

"Fuck me!!" I can't stop hitting the steering wheel.

I know she isn't here anymore. When we reach her old apartment last night, she was gone. The front door was open, all the lights were on, but there was nobody. I checked the bedroom. It was a complete mess. There were clothes everywhere.

In the bathroom all their products were gone, and in the living room and kitchen was another mess.

All her baking tools gone, mostly all the toys, too.

It seems like she passed by, took the most important things and left.

"Where are you, Ruby?" I murmur to myself, I heard the sea last night. She is somewhere near the beach.

"She can't go so far on a bike and with two kids," Matteo says.

"Someone is helping her. She is not in London. They are by the seaside," I assure, driving away from the city.

Checking my rear mirrors I can see the boys following me, I haven't told them yet where we are going, but they know we won't found them here.

We have ran every house, road, even went to London.

"Ruby will have to come out today. She has orders to deliver." Matteo gives me a questioning look. "She mentioned at the summer fair that at least three orders were for today."

"Do you know where the orders are?" he asks.

I just shake my head and sink into my seat.

"I will put more boys on the streets," he assures me.

Matteo knows more people than I could have possibly imagined, and all of them will protect us all.

After three hours, we reach the coast. I step out of the car at a petrol station on the side of the motorway.

"This is the middle point, we will divide and inspect every single village, town, house, hole in the fucking ground until we found them," I explain every single man Matteo has brought with us on top of my over forty security men team, "spread the word, show their pictures, alert police, I don't fucking care!"

No more words are need it. We split in half—I go East, and as we drive the motorway, I see how each car leave on every town we pass by. My exit is Sunderland.

Nearly home, Matteo and I spend the day talking with locals, asking questions. Matteo has been all morning in contact with an ex-girlfriend cop, checking every street camera, trying to find her.

She sent us the CCTV back in Blue Valley. I saw her leaving my house—I saw her riding for her life, but she suddenly disappears, there no cameras where she left.

In the late afternoon, Calvin and Logan join us.

Low head meet us. There is no news from her.

"Sorry boss, they keep looking," Logan says.

"Go home, rest. I want to be alone." No matter the hour, I just call her. I know she sees my calls.

"Where will you go, *hermano?*" Matteo asks.

Without answering, I stand from the bench near the beach, seat on my car and speed away.

I ain't thinking, just driving my body is heavier than usual, my mind is blurred and I can feel my chest broken into a million pieces.

Three hours later, on the horizon, my home rise in the green mountains, the fortress, the castle, the only place that one day held happiness.

I've been here hours ago, but alone, in the night seems mysterious.

Pushing the front heavy doors, I step in, resting my back on the door, closing my eyes and taking a deep breath.

Standing in the foyer, lost, in pain, in silence, it isn't quiet, I can hear my past, the voices, the steps, the movements, this castle is alive, awaiting my return, ready to shallow me on the deepest murkiness.

I push myself away from the door and walk to his bedroom, is dark and dusty, but I step in, walk until his bed, and lay down.

Letting the night take away everything, I close my eyes and disappear.

The sun rising through the mountains burns my eyelids. I turn and found myself in the old sheets, cover in dust, spiderwebs everywhere, but everything is intact.

Getting out of bed I head to the bathroom, twist my lips as I see the mess, disgusting situation here too, so I walk to the kitchen, brushing the walls with my fingertips all the way there, the paper is damage—the stones are cold as ice, and the wood is dry.

As I enter my tummy roars, but there is not a single item

piece of food here. Checking under the sink, I found what I was looking for, but is expired too.

I can't have a shower on a dirty shower, I can't clean with expired products and I can't drive this way to town.

Remembering a hose in the back garden, it's July, I should be fine with that, forgetting how cold water can be in the mountains, just realising I don't feel the pain, the burning feeling, my soul is destroyed, there is no more pain that can hurt.

Getting a hold of some spare clothes in the car, I seat in and drive back to town; the roads are quiet—the shopping is quick and I pass unnoticed over every store.

After getting a muffin and coffee at the local café and with a car filled with food, cleaning products, building tools and paint, I head back home.

If I need to take Ruby and the children out of my mind and heart, I am going to need a lot of distractions, a ten master bedrooms, each with their respective en-suite bathroom, five employees bedroom, a kitchen the size of my entire apartment in Belgravia and three-level staircase, just for start should distract me enough.

This house was my safe place, the only space I could be me for a while, it was bright, filled with laughers and love, especially when we were all here, melancholy surrounds me, making me realised I lost the opportunity to have a father, just because of how similar we were, just because he wanted to me to become a better version of himself.

Fucking ungrateful, spoiled Samuel!

By the end of the day, the master bedroom is cleaned, freshly painted, the bathroom is disinfected and the curtains are back after a well-deserved wash.

Other two more bedrooms are done and the staircase that connects the ground and first floor is clean and varnish, the wood shines so much that I can see my reflection in it.

The house has a special scent of homemade roast and I seat at the spotless kitchen island and have some dinner.

Getting filled of new energy so I can continue working tomorrow, at this speed in the next three days the inside will be done, and I am already planning the transformation at the rear garden, that was Grandpa and then my mother's favourite spot, and in their honour I will turn it on a magical place.

Filled with flowers, the thought of them reminds me of Ruby, her passion for them, how gorgeous she looks.

Gosh! I miss her so fucking much!

CHAPTER TWENTY-FOUR

Samuel
Nineteen years ago, Edinburgh.

I take off the keys from my bike, opening my leather jacket and removing my helmet.

Rosita is by the front door with arms folded under her chest. There is something on her beautiful Latina face that makes me pause.

Suddenly I hear some trotting behind me and I can see my beautiful sister galloping my way.

She doesn't greet me as usual, just stare at me, raises her chin and gallops away again.

"It's the way to greet someone? Where are your manners, ladies?" I ask exasperated at their attitude.

I walk pass by Rosita and head to the flower garden where mother should be reading under the sun as usual.

"Samuel," Rosita calls me, rushing behind me.

Ignoring her, I reach the garden, but it's empty. Searching around, I can't hear her, see her, or find any sign that she is here.

My entire world falls on my shoulder when I turn to face Rosita. Her eyes are as red as the fire, her cheeks are wet with thick tears.

"There are gone," Stella says, walking into the garden by the side, after she walked Storm back to the stables.

"What the fuck are you talking about, child?" I scream at her.

"You fucking left!" She screams back.

"*Mi hijito,*" Rosita can barely talk, she just murmur the words in between sobbings, "they looked for you, they went after some news of where you were, but they never came back," she covers her mouth, trying to control herself.

"Look for me?" I ask, confused, "How? When?" So many questions are rushing on my mind, "Why now?"

"They run behind you since you left arsehole!" Stella spit.

"Shut the fuck up Stella!" I scream at her, letting all out of my system.

"They are gone because of you!" She throws at my face.

My entire body trembles, I feel cold—I feel emptiness and how what was left of my heart unharmed break into million pieces.

I just lost the women I loved the most in my life, my mother, the perfect, kind, unique soul that made our existence a better place.

With heavy foot, I walk inside, not sure where I am going.

I reach my father's office, memories of the last time I was here.

Do I feel hurt he is gone?

Why would I be? He took my grandfather away from me, didn't let me say my goodbyes, spend the last minutes in the bedroom.

I am actually thankful he is gone, that I won't ever have to confront him again.

We must leave. I step out of the office and walk around, searching for Rosita. She is preparing the dining table for supper.

"Get everything ready, we will leave first thing tomorrow," I inform her, turning away and heading back to what now has turned to be my new bedroom.

CHAPTER TWENTY-FIVE

Ruby

The children woke up at around 8 a.m., straight running to the porch where I wait them every morning with fresh orange juice and this morning, pancakes.

"Buenos dias mama," Naima says.

We have been practicing a lot of Spanish for the past few days. Miguel suggested we play the Latina niece, visiting my uncle with the children.

After over a week here, we have agreed it's safe for us to take a walk by the beach, enjoy the Thursday farmers' market.

"Today is going to be a really warm day. I need everyone wearing hats, sunglasses, fresh clothes and comfortable shoes," I say, it's not just for the warm weather.

It might sound paranoid, but the hat and glasses are more of a *hide who we are* purpose.

Few minutes later we are ready to leave. There is a fifteen minutes' walk to the town center.

As we approach, our spirits cheer up. It won't be so bad to

socialize, see something different, and buy some fresh food.

Miguel has been extremely kind, dropping groceries, making sure we have all the clothes and things that we might need.

Collecting and delivering my orders, he was coming every other day, and leaving before the sunrise, the only way to not be seen.

This town is way more beautiful than I imagined. Flower stalls open the road market, they are selling any type and color of flower you could imagine.

Holding hands, we check every stall. They have fresh fruit and vegetables, homemade craft and the one that calls mostly my attention is the bakery one.

They have bread, cakes of many flavors and colors, pastries, even homemade pizza.

"Morning," I greet on a thick Western accent. If I want to play my part, I better do it right.

"Morning sweetheart," the lady says, giving us a beautiful smile, but suddenly she frowns, and all my body alerts are on.

"*Mama*, can we get something?" Naima asks.

"Yes, of course. What would you like?" I ask, letting them have a look at everything Aidan can't barely see, so I hold him up on the arms, what accidentally made my summer hat fall away.

I quickly bend to take it, dropping my sunglasses too, *oh gosh!*

When I stand, the lady's expression totally changes, the line of her frown dipped, and she looks around.

"Leonardo!" She calls. I rush to put everything back on, searching around for a quick escape, but we are in the busiest area of the market.

Naima can feel my stress. Aidan holds me tighter, turns around, but it's too late. A gentleman is right behind us, staring at me with a big smile, making me extremely uncomfortable.

Turning back to the stall, the lady snaps a picture of us. I shake in panic, but unaware of what to do.

Miguel was right, we shouldn't have left the house, I shouldn't have insisted.

"It's the lady of the magazine!" The lady exclaims.

That makes sense, I absolutely forgot my face is all over the internet, on the cover of one of the most important magazines in the world.

Was I really thinking people will never read it, or recognize me?

"I read that magazine since I was a teenager," the stall lady exclaims.

"Stop it, woman! You are petrifying them with all that noise."

I turn back and forth between them, turning red as I see that this brief scene has called way more people's attention.

"Can we get a picture?" Another lady in the crowd asks.

I tense. Naima holds harder with my hand, and I look back at her.

"*Mama* it's okey," she assure.

So I do it. One picture turns in over twenty, but I smile. I help the local magazine little store sell few more of SaStel magazines and they ask me to sign them, just a simple;

Ruby♥ x

Once we are done, the baker gift us some pastries. I feel horrible to don't pay for them, but she clarified it was a baker supporting a baker, and how much she looks forward to try my own creations.

With three tote bags filled with fruit, vegetables, flower and pastries we head back home.

Before I can close the door, my mobile rings. It's Miguel.

"*Hola* Miguel," I cheerfully say.

"What have you done?" He asks. I can hear the roar of his car in the background.

"What do you mean?" I feel extremely confused.

"They found you!" He exclaim, way more alarmed than usual, never heard his talking this way.

"What?!" I can't believe what he is saying.

"Pack everything. I am on my way!" he exclaims.

"But Miguel," I complain.

"Not another word, *hijita*!" He orders and hung up.

Making sure every door and window in the house are locked, I head to the bedroom, pull out the luggage, and start taking everything out of the drawers and cupboards.

"What are you doing, *mama*?" Naima asks.

"Miguel is on the way," I murmur. "We must leave as soon as he arrives."

No more words are need it, she just walk away.

I hear her in the bedroom, closing drawers and hurrying

to the bathroom. Sadly, I told her well how to pack and run away.

When will I stop running?

As I drop the luggages at the front door, Miguel appears with an expression I have never seen in him.

"We must talk," he says, walking towards the kitchen.

As we enter, he drops a set of unknown keys on the dining table.

"Congratulations, the cottage is yours," he sighs.

With everything happening, I have put out of my head the cottage—us getting a forever home, a fresh start, especially in Blue Valley.

"How can you be so careless?" He asks, sounding exasperated.

"What have I done?" I ask, confused how getting the keys of the cottage is me making any type of mistake.

"You know what happen the day I dropped you here? Who came to me the minute I put a foot back in the village? Who question all my movements after I dropped your orders?" He asks, and shock paralysed my body.

"Advik?" I ask, nearly puking at the mentioned of his name.

"Thankfully for you not," I exhale of relief, "Samuel's security team, Rosita, even a police officer!"

"Why they came to you?" I ask confused.

"Because they followed me. There were everywhere I dropped an order, but the wait until I was back at my store, then is when they all showed." He says, explaining all what has happened.

"What did you tell them?"

"I denied it all, but how can I hide you when you let yourself be photographed and posted on the internet with the location of the place," he explains.

"Do you...? Use social media?" I can't imagine Miguel chatting or scrolling.

"I didn't have to! They showed up on few hours ago. Your face is with the children, over the internet and in the farmers' market!" He points out every aspect, my entire body tense.

"Samuel was there?" I ask.

"Is that what you care? If Samuel will rush on his white horse, rescue you from the tower and take you away to live happily ever after? Wake up Ruby!"

"We didn't plan it," I say, and he raises a thick eyebrow. "We covered ourselves. It was an accident. We didn't have a way out," I explain. Honesty will help us more.

"Accident or not, they know you are here. I rush as much as I could, but you know..." he sighs, raising his shoulders.

"They will be here soon, anyway is not like they can take me away. I don't belong to him." I declare, sick of feeling I need to run away from Samuel too, or be forced to be with him. "Let them come!" I declare.

Walking out of the kitchen, into the hallway, and grabbing my luggage.

"We ain't leaving," I announce Naima and Aidan when they show their little faces out of their bedrooms.

They might know the town we are hiding in, but not the house we are staying in.

I have a quick shower, change my clothes, and march out of the house.

Miguel rush behind me, "what? *Hijita!*"

"They don't know our exact location, and I intent to keep it like that for few more days." I say, turning and walking away.

I take the beach way and arrive at the town by the fresh, beautiful, wet sand.

Casually walking around, looking at the sea. This time, I am not covering myself. My mane is flying away, my pale skin warming up with the afternoon sun.

Once I reach the busiest spot, I walk to shore, found a free space on the stone bench facing the water and seat there.

Before expected I can feel all the eyes are on me, but there is not scary or special goosebumps, there is not paralysation on my body, there is just the simple feeling of been seen.

"Hello Ruby."

I don't turn, but I know who is behind me. He slowly lowers and takes a seat by my side, but he is looking at the town.

"What are you doing here?" I ask Matteo.

"Make sure you and the kids are fine," he says simply.

"Been paid to spy on me?" I am grateful they care for us, but I can't let Samuel have the power over us.

"He is gone, Ruby," he says, and I turn my head in shock.

"I can't believe that." he wouldn't give up on us, *seriously?*

"We start the search as soon as you left *Little Castle*, team up with police and some other friends to search for you in every village, every town near the ocean," I raise an eyebrow in question, "you call him and he heard the water," I just nod in agreement and let him continue, "we reach north, he sent us away and disappear, mobile off, no calls, no texts, nothing but silence, he did it again."

I look away, hurt. It's ironic—I didn't want him to rush behind me and come to rescue me, but I did at least show up, throw his power over me and let me fight back.

Without another word, I jump down to the sand again.

"Ruby?" Matteo calls, and when I turn, I see them all, Matteo, Logan, Calvin, and some unknown men.

"Go home guys, we are fine," I say, walking away.

I won't lie, that hurts, how someone can love you and need you so much one day and the other be gone, well that apparently is really common in Samuel, anyway.

They questioned my run away with Advik, but every time something hard has happened, Mr. Samuel has run away for as long as he pleased.

I walk back into the house, passing by the kids and Miguel, that were having something to eat at the front patio.

My expression must say everything when they didn't say a word, I walk away and get into my bedroom, lay in bed and close my eyes, traveling away from Advik, away from Samuel, away of all of this, wishing I could just take my children and run back home.

It's dark outside when a soft knock kick me out of my drowsy state.

"*Mi hijita*," Miguel calls from the door.

"I want to be alone," I mumble to the pillow.

"The children need you; Scott needs you," he says softly, reminding me of the party, the one thing that start all of this, damn you Samuel for finding me, fuck me for accepting the booking, everything might have been easier if I didn't accept it.

"We will travel back tonight. The cottage keys are in the kitchen and Samuel's team moved all your belongings there," he explains.

Breaking my heart slightly more, making me understand he has completely kicked us out of his house and life.

We reach the cottage nearly at dawn—the streets are quiet and I can't resist looking at *Little Castle,* it's not a beautiful bright castle anymore, the walls look darker, abandoned as it was months ago, way before Samuel storm into our lives.

The children are at their brand new painting corner, while I finish the breakfast.

I am about to call the kids to wash their hands when my mobile rings. It's an unknown number, so I ignore it and a message comes through.

Before I can open it, my entire body tenses, my heart stops, my lungs are empty—I can't breathe. I press the message and there he is.

You are even more beautiful after these months.

Can't wait to be back home.

Love, your husband

My hands are shaking. I look around the room—we have been extremely cautious.

We have been gone for a week, but he hasn't given up. I better get the things ready and plan our departure from London for good.

CHAPTER TWENTY-SIX

Samuel

I walk to the front heavy doors. This is a proper castle, one that my great-grandfather built, one that holds more secrets than even my father could imagine.

When I was a kid, my grandfather used to take night walks, opening and closing things everywhere, disappearing into thin air.

He tries to tell me something before he passed, and after a week here, cleaning everything, getting this entire place ready to be habitable again, I am ready to find out everything.

Ruby could show me secrets that were never mentioned, people that were never spoken of, but that end today.

I walk to the corridor he mentioned, the one that heads to the kitchen, brushing my palm over the wall and as I've learned in *Little Castle* nothing it's as it seems.

After three attempts, the wall opens in front of me. I hold my breath.

Stepping into the darkness, I follow the path. There is light at the end, it's natural light. It's a secret office, the ceiling made of glass. *How can we miss this place from the outside?* I think, which makes me realise there are bushes surrounding the window that, after many years of not being taken care of, nearly keep it hidden.

That's the next project, the garden, but this is way more important.

I check every inch of room, taking every pile of documents that I found and brought them to my office back at the house, hours later the entire space is clear, there is not a since paper visible and all the books are now on the library room.

These were the family antiques, not the shit that they stole the last time. I knew grandpa or even my father wouldn't be so careless with our family belongings.

But I haven't found what I was looking for.

Where did you hide her, grandpa?

I stand near the first bookshelf, knocking the back wood panel. I hear what I suspect echo.

That can only mean one thing. I touch the borders of the old wood for a little button that will move it.

A loud crack happens, and I step away, letting the shelf do its job.

"For the love of God!" I exclaim.

I am facing a secret family treasure. There are pieces older than my grandfather, but what paralyzes me is a portrait. It's of a young lady, dressed in a beautiful light yellow gown.

Looking away, I see my skin and Stella's eyes. Ruby was absolutely right.

"Catherine," I say.

I step closer and found there are multiple of them, inspecting what else is inside her. I realise it's safer to keep it hidden. I just take with me a pocket portrait, step out, lock the bookshelf and walk away.

Observing her while I finish my coffee at the office, she was gorgeous, thick black waves, same as mine, and the ones that Stella been trying to hide away since she was a teenager.

Brights, deep, beautiful turquoise eyes, innocent smile, olive smooth skin, slightly darker than mine, more like my father's, but I can see Stella in her.

"What happen to you, Catherine?" I ask the portrait.

Since I can remember, they did not mention her. My father never had an answer about her, and Grandpa absolutely avoided the questions.

Not losing any more time, I separate documents per date, topic, importance even.

It's extremely dark outside when a knock on the door force me to stand away from the good work I was doing here. The knock persists.

"For God's sake give me a fucking moment!" I exclaim, opening the heavy door to confront Helena.

"Evening, Samuel," she says sarcastically.

"What the fuck Helena?" I ask, *what is she doing here?*

"Are you fucking kidding me?" She asks, following me when I turn around, "it's Saturday Samuel! Did you forget?"

You don't know what has happened. I'm not in the mood for this visit, I think.

I look over my shoulder as I enter the kitchen, and she rolls her eyes.

"It's Scott's birthday party. Stella is back home, the boys found them, you know, the regular," she says, giving me an instant headache.

"No one will miss me at that place," I answer, taking some wine glasses and red.

"I am driving, and so are you," she says.

"Don't have the intention to go anywhere," I argue back.

"You make everyone look for them and then ignore all the calls and messages once they find them?"

She is irritating every pore of my being. That tone is killing me.

"Are you going to have a shower, get ready for the birthday, and drive us back to London?" She asks, raising a questioning eyebrow.

I have no answer for that. I take a seat on the island and rest my head on my hands, looking at her, waiting to finish and leave.

She turns on her heels, head to grab some water and turning back to me.

Before I realise it, she throws the water on my face, kicking me out of this misty mind set I have been for over a week. "Helena!!" I exclaim.

"What the fuck is wrong with you?" She asks.

"You!" I scream.

Standing and leaving her, walking back to my previous

task, the files, that by now I can read as they are all separated.

She rushes behind me and comes to a halt at the door.

"Holly fucking shit," she exclaims. "They didn't take them away."

"Did you know about all this stuff?" I ask her.

Are you telling me she knew of all this stuff's existence and never said a word?

She walks to the table and grabs the portrait.

"Catherine," she whispers, and I look at her in shock.

"What do you know?" I ask.

"She is your grandmother," she answers so naturally that I can't believe it.

"How do you know?" I need responses.

"Because your father disappears shortly after he found out," she explains, brushing her fingertips under her eyes avoiding a tear to messed up her makeup.

"Rosita knew it..." I mumble, and she nods, "I will be ready in ten minutes," I scream rushing to the shower, the only person who can give me any information is in London, scared to talk, but this secrets end today.

It's nearly 11 a.m., when I reach Stella's house. It has been a long ride. We left after we hide everything again and secure the castle.

As we park in the street to leave space for the guests to enter, I see Stella walking toward us.

"Welcome!" She has a beautiful, bright smile on her perfect face.

I give her a hug and turn to help Helena out of the car. There is no chance to talk anymore as they walk away for help and support.

At the front door, I see Scott waiting for me.

"Mom said we need to hide," he says and I follow him upstairs, but come to a halt when I see Naima's profile seated at the dining table at the back.

Naima? Fuck Ruby is here!

I can't hear or see Ruby, but the idea of being under the same roof again stops my heart.

We walk to his bedroom and get consumed with video games. Matteo joins us shortly after, giving me the opportunity to leave.

I rush downstairs and enter the kitchen like a hurricane, which brings everyone's attention to me.

Ruby is at the furthest counter taking care of the cake, but she turns when she hears my heavy footsteps.

I can see fear in her eyes. They are dark and red—she has been crying—and she hasn't slept well either. She looks gorgeous and sweet, but also in pain, sad, and scared.

I want to get closer, hold her, protect her, but everyone in the room is looking at us. Nobody talks, they just stare at us.

Helena gets closer and whispers in my ear, "She is even better in person," she says, dropping a kiss on my cheek and walking away.

"Ruby, is everything okay?" Stella steps closer, holding her softly by the arm, and she breaks our gaze, looking at her, giving her a small smile and turning back to what she was doing before I arrived.

She doesn't turn back to me. Stella is acting weird, just like she doesn't remember all that has happened, and Rosita is trying to keep calm while preparing drinks.

I turn around and I see Naima and Aidan—she is looking at me, and he is calling for my attention with his arms.

Without thinking, I head straight to him and hold him as usual. His small hands fist my white shirt, making sure it will be no simple job to put him down.

Clearing my throat, I find the courage to speak. "Scott would like to know when he can come downstairs."

Now that I know they are here, I can't leave. I will wait for the moment I can talk to her again.

"Ruby, how much longer?" Stella asks.

Ruby doesn't answer at once. I can see her moving from one leg to another, uncomfortable and so I am.

Stella gives a slight cough and Ruby comes back to life.

"I will say five minutes," she hisses. Turning to find Aidan in my arms, the spatula in her hand drops, and her head turns, trying to avoid me.

"You heard, thank you, Samuel." Stella just dismisses me, like I'm in the middle.

"Sorry baby," I place Aidan back on the chair, and little Naima's hands meet my arm.

"She needs you," her whisper is the saddest thing I've ever heard. "We need you Samuel, you promised." I did.

"I will get her back. I just need to be alone with her." That will be the only way.

I was thinking of going back upstairs, but I can't. Instead, I head to the front door. I need some fresh air. A part of me would even like to run away again. She might refuse me, and

God knows that will definitely ruin me forever.

Helena is outside, talking over her phone, and looks shocked when I step outside.

"I will call you later, babe." Natasha must be the one on the phone. "Why aren't you inside?" she asks.

"Are you fucking kidding me?!" I just raise my arms to the sky in desperation.

She won't give me space, but I need fresh air. I step away but I can hear her heels following me, and then are parents. I can see them parking the cars, and I don't want anyone questioning why I'm out here, either. I consider maybe going back inside, knowing soon more people will be around—yes, that will be the best choice.

"Samuel, wait! Stop being a child and behave." She runs to my side and we both freeze. We aren't alone. Ruby is at the front door.

Not saying a word, she heads back inside the house. I'm on her heels when we enter the kitchen. Stella is preparing a tray of mugs and small glasses for juices, and the kids are in the garden playing with Scott.

"Let me help you with that," she says.

"I will make sure everything is perfect in the garden," Stella says, stepping outside, giving me a killing look as she passes by me.

Ruby heads to the sink and refills the kettles, ignoring the fact that I am right behind her, on a short distance.

"Ruby...." I whisper, making her entire body tremble, "Baby, I am..."

"Samuel, let's go outside and have a drink," I hear one of Stella's disgusting fake friends calling me

"*Mama!*" Aidan calls Ruby.

"Yes, baby," she turns and bends down, trying to avoid looking at me.

"I want you to play with us, *mama*," he murmurs. I saw a few people coming in—I bet they were feeling a little overwhelmed and uncomfortable.

"*Mama* is helping Stella with the drinks, and I will be in the garden in a moment."

"Why don't you have some fresh air?" Rosita is by my side. I didn't even notice her. "I will finish the drinks and help with the oven."

"*Gracias* Rosita," she murmurs, walking away.

And I stand there, while everything happens around me. I am absolutely invisible to her. She is done with me.

"You did it again *hijito*," Rosita whisper, "she is not a normal woman, I warn you."

Yes, she did.

But, I won't give up. She loves me, and I will do anything to have them back.

I walk outside. It's a beautiful day, really sunny, but fresh at the same time. There's half of the garden that will hold shadow for a few hours, before everything from the buffet table will have to be moved.

"Ruby!" I hear Stella calling her. She is with three of the biggest witch fake friends she could have. "Please, come! We were just talking about you," she says, giggling.

Ruby approach them, chin up high and I spot a white

wineglass in Stella's hand. It's nearly 2 p.m., and she is on medication.

"They couldn't believe you have made all these delicious nibbles," she giggles and looks at them, making them giggle, too.

"You are so..." Sofia says, not looking at her, until she does from top to toe, "sweet." More giggles.

Not saying a word, Ruby just turn around and walks towards the kids. Scott is with them.

They are at the craft table, with baking activities and cookie decoration.

"My deepest apologies, Ruby," he whispers, and I smile at the big-hearted nephew I have.

Other kids start joining them, asking Ruby for more ideas, ingredients, and colours.

I bet you can hear the giggles and laughs from the entrance of the house.

But my joy doesn't last long. Sofia is right behind her in no time.

"Roberta! Look at the state of your clothes!"

I quickly spot her daughter. She is sitting by the other side of Scott—she has her long blonde bouncy hair, with an enormous bow on the top, gosh that thing is nearly as big as her entire head.

Her gaze fixed on the beautiful cookie she was decorating, with a perfect rainbow, but her hands were shaking. I can feel how bad she feels, the anger, the annoyances.

Ruby rise and turns around. Sofia looks nervous about

being this close, but Ruby is not intimidating it.

"Would you like an apron?" Ruby asks, making me laugh.

Well done baby. If she wants to behave like a child, we will treat her like one.

Her chest rises, her nose nearly pointing to the sky. I can see full anger on her face, her nostrils inflate, her arms raise, and Ruby should back up, as Sofia might be about to slap her, but she is not afraid of anyone anymore.

"How dare you, you little bitch!"

Did she just call her *bitch* at a child's party? Ruby stops her hand millimetres away from her cheek. "I don't think this is the place to use that language ma'am."

"Who the fuck do you think you are to tell how I can talk?" Gosh this is getting worse. I get closer. "Who gave you permission to even talk to us?!"

Since when Ruby needs permission to talk to someone?

"Sofia, that's enough," I cut her off from behind Ruby.

"Samuel, call. What's her name?" She giggles, pointing around, "ah yeah, Rosita and ask her where the servants' space is."

Did she just call Ruby and Rosita servants?

I step closer until my chest is brushing Ruby back. I am using her as a shield, so I won't kill this crazy woman.

"Sofia, take Roberta and leave the party immediately." I can feel the anger leaving my system.

As Sofia turns around offended and leave so does Ruby, instantly seeing her running away from me again, and just Scott screams bringing me back to life.

"THE PARTY IS OVER! EVERYBODY OUT OF MY

HOUSE NOW!" He screams running away.

I run to the front door. Scott is there, crying like he has just lost one of the most precious things in his life. I've only seen him like this before, when Donnie passed away.

I run outside to the driveway, but she is rushing inside a car.

"Ruby!" I call.

Freezing, she turns around. Her eyes fill with tears. So does mine, and my vision becomes a blur. This is way more painful that I could imagine.

When she disappears over a week ago, it broke me, but I lose her. Now it's like the need of me to say goodbye. I can't, will never give up on them.

She gives a small step, letting me know she wants to stay, she wants us, but when she tenses and looks around, I can feel it too. We are not alone.

"Please, don't." I say.

In a second, she is in my arms, holding me. She hides her face in my neck. Her hands fist my shirt, her arms try to hold me strong, not willing to let me go.

"Let me go," she murmurs in my ear, kissing me. That kiss would have to send me to heaven a few days ago, but now it is my death sentence.

Pulling away, I can't see her anymore. My eyes fill with tears, not capable of holding them anymore, and that's when her lips meet mine again, in a soft, meaningful way. I can taste our tears mixed with pain. I break our kiss, not capable of holding this painful moment any longer.

She turns around, and I step away, letting her jump into the car and leave. I walk away, away from the *Love of My Life*.

I head upstairs first, where the people that I care for is hiding.

Rosita seated on a couch by the window, Scott in her arms and Matteo by the wall.

"How is my birthday boy?" There's sadness in his beautiful little face. Which makes me want to kill Stella and all her fake friends.

"Can we celebrate it with Naima, Aidan, and Ruby?" He asks.

"*My hijito*, Ruby needs her time now, but soon, sooner than you imagine, they will come back. I promise." Rosita explains.

Goddam Ruby, one woman has broken all of us.

"But she is in the cottage now!" He declares angrily.

"What did you say?" I ask in shock.

She has moved there already? Where have I been? Why hasn't Matteo said a word?

When I look at them, Rosita turns her face to Scott, and Matteo pushes himself away from the wall.

"We found them, bro, but you didn't answer your phone or the door." He looks in pain but especially angry.

"The other day when Mum came back, I saw shadows inside, like they were inside, but didn't want anyone to know." Scott explains.

"Are you sure?" I can't just show up there and find another empty house.

He just nods in response, and so do Rosita and Matteo.

"Goddamn you guys!" I scream, running out of the room,

heading downstairs.

When I am about to reach the front door, something else calls my attention.

I walk towards the clutter of noises. There Stella is, in the kitchen, out of control, throwing and breaking everything on her way. It's like I'm travelling back in time, back to when we were kids, back to when she lost her husband, too.

"There you are!" She sounds drunk, gosh not now, "What the fuck is wrong with you?!"

"I beg your pardon?" I ask, *is she really going to blame me for this one?*

"The party was perfect, everyone was having fun, but no! Samuel can't let things be! He needs to be the centre of the attention." She can't hold herself straight without holding a hand on some counter.

"Stella, you aren't at your best to be having this conversation." We need to have it, but with a clean system.

"My best? I was finally having fun, feeling myself again, and you just ruin it, like you fucked up everything!" She doesn't know what she is talking about.

"Were you having fun? Or were those bitches you keep trying to call friends?" I've hated them since we were in college.

"How dare you?!" Another deep sip of wine, directly from the bottle.

"Where are they all yearlong? They aren't your friends Stella, they just come here for gossip, to have something to sell the press and pay for their rest of the year's miserable life." It is not the first time they've done it. Last year was humiliating.

Thank God that Scott doesn't have access to much press yet.

"They've been by my side every time I need them!" She is mad, absolutely mad.

"What the fuck are you talking about?! They came when? At our parents' funeral? Nope! That wasn't juicy enough. When you lost your husband? Nope! He was a nobody, so no interest, when you had your last breakdown? Nope! Because I kept it as a fucking secret trying to protect you. They just come to Scott's birthdays, especially now! You moved out of the spotlight. They need to have the correct information to sell." She doesn't want to listen—just shaking her head.

"That's not the truth, they... you know... they are busy, Samuel." *Oh God.*

"You are delusional, and I won't be having this conversation in this state. You found the perfect person for the perfect party. She busts her arse to deliver it. She risked everything for this party and how do you pay back? By humiliating her!" I can't let that slip away.

"Oh yeah! I forgot, Ruby, she is your what? Your new..."

"Careful Stella!" I warn her.

"You fucked her and think what? She is now part of the family?" She laughs.

I haven't seen this side of my little sister in a while, but I won't tolerate it against Ruby.

"I will let no one humiliate her." That's a promise. "How selfish and ungrateful you are, sister."

She doesn't look ashamed of it.

"Haven't you seen all she did for you, for Scott?"

"I paid her a fucking fortune. The little rat was inside a

muddy hole when I found her."

My fist grows on my side. I need to take a deep breath and control myself. She is my sister and has drunk a lot.

"Even with that, you humiliate her! But she is way smarter than you. She used it to grow and save her children." She laughs again.

"Safe her children," she mimics me. "Gosh Samuel, one fuck and you lick her feet. How sad of you."

"Stella, I warn you, measure your words," I growl between my teeth.

"Can't you see it? She took advantage of you! She took advantage of all of us!" She is mad.

Rosita comes to my side, rubbing my arm, trying to calm me down. She knows well we can't get close to her like this. We just need to let all the poison come out.

"*Mi hijo*, Helena been waiting, and I think is better you go."

"*Mother Teresa* is here! In perfect time and ready to save the world!"

Rosita is immune to her. She has done this multiple times—Stella knows what hurts us and will use it against us to make herself feel better.

"*Mother Rosita* is going to take baby Stella to bed," she approaches her, cautious, used to be attacked in this condition. Rosita puts the bottle aside and holds her gently by the arm.

Stella doesn't fight back or complain, she just follows Rosita's guidance, and I head to the living room where Helena is waiting for me.

"I apologise. Let's get you home." She stands as I wait in

the doorframe.

"You don't want to drop me home Samuel," she kisses my cheek. "Go to her. Natasha is outside anyway."

I'm thankful to Natasha right now. Without another word, I jump in the car while Helena and Natasha drive away.

Deep breaths and ready to clear everything up with Ruby.

CHAPTER TWENTY-SEVEN

Ruby

We drive back in silence, but I can see Naima clearing away some tears.

I can't blame her. We were all hoping this day would have ended better, but *what was I thinking?*

That Samuel will run inside the house, take us away and live happily ever after?

Fuck off Ruby! There ain't no Prince Charming!!

Miguel waits for me while I take each kid out, change them, put them in bed and return, but I come back one last time alone.

"I promise it's not that bad," I assure him by the window.

"They were your safe place Ruby," he says, placing his hand in my arm by the window. "Nobody should run from a safe place. Now you did it twice."

I nod, ashamed and hurt after his words.

"*Buenas noches señor* Miguel," I say, "go home and rest, tomorrow we have a barbeque with Sarah and her children," he raise his eyebrows questioning.

"That was quick," he says.

"I know, I was so surprise when she call me. They prepared the documents faster than expected and we are trying to prepare things for the next school term," I explain.

"Let me know how I can help, and of course I will be here, *un asadito*!" He sings and I giggle.

I wait on the pathway until he drives away and walks inside the house, make sure it's locked, go to the children's bedrooms, make sure they are cozy, drop a kiss on their little foreheads and have a quick shower.

I take a big T-shirt from a box and walk back downstairs.

There are boxes everywhere, so I have a look around and arrange them for rooms, that I think will make my life way easier.

After a few minutes, I am left with around five, maybe six boxes downstairs.

I pour some iced tea from this morning, play some music, and start with the kitchen. Scott's party is over. There are orders I need to take care of, but not while I'm surrounded by this mess.

The beach house kitchen was stunning, but this is the cutest one I've ever been in. Everything is old-fashioned and rustic.

It might look like it doesn't have much space, but there are multiple secret spaces where I can store most of my baking tools.

My tummy growl and with all the craziness of the party, I just realized I haven't eaten at all, so while I finish another box, I prepare a quick evening snack.

Grab a fresh glass of ice tea and step outside. We have a

cute little garden, with a little vegetable plot, which will be amazing for us and the business.

I stay there on the wooden patio bench, eating bite by bite, enjoying the silence and privacy, but I miss the noise that the waves made when they hit the cliff.

Finishing my tea, I walk back inside, ready to be busy. I need to stop thinking about all what has happened the last month.

After a few minutes, I empty another four boxes. That means the entire kitchen is done, books are on the shelf and all the toys, too.

Tomorrow is collection day and we have to make space, well two little ones we have converted them on a boat and a space machine are staying, but the rest need to be in the trolley by now.

I open the front door, making sure the door stopper is in place—I step out in the fresh summer night. I can't help but look to *Little Castle*. It's dark, he isn't back yet. He might not be back for the night, he might disappear again, but we miss him.

Putting all the boxes in the correct bin and putting it back on the pathway, I turn around and try to move the stopper, but suddenly the lights turn off. Everything is dark.

My forehead is on fire. I can't feel the back of my head. My entire scalp is wet, and my arms hurt. I can't move them. Cut open the flesh on my cheek, and I can't open my left eye but the right one shows me my worst nightmare is kneeling on top of me.

He is smiling in that disgusting way he used to—satisfied

with what he is doing to me. My T-shirt ripped, my arms tided above my head, and my mouth and nose taste like blood. *Is that normal?* I can't feel pain anymore. He broke me years ago.

Because he couldn't handle that I want to succeed in life, have a better future for my children—oh my God, the kids, I can't let him win. The kids need me. I need to fight, and I need to stay alive.

"Before I end you, sweetie, I want you to know I will take your children, bring them to India and make sure they know the way bastards are treat it."

I can't let him take them. *Please somebody help me, please someone save my children.*

I can see his fist raise in the air and all goes black. I can't breathe properly, I can't open my eyes anymore, I can't move.

A part of me is trying to fight, but my body isn't responding to me. I take a deep breath and focus, but it's hard when my children are in jeopardy.

CHAPTER TWENTY-EIGHT

Samuel

I am about to leave when my phone rings. I frown when I see Nathaniel Lennon's name flashing.

He has been the family lawyer after his father passed, who was Grandpa and my father's lawyer too.

"Nathaniel, to what do I owe this pleasure?" I have a sarcastic tone, as usual.

"Samuel, don't use your sarcasm with me."

We are the same age—known each other our entire lives.

"We a delicate situation." He assures.

"Have you been in a cave lately? My life is pending on a thin thread over delicate situations."

"This is way more..." I pull the mobile away from my ear when I see Scott running outside. Matteo tries to stop him.

"Uncle Samuel!!" I've never seen him this nervous. "You need to go! Ruby, she needs you!"

I look at my nephew. He is pale, his eyes wide open.

"We saw something on Little Castle CCTV. Run *hermano*!" Matteo screams.

I don't stop to ask questions. Don't check the road. Just

drive away as fast as I can, passing some cars on my way.

What have they seen?

My mobile is in my hand. I'm trying to log into it, refusing every call from Nathan.

I try to rewind to a few minutes ago, but before I can see or understand anything, I drive over the road that joins both of our houses, and I jump out of the car.

Something weird makes me pause. Ruby's front door is open. I can see a small light on. Sprinting up, I immediately hear noises upstairs. It's Naima. She is screaming, so I slowly start climbing the stairs. All the lights are off.

I can hear her, but there's a clatter that scares me the most. It must be Aidan, but he isn't screaming and when I have a look inside, I see a male. He is holding a pillow over Aidan's little head. His body is moving. He is alive, but not for long if I don't move.

The fastest action is to jump over him and throw my fist over any part of his body I can find. He tries to fight back, but after what I've just seen there's no way I will let this bastard leave here alive. I throw another fist, knocking him out for a while.

But Naima's screams bring me out of my trance. When I look up, I can't see her. She was in the corner screaming when I jumped on this bastard, but now she sounds further away.

Aidan sits in the bed, his face wet. I quickly hold him in my arms, taking him away, towards Naima.

I pull my phone out and start calling 999, while trying to find Naima, when I arrive at the bottom of the stairs. She is there, calling Ruby, who is unconscious on the floor.

When I get closer, I realise there is a pool of blood around her head—she doesn't look like herself. This bastard has punched the life out of her, but she has a pulse.

"I'm here baby, please don't leave us," I reach Naima and pull her to my chest, she quickly hides her little wet face in my chest. Her little hands fist my shirt, making sure I can't move away from her, and I make sure Aidan can't see his mom like this.

"Please save her, don't let *mama* die," Naima mumble on my shirt.

The ambulance and police appear immediately and while they prep her on the gurney, I step aside.

Making sure I get what I need to cover the kids and take them with me, giving a quick call to Matteo.

"I need you here with the other car," I say.

"On the way, bro."

He appears before everything is ready, moving my car aside and handing me the keys of the bigger car with the kids' car seats.

Matteo drives behind the ambulance all the way to the hospital—I requested for her to be taken to St Marcus's hospital.

William is at the A & E entrance waiting for us. I jump out of the car before they even take her down.

"We will make sure she recovers in no time. She will have her own private suite, where the children and you can rest too." William explains, and I nod.

"I'm not leaving her side ever again." I assure him.

Holding the kids again in my arms, I walk behind her gurney.

"Is she going to be, okay?" Naima asks.

"Your mom is the strongest woman I've ever met. She knows we need her." I assure her.

"Thank you, Samuel." Her eyes fill with tears.

"For what baby?" I ask, kissing her little face.

"For loving *mama*."

"Forever baby," I assure, and she rests her head back on my shoulder.

I just hug them tighter, trying to hide the pain in my chest, the worry of anything happening to her. We can't lose her.

Ruby is the only person I can't afford to lose. She has helped me heal, be a better person, be an actual normal human being, she has helped us be a better family. I can't lose that.

We spend the rest of the night in the suite—the kids are sleeping in my arms, not allowing me to put them down. Naima is trembling while she dreams, squeezing me now and then.

Ruby has been in surgery all night, many tests have been done, and they will clean her in another room, so the kids will see her in as good of a state as possible.

By breakfast time, the nurse brings a tray for the children. I can't even put a coffee in my stomach, seen her bed empty it's keeping my anxiety on high levels.

It's been many hours and we have no news from Ruby. I was about to leave the room and confront someone when William comes inside the room.

"She is fine, we just need to make sure she rest, that's why she has been in the recovery room for the past few hours," my gaze must burn his skin, "as soon as she get out of the anaesthesia, we will take her here," I nod, "I think you want to have a look at this."

He hands me a thick reports folder, opening the first page I found her name *Ruby Rao*. I nod and he leaves.

I take a seat on the armchair near the table where the children is having lunch and start checking her report;

MEDICAL REPORT

Shepperton Central Hospital, this report is confidential.
The details of the patience will only be shared with other health and safety facilities on the intention of helping the patience.

Patient; <u>Ruby Maria Rao</u>
DOB; March 15th 1992
Age; Fifteen
Nationality; American
Sex (Gender); Female

"What is the Samuel?" Naima ask, giving another bite to her burger.

"Grown-up boring stuff," I answer, closing the folder and resting it aside. I will have a look later on.

The sun is gone when the door opens and Ruby comes in. There are two nurses moving her bed around. She is sleeping or sedated, her beautiful face is all bruised. She has few cuts that needed stitches over her cheek.

Putting the kids down on the guest bed in the corner, I

walk to her. I sit by her side, holding her hand I can see bruises on her wrist from where the bastard held her. I kiss her knuckles and rest her palm on my cheek—I miss her so much.

Her fingertips move around my cheek, her eyes try to open, but they are swollen.

"Please, don't." I move forward to her face and kiss her cheek. "The kids are here. We are all fine. I just need you to be strong and get well soon." My voice is trembling, tears are pouring out, making her face wet.

Tears fall on the side of her face too, but just with those words, she goes back to sleep.

She must be in so much pain and tired that sleep will be her best cure.

I move the armchair to her side and rest back with the folder in my lap, after the regular reports over her childhood, William has found everything since she ran away, there are reports from all over US, down to South America, Africa, Spain, and then UK.

They travelled a lot, but seen the routes I can tell he was travelling from low-profile countries around to make sure Ruby wasn't located easily.

She has been in hospital over a thousand times in the past years—she felt down the stairs multiple times, broke one rib and wrist, multiple visits to the GP just for minor issues.

But what shocked me the most is reading a gynecologist reports, she has multiple miscarriages before she was pregnant with Naima, both pregnancies went well, but after them, he injured her so badly she reported nothing so when doctors finally treat her months after—he had caused her so much damage she can never have children again.

Most of her serious injuries were found out six months ago, a police report is attached to her last medical report, the children and Ruby report been locked for weeks inside a room, sometimes locked inside the house, but that they couldn't remember the last time they left the house.

I walk to the toilet as a few nurses come and change some stuff around, apply more creams to her wounds. They say that will help with a faster healing.

I have a quick shower, wash away my anger and pain, and exit the room to find Ruby awake.

"Baby," I whisper, "I am so sorry."

She just nods and gives me a small smile. Her wound cheek won't let her smile any more.

"It's the middle of the night, please rest," I order and she closes her eyes.

At the next morning a police officer comes around, while I was helping the kids with their breakfast.

He asks a few questions, not about me attacking him, more about if we recognise him.

We explain everything we were through for the past weeks and he informed us that, Advik has been arrested, they been working with the Indian government and they will deport him.

*****

We've been here for two weeks. Ruby scars have turned in dark shadows. The children are back in *Little Castle*.

"Are you ready?" I ask nervously.

"To be outside?" she asks. "I am not scared anymore."

Brushing her cheek, I drop a soft kiss on her lips.

"I meant to move with me," I assure.

"Are you sure?" she asks.

"Do you really think I will ever let three of you to leave my side again? Never, I will have to be dead."

"Well, my business could grow faster with that kitchen," her eyes brighten up at the mentioned of the kitchen.

"Are you accepting my proposal because of a kitchen?" I ask in disbelieve.

"I will actually be happier with the cottage kitchen style but the size of *Little Castle,*" she assure.

"Do you know I own a castle in Edinburg?" I ask.

Her eyes become wider, wondering about more information.

"And since my great-grandfather build it over a hundred years ago, it has the original kitchen, and let me tell you baby," I get closer to her lips, "it's bigger than *Little Castle's.*"

A perfect smile grows on her beautiful face. I need to take them there.

At late afternoon, we exit the hospital, and I help Ruby into the car.

A short ride home, and I sigh in relief seen our safe place in front of us.

Everyone is at the entrance to greet her, jumping over us as we exit the car. A sense of calmness comes to me, something new, as we are finally together.

CHAPTER TWENTY-NINE

Ruby
Months Later.

Life is way better and easier now. We are free—we aren't scared—we are stronger. For the first time in nearly my entire life, I wake up and go to bed smiling.

The house is 24/7 chaos, people running around doing multiple things at once.

Samuel is working from here full time. Helena is our assistant, right hand, and the one who makes sure we follow our schedules as much as possible.

But she also makes sure Samuel and I get a good break through the day, exactly when we reach our limit, before we need to join the madness of parenthood and school runs, to have time for us, and gosh we enjoy it so so so much.

Naima and Aidan are doing fantastic at school. In the beginning, I didn't want them to go. I was afraid—I was paranoid, but now we are sure there's no way anyone can get to them. Samuel made sure they were at the most secure, private school, with a limit of people allowed around them. It might be too much, but it gives us all an essential peace that, at least for now, we need.

They sent Stella to a mental health hospital/recovery center for wealthy people after the episode on Scott's birthday. Apparently, she never coped with life so well. Rosita tried her best after her grandfather passed, and after her parent passed. But nobody could help when Donnie died. Logan has visited her. They can't deny there is something going on, but we already have enough around. That will be an adventure with this family soon.

Matteo has been gone on a business trip for over two months already. It's all been really secretive, but it's a personal matter that I'm sure when he is ready, he might share with us.

Natasha has joined the team full time. She doesn't look very social, but actually is the funniest woman I've ever met, so it's clear why Helena is obsessed with her. She runs my entire new social media. There are so many platforms I have never heard of. Now I have a proper, worthy to spend time and order from website. I'm even filming small video recipes. She has the camera on all day around me, and that has sent the sales to the sky.

I never stop baking, and everyone loves it, because that has created an incredible homey scent and they get to eat delicious treats all day.

Rosita has delegated the kitchen duties to me. She takes care of getting all the items I need for each order, helps with the baking in the evenings. We pack things when everyone is sleeping and enjoy a cup of tea talking about anything.

I guess is has something to do with our family happiness and with Miguel.

He has been visiting her, sending flowers, notes, inviting her for a walk at the park, with the big excuse that he is the one in charge of all the printing and designing, so he comes frequently to the house.

Samuel didn't like it at first, but we all deserve our own privacy, to be loved, to be special for someone else, and she has given her entire life to Samuel and Stella. She has no husband, no children, only them, and now they are grownups, so it's her time.

Today's schedule is chaos. We won't finish until nearly dinner time, but Helena has booked a family movie time, the one I'm so looking for.

Rosita and I are preparing colorful popcorn and mini pizzas for them. But first I need to finish a wedding order. Our delivery guy will be here at 6 a.m. He is someone that will collect, deliver, and prepare the order at each event, all without me.

"Rosita, have you seen the..." she automatically hands me the little pearls. They are the last detail of these incredible three tier cakes. All have a broken white buttercream. I've made minor details like lace with different shades of gold.

"Thanks," I say while she hands me the container of pearls. I don't look at her. She doesn't take it personally, nor do the rest of them. They know when I'm focused, everything around me is gone.

I step away from my masterpiece and smile. When I turn

around, everyone is smiling too.

"That's so beautiful." I frown and Helena laughs. "That's spectacular." My smile grows again.

After Natasha does her video and camera duty, Rosita hands me the cover and we close it down, ready to go in the walk-in fridge/freezer.

"Okay, so with this, you just have to make sure you have wrapped the two hundred cookies for the gifts, I counted hundred and fifty before Samuel disturbed me," Helena says, and I roll my eyes, we all know he doesn't mean it, but it can be really inappropriate.

I check my watch. The kids' pickup time is over. He should be there by now. Apparently Mr. Winkles is with him. Which gives us twenty minutes to get everything out of the way.

Natasha moves to the movie theater room as she wants to find Scott's choice for this week, which is a mystery except for both of them.

Everything looks spotless when I hear the noise of the keys, Mr. Wrinkles' paws hitting the marble, and giggles coming toward us.

"Mama!" Naima and Aidan run into my arms. I hold them tight, as I missed them, making them laugh and push me away.

"How was your day?" I ask, brushing messy fallen pieces of hair with my fingers.

"We did a really fun activity in the playground. We had to crawl under ropes, climb a wall, it was messy, but funny." She is excited about it, so who am I to ruin it for just a messy mane?

"How about your day, Scott?" I ask walking to him, giving him a hug and brushing his cheek.

He looks at me, holding a smile away, failing, and when I'm about to ask, he just runs away.

"Okay, that was weird." It's fine, I will find out later.

"Kids, follow me, please. Let's get those dirty uniforms into the laundry room. Today will be a quick shower for everyone," Rosita orders. It is still early, but I'm really looking forward to them to be clean up, and I guess so is she.

Once they are out, I finally turn my attention to Samuel. He is quiet, his hands are hiding in the pocket of his denim, gosh he looks hot. I walk slowly towards him, and when he is really close, I wrap my arms around his waist, resting my cheek on his chest. His heart pumping extremely fast, so I raise my head, questioning what is happening, but he just smiles.

"We need to get you cleaned up too," he says, brushing his fingertips on my cheek and revealing a white paste. "So sweet like always," he murmurs, licking his fingers.

And just like that, he grabs me under my ass, raising me to his waist.

He carries me upstairs, and I kissed his lips. I guess he understands I must be tired and the thousands, more like maybe twenty steps that will take me upstairs, will be an enormous challenge. I love this house, but gosh these stairs seem to never end, especially after a tiring day.

We get to the bathroom—I don't even realize what is happening until my back hits the wall. His head on my neck, kissing, licking, biting, all while his hands work on taking my shirt off. My back curves with every movement of his mouth. As I feel him pulling my shirt down my arms, I work on his T-shirt. I break his mouth from my neck, giving me a delicious view: his lips parted, his eyes foggy, desire pouring from every pore of his perfect figure.

I jump off of his waist, determined to get rid of our clothes from the waist down. We quickly help each other. As soon as my trousers and knickers hit the floor, I jump on him like a chimpanzee, devouring his lips.

Straight to the shower, the water starts extremely cold, but we don't move, we don't complain. My body is on fire and nothing can take that away.

My back hits the wall again, but this time I scream as his cock brushed my clit, and before I can move, he enters me at once. No slow moves, no adjustments. I haven't realized how much I need this hard delicious Samuel until now.

His hips move forward, faster and faster every time. My hips roll with every push, sending each other to another level. We don't kiss, we just look at each other, enjoying the other's pleasure.

I can't take my eyes away of this Adonis, wet, savage, moaning, growling, murmuring.

My hips lose control and turning faster and faster, my walls are squeezing his arousal hard, as his thrusts are getting deeper and deeper.

His forearms hit the wall on each side of my head and his forehead meets mine. I can hear his whispers, his hot breath brushing my skin, his hips move harder and mine rotates faster.

The room spins around, so my hands reach for the back of his head and I devour his mouth. My tongue fights with his.

I bite his bottom lip and push my head back, breaking our kiss as I scream. Samuel growls, murmurs, and draws small kisses around my face.

Gosh, that feels so good. All the stress, tiredness, nerves I've been carrying around all day are absolutely gone.

Samuel brings us out of the shower and places me in the sink. A towel is under me, and he quickly pulls it up to my shoulders, drying my body with soft brushes and squeezes, trying to take the water away, but my skin is waking up again.

"Stop," I whisper, and he just laughs, more than aware of what he is doing.

Handing me my toothbrush and getting his, we brush our teeth, apply some cream, and brush our hair, just doing our thing.

"How was your day?" he asks, hanging his towel and walking fully naked out of the bathroom.

"Productive and extremely long," I answer, walking out too, heading to where he is, the walk-in closet. Getting some comfy clothes, he hands me mine. "So kind." I smile.

"The wedding order is all done?" I just nod, pulling a big T-shirt over my head. "Let's go."

Suddenly, we are in a rush. He is pulling my hand out of the bedroom. Just then I realize how quiet the house is. Everyone must be in the theater already.

When we enter, everything is pitch black. Suddenly, Samuel is not at my side anymore. I can't see or hear the kids.

"What's going on?" I ask.

Before I can get an answer, the screen comes alive. I frown.

It's Samuel, as a baby, a toddler, running, laughing. I see his grandpa, dad, gorgeous mom, and then it's me, as a baby, my first steps, my adventures with the animals.

My throat is closed, my palms hold my heart in place. The video is full of our childhoods, teenage years, but only Samuel growing older. In me there is a tremendous gap until I can see myself in the stores, at the old apartment kitchen, the pictures Samuel never used for the special edition. They were his private collection.

I'm not aware I am crying until the entire screen becomes a blur and something hits my thoughts. "How did you get my pictures from... good God," I stop.

My parents are on the screen, talking to me, but I can't hear them.

"I can't hear them!" I cry in panic, in distress, I choke on my own tears. I can't hear them. "Samuel please, I can't..." the light turns on and I nearly fall on my ass.

Everyone is here. The kids, Samuel by their side, Matteo is back, Rosita, Helena and Natasha are sitting on the velvet couch.

I see Miguel. What is he doing here? But realize there's someone else.

I can't see who it is. Everyone is looking at me, some of them crying, some seem uncomfortable.

Stepping forward, I turn my head to understand who is behind Matteo and Samuel. They immediately move and I scream, holding my hand to my mouth, trying to hide away any more possible screams.

I can't believe what I'm seeing—it's my parents. I fell on

my knees, hiding my face, crying and laughing. My entire face is wet, and when I'm about to raise my head to look at them again, hard, powerful hands touch my back. My body receives an electroshock that puts me straight immediately.

And there I am, kneeling in front of my parents. I get a hold of my father's leg. "Forgive me, dad."

He caresses my hair, not saying a word, but when one of his tears hit my crown, I understand he can't talk. I move to my mom and beg for her forgiveness, too.

"There's nothing to forgive you for *hija*," she says in a soft, calm voice, offering her hands. I raise to my feet and throw my arms around both of them. We hug, we sob, we laugh, we kiss, we inhale each other, taking back their essence that I forgot so long ago went away from me. "Thank you *hija*."

"Thanks to you, mama." There's nothing they have to thank me for. I have done nothing more than hurt them.

"Thanks for surviving, thanks for never giving up, and thanks for coming back to us."

I never would have imagined Samuel would do something like this, but it's been more than clear after all these months that our happiness is his own happiness.

Now the time Matteo was gone makes sense, the mystery every time I asked about all the whisperings.

I break the hug, cleaning my face and call Naima and Aidan, "Let me officially introduce you."

My mom is trembling, squeezing her hands on her chest, trying to remain calm, but failing.

"This is Naima, and Aidan, kids, this is Abuela and

Grandpa."

They all look at each other, just smiling widely. The kids can't hold themselves still any longer and just throw themselves in their arms and are all hugs and kisses until Samuel gives a little cough.

He just walks closer to me. "Don't worry, I already introduced myself this morning."

What? How long my parents have they been here? Where? So many questions, but Samuel holds both of my hands and turns me to face him.

"There's something I want to say," he is playing with my hands, nervous too.

I frown at him, questioning what he could say right now, what will happen that has to be taken so seriously.

"Ruby..." he coughs, clearing his throat, "months ago I found you in the streets of London. I was lost, and I saw you, but it was so briefly I thought it was a dream." His voice trembles. "I thought I would never see you again. I found you at the park taking care of Scott while I looked for him like a madman." He looks over his shoulder back at Scott and we all laugh. "Since the moment that I saw you, I couldn't help it. I was madly in love with you, couldn't take my eyes away from you, didn't want to be away from you," he smiles shyly. "And the moment I enjoyed your spectacular food," he smiles widely. "Gosh woman." everyone laughs.

He holds my hands tighter—they are trembling. I try to look into his eyes, but he so nervous, he can't look straight at me. I reach one of my hands to his beautiful face and push it up. He rests his head on my palm and closes his eyes slightly, taking a deep breath.

"You always thank us for anything that we do for you." There's a little pain on his face. "But you've changed our lives. I'm a better human, thanks to the three of you. My life has a purpose thanks to that, no matter anymore what happened before. I want to close those chapters. I want this, and I want it forever." He has a nervous smile. "Would you Ruby..." my breath stops when he kneels, "be my forever?"

There's a little black velvet box in his palm. He opens it and automatically holds me again. He knows I'm about to faint.

There's a breathtaking ring inside it, so sparkly it might hurt my eyes, a huge ruby in the centre. Around it are multiple small bright diamonds. I can't breathe. He smiles widely, his perfect smile, the one that he just gives me, biting his lip nervously, waiting for my answer.

"I will be your forever Samuel," I answer, jumping into his arms. Everyone claps, laughs, and cheers for the moment.

For an instant there is only us, locking our gaze, smiling, saying millions of things in our secret silence.

He places the ring on my finger—fits perfectly.

I've never had a ring, especially not one like this. I raise up, hugging the kids, hugging my parents. This is a very important and special moment. I finally have my entire family together and safe.

CHAPTER THIRTY

Samuel

One year later, Edinburg.

I couldn't sleep all night, the nerves of today couldn't let me sleep, especially when Eva our wedding planner has to be replaced by Marsha—Eva's baby has decided to born three weeks in advance.

We came to Edinburg nearly two months ago, as soon as the children were on summer holidays, and as it seems, Ruby loves live here more.

Considering even to move here, run her business from here and let the children have the life I once enjoyed, surrounded by green mountains, animals and nature.

Marsha has come three times into the room already. She is extremely nervous and apparently Ruby has forbidden her to return to her room. *Can't blame my gorgeous wife to be.*

"Marsha, have a drink. Everything is under control. Give us a break," I order, giggling when she gives me a shocking face.

"Come with me," Calvin says, taking her away, knowing I won't be so nice the next time she comes to bother us.

I step outside and take a seat on one of the patio chairs, finishing my coffee while I enjoy watching the kids and the boys playing around.

We still have a couple more hours until we get ready. My hair is perfect. I'm just wearing some comfy joggers and letting the sun warm my olive skin.

"Pa!" Naima calls me.

She started calling me *papa* months ago, the first time came out so naturally that even though we were all shocked, nobody said a word about it.

But my poor wounded heart jumped on gratitude of the love this two little creatures has given me in this time, asking nothing in return, more than what any human deserve, respect and love.

One night, while I was reading a story to them about a little girl losing her parents, she asked me if it was possible to find a new family, and if it would be appropriate to love them more that your blood family.

I knew where she was coming from. She never felt loved by her biological father. Never experienced what a family was until we came into her life, and suddenly we were a lot of us.

She has given same the love, respect, attention, and kindness to each one of us.

But her favourite out of all of my boys is Logan, and I can't blame her. He is as big as a double cupboard. But with her, he looks younger, smaller, softer, unless we are in public, surrounded by others, then he becomes bigger and will protect her from anything.

Lately distracted with the concerned of Stella leaving the clinic, even if my blood boils, I know there is something going on between them, not concern and calm knowing I will always have eyes and ears around her.

Scott has refused to return to live with her. We are working on it.

But my mood change when my lawyer enters the patio area.

"Nathaniel, do you understand is my weeding day, right?" I ask sarcastically, avoiding him.

Matteo stops playing and stands looking straight at me, giving me goosebumps.

"Samuel, I contacted you multiple times," he accuse.

Yes, he did. The night Ruby was attacked and many times after that.

"I've been trying to get hold of you for a year Samuel," he sounds irritated.

"Let's say I had been extremely busy."

I have been avoiding him. Every time he calls, there is bad news on the other side of the line.

"That is why Helena and... Matteo..." I stop.

"Yes, Matteo was the only one available to answer my calls."

That would explain why he is looking at me like that. Irritated, I stand and face him.

"What is it so important that it cannot wait another day?" I ask, and he hands me an envelope.

I open it and take the few documents out.

There is a marriage certificate, a birth certificate, and a

lawsuit.

"What do you know about Colton and Catherine Murray?" He asks, taking more documents out.

"Catherine Thomas was my grandfather's lover."

We all been working hard on founding as much information as possible, but there are so many questions we can't find the answer.

Rosita has refused to tell a word about it. That might have helped, but with time I know we will find all the information. There is nothing to worry about.

"The Murray's family claimed Colton is your grandfather," Nathaniel is trying to explain a nonsensical story.

"Your grandfather took everything away from the Murray's after Catherine died."

"What are you fucking talking about?!"

"Was your father a legitimate Smith? Or are the allegations right and he was a Murray?" I nervously pull my waves. "All was a secret. They built the SaStel Legacy on a lie."

My fist hits the patio table, my entire system burning in anger.

"You don't know what you are talking about," I argue back.

"Samuel, take a genetic test. Prove you are who your father many years ago fought the world for." Matteo says.

"My father was a Smith, and so am I."

"Colton knew of Catherine's infidelity, of all Scott senior gave her. We are talking about this castle, Little Castle and a percentage of the companies Samuel," he explains, "are you willing to lose everything?"

This is the most insane situation I could imagine, but that makes sense of what has been happening for the past few months, breaking on the houses, stolen items.

"They are the ones who broke into the properties. They were looking for more information." Matteo accuses back.

I get no more answers, just a simple nod.

Matteo rests his hand on my shoulder and applies some pressure on it.

"We will fix this *hermano*." I look straight at him, seeing his determination. "We will protect the SaStel Legacy."

To be Continued…

Thank you so much for reading Samuel, Book I of the SaStel Legacy Series.
DON'T MISS BOOK 2, STELLA AND BOOK 3, THE SASTEL LEGACY.

About the Author

Nadia Marsoli was born in Spain and raised in Madrid.

In 2015, she moved to London planning to start her dream
family and pursuing growing in her career.

Since she was young, stories will come to her in dreams, or
experiences in life will leave her with the feeling a most
excited end would have been incredible. One day she wrote
to take those thoughts out of her head, and found herself
with an incredible, mysterious romance, creating powerful
characters has become her addiction since then.

Acknowledgment

Thanks for reading! Please add a quick review on Amazon and let me know what you thought!

I dedicate this story to my children, for all the patience over my long working hours on developing this book, and give me the courage to never give up.

To all those mighty mamas that fight every day to give the happy ending to their children, that will do anything and everything for them and will never give up.

To my beloved besties couple for the love and support becoming Ruby and Samuel for a day, we had so much fun, and let me tell you, the fire was there, no pretending on that one ;)

LINKS TO SOCIAL MEDIA

Instagram
@author__nadiamarsoli

Facebook
www.facebook.com/nadiamarsoliauthor

Spotify
Listen to the full playlist while you read
www.open.spotify.com/playlist/3l1A7xAqcglHHCSOqA0w
EH

Feedback and Suggestions for next books?
Email it to me; team@nadiamarsoli.com

Books and Merchandise
www.nadiamarsoli.com